Unjust Conviction

Shane Reed

Copyright

Copyright © 2024 by Shane Reed

All rights reserved.

Chapter 1

The bass throbbed like a heartbeat through the night, reverberating off the river's surface and mingling with the cacophony of laughter and chatter. Chris Matthews moved with a relaxed ease among the throng of dancers, the flickering bonfire casting a warm glow on his earnest face. His short, dark hair was tousled from the playful tugs of the night breeze that swept in from the water's edge.

"Chris! Over here!" Angie Thompson called out, her voice slicing through the din like a beacon. Her wavy blonde locks caught the firelight, turning into strands of molten gold as she waved him over. The crowd parted as Chris made his way to her, each step bringing him closer to her infectious energy.

"Thought you'd get lost in the sea of partygoers," Angie said with a teasing sparkle in her eyes, handing him a drink. It was a simple plastic cup, but from her, it felt like an invitation to join in the revelry.

"Never," Chris replied, his words underscored by a smile that was both grateful and adoring. "Not when I have the most vibrant person here as my anchor."

They clinked their cups together, the hollow sound lost amidst the booming music, and took synchronized sips. Chris watched as Angie's gaze flitted across the crowd, her bright eyes reflecting the flicker of flames and the moonlight overhead. She danced with an abandon that drew others into her orbit, her laughter a melody that blended seamlessly with the pulsing rhythm of the party.

"Come on, dance with me!" Angie grabbed Chris's hand, pulling him toward the makeshift dance floor. He let himself be guided by her enthusiasm, feeling the weight of his worries lift with each step they took together.

Surrounded by the pulsating bodies of fellow partygoers, Chris matched Angie's movements, their dance a silent conversation that needed no words. They spun and swayed, two friends united by an unspoken bond that had been forged through shared experiences and mutual respect. Angie's vivacity was a contrast to Chris's more reserved nature, yet together they found a balance that resonated with the very essence of the night.

"Thanks for being here, Chris," Angie said during a brief lull in the music, her voice soft yet clear. "You always know how to make a good night great."

"Wouldn't miss it for the world, Angie," he replied, sincerity lining his words. His optimism, usually a shield against life's cruelties, now shone brightly, fueled by the genuine connection he shared with the girl before him.

Their laughter mingled with the crackle of the bonfire, and for a moment, all was right in their world. But as the night wore on and the stars climbed higher, the shadows seemed to stretch a little longer, whispering of the impermanence of such perfect moments.

Laughter erupted from a group huddled around a picnic table, where Jason, with his mop of unruly curls and the perpetual grin of a prankster, was holding court. He regaled them with tales of escapades that were only half-believable, but entirely entertaining. Chris chuckled as he watched Jason animate his story with wild hand gestures, drawing even the most reserved attendees into his orbit of mirth.

"Man, you're too much!" Chris called out to him. Jason tipped an imaginary hat in response, his antics a staple of their gatherings.

Nearby, Lila leaned against a tree, her arms wrapped around herself in a self-imposed barrier that kept the world at arm's length. Her sharp wit was often masked by a quiet demeanor, but Chris appreciated the depth behind her observant amber eyes. They shared a quick, knowing glance – a silent acknowledgment of their shared trait of being watchers in a crowd.

"Care for a dance, Lila?" Angie teased, beckoning her friend towards the jubilation.

"Maybe later," Lila replied with a small smile, her voice barely rising above the music, yet carrying a warmth that echoed Angie's earlier invitation to Chris.

The air was thick with the scent of grilling food and the earthy perfume of the river. Music notes floated on the breeze, intertwining with the babble of conversation. Shadows danced along the ground, mirroring the revelers' movements as the flickering light from the bonfire cast an otherworldly glow over the scene.

But as the fire's embers popped and crackled, a sudden chill brushed past Chris, like the touch of a ghost amidst the heat. It left an uneasy prickle on his skin, a dissonance in the night's harmony that whispered warnings he couldn't quite understand.

"Did you feel that?" Angie asked, pulling her cardigan closer.

"Yeah, just a cold draft, I guess," Chris said, though his heart had begun to keep time with an anxious rhythm.

"Let's not think about it," she laughed, though her laugh didn't quite reach her eyes. "We've got a night to enjoy!"

The party continued to surge around them, a tidal wave of carefree spirits, but the nagging sensation lingered in Chris's mind. As the moon climbed higher, casting its indifferent gaze upon the throng of youth, the sense of foreboding grew. Unseen and unheard, the threads of fate were tangling, readying to pull one of them into its snare.

Sunlight filtered through the half-closed blinds, casting striped shadows across Chris's face as he fought the pull of consciousness. The last remnants of the party's euphoria clung to him like a second skin, sticky and sweet. With a groan, he rolled over, fumbling for his phone amidst the tangle of sheets.

"Chris," came the choked voice on the other end, "It's Angie... she's dead."

The words landed like a punch to the gut, scrambling his senses. Disbelief tethered him momentarily in the safe harbor of sleep before reality dragged him under its riptide. "Dead? Angie? No, that can't—"

"Man, I don't know all the details. Just come over to her apartment, now!" The line went dead, leaving a haunting silence in its wake.

Stumbling out of bed, Chris grappled with the weight of those words. The vibrant image of Angie laughing by the river clashed with this new, grim portrait. He couldn't reconcile the two. It was impossible; a cruel joke.

Outside Angie's apartment, chaos reigned. Police tape flapped lazily in the morning breeze, an unwelcome banner marking the entrance to a world turned upside down. Uniformed officers moved with purpose, their faces set in professional masks that did little to hide the tension beneath.

"Sir, you can't go in there," an officer blocked Chris's path.

"Angie's my friend," Chris said, his voice a mix of desperation and defiance. "I need to know what happened."

"Let me handle this," another voice, calm and authoritative, came from behind him. Detective Ramirez surveyed the scene, his eyes sharp and probing. "Why don't you tell me how you know the deceased?"

"Angie and I—we were at a party last night. By the river." Chris's words felt fragile in his mouth, each one threatening to shatter. "We left together, but I went home. She was fine."

"Fine," Ramirez repeated, the word hanging between them as he scribbled notes.

Chris watched as officers streamed in and out of Angie's apartment, emerging with bags that held unseen evidence. Flashbulbs punctuated the tense air, capturing snapshots of a narrative Chris couldn't read.

"Chris Matthews?" Ramirez's gaze fixed on him, searching, evaluating. "We'll need to ask you some more questions later."

"Of course, anything," Chris managed, his resolve anchored only by the need to understand, to find truth amid the ruins of the night before.

As he stepped back, allowing the investigators to work, Chris's mind whirred. He replayed every smile, every word exchanged with

Angie, hunting for clues in memories that refused to align with the harsh daylight reality. But the truth remained elusive, slipping through his fingers like the river's current, leaving him cold and gasping for air.

Chris fidgeted in the hard plastic chair, the sterile light of the interrogation room casting long shadows across his face. The table before him felt like an ocean, wide and expansive, separating him from the officers who fired questions like bullets.

"Where'd you go after the party, Chris?" an officer asked, pen poised above a notebook.

"Home," Chris replied, his voice steady but thin. "I told Angie I wasn't feeling great."

"Alone?"

"Y-Yes, alone." His brow furrowed, confusion creeping into the lines of his young face. He couldn't shake the sensation that the ground was shifting beneath him, that every answer nudged open a door he didn't want to enter.

"Did anyone see you leave? Can anyone vouch for your whereabouts?" The questions were relentless, chipping away at his composure.

"Look, I don't know, it was late, and—" Chris started, but his words tangled, choking on the growing unease.

"Let's pause for a moment, shall we?" Detective Ramirez entered the room, bearing an air of control that seemed to sweep the tension aside. He took a seat opposite Chris, removing his glasses with one hand while setting down a file with the other.

"Chris Matthews," Ramirez said, his tone deliberate, each syllable measured like the tick of a clock. "I understand this is difficult for you. But I need to know everything about last night. No detail is too small."

Chris looked up, meeting Ramirez's gaze. It was sharp, piercing—the kind of look that saw through facades and unearthed secrets buried deep. And yet, there was a flicker of something else, perhaps a glint of compassion or understanding.

"Detective, I didn't do anything wrong," Chris said, his resolve finding its footing again. "Angie was my friend. I want to help however I can."

"Good," Ramirez responded, jotting something down in the file. "Because someone took Angie's life, and I'm going to find out who. If you're innocent, you've got nothing to worry about."

The detective's determination hung heavy in the room. It was clear that Ramirez would turn over every stone, follow every lead until justice was served. Chris wanted to trust in that resolve, to believe that the truth would shine through the murky waters of doubt and accusation.

"Can I go now?" Chris asked, his hands clasped together as if holding on to the hope that he could wake up from this nightmare.

"Stay available, Mr. Matthews. We'll be in touch," Ramirez instructed, signaling the end of the questioning.

Chris stood, his legs unsteady, the weight of suspicion resting squarely on his shoulders. As he exited the room, the click of the door closing echoed ominously, a stark reminder that Angie's death had irrevocably altered the course of many lives—including his own.

Chris paced the cramped confines of his apartment, the early morning light casting long shadows that seemed to echo his growing unease. His every step was heavy, weighed down by a sense of loss so profound it threatened to crush him. Angie's laughter, bright and infectious, still rang in his ears, a haunting reminder of the void her death had left behind.

"Angie," he whispered, the name catching in his throat as he ran his fingers through his short, dark hair. He could still see her dancing by the river, vibrant and full of life. The memory stung, fresh and raw, a stark contrast to the empty stillness of the present.

The ring of his phone jolted Chris from his reverie. It was Detective Ramirez on the line, requesting another meeting. The detective's tone was cordial but insistent, and Chris's heart sank further. The call ended with an unspoken message clear as day: he was far from being cleared.

Stepping outside, the city seemed different to Chris—a labyrinth where every turn brought more questions and the answers lay hidden, just out of reach. He watched the police move methodically in and out of Angie's apartment, collecting evidence with a clinical detachment that felt alien to him.

"Can't believe this is happening," muttered a bystander, shaking his head. Chris overheard snippets of conversations swirling around him, each word like a knife twisting in his gut.

"Did you see how close he was to Angie?" one voice suggested, a whisper loud enough to carry.

"Never know what people are capable of," another replied, suspicion tainting the words.

Chris felt their eyes on him, judgmental and accusing, as if his very presence was an indictment. His resilience faltered, his optimism dimming under the weight of their stares. He tried to muster the strength to confront them, to assert his innocence, but doubt crept in, silencing him.

"Mr. Matthews, we'll need to speak with some of your friends, get their take on last night," Detective Ramirez said, approaching Chris with a notepad in hand. The detective's expression was unreadable, a mask that gave nothing away.

"Of course," Chris replied, his voice barely above a whisper. "Anything to help."

As he watched the police work, Chris couldn't shake the feeling of being trapped in a web spun by fate. With each witness that spoke to the detectives, each item bagged and tagged as evidence, his isolation grew. The connections he had cherished now felt like threads pulling him into a dark abyss he couldn't escape.

"Chris, man, this is messed up," a friend said, clapping a hand on his shoulder. "You good?"

"Trying to be," Chris admitted, his earnest eyes searching his friend's face for any sign of doubt.

"Hey, they'll figure it out. You didn't do anything," his friend reassured him, but even those words felt hollow, floating away on a breeze of uncertainty.

Left alone again, Chris watched the sun climb higher in the sky, its rays doing little to warm the chill that had settled inside him. Each passing moment added to the tension that curled tight in his chest. The truth was his ally, he reminded himself, yet the truth seemed obscured, mired in a fog of suspicion and fear.

"Mr. Matthews, you can go now," Detective Ramirez said abruptly, closing his notebook with a snap that echoed in the quiet room. The words, simple as they were, hit Chris like a gust of wind after hours in stifling heat. He stood up, his legs weak and wobbly, not entirely convinced he'd heard right.

"Go?" Chris repeated, his voice tinged with disbelief.

"Until we need to talk again. You're free to leave," Ramirez clarified, his eyes sharp but not unkind.

A sigh of relief escaped Chris's lips as he stumbled out of the interrogation room, the fluorescent lights of the hallway feeling less oppressive now. His mind spun, relief tangled with confusion. Was this how it was supposed to feel? Angie was gone, and here he was, walking out while she couldn't. The air outside seemed fresher, but it did nothing to clear the fog of his thoughts.

Chris's phone buzzed relentlessly in his pocket, a barrage of missed calls and texts awaiting him. But he ignored them for a moment, leaning against the cool brick wall of the precinct. He needed to breathe, to understand why the fingers of suspicion had loosened their grip enough to let him step away.

"Is this what justice feels like?" he murmured to himself, glancing down at his hands, half-expecting them to hold some secret clue to the puzzle that was Angie's death.

As he finally began to sift through the messages, words of concern, and even veiled accusations from friends and acquaintances, the weight of the situation settled back onto his shoulders. Each notification was a reminder that Angie's light would never brighten another party, that her laughter wouldn't echo by the river again.

"Chris, where are you? We're all freaked out here, man."

"Did the cops really think you did it?"

"Can't believe Angie's gone. Do they have any leads?"

"Stay strong, brother. Justice will come."

The messages blurred together, a cacophony of voices in a world suddenly muted of color and warmth. Chris pocketed the phone, knowing well that the road ahead would be fraught with tension, each step subject to scrutiny.

As he walked away from the station, Chris felt the gaze of the city upon him—the whispers of passersby, the sideways glances of those who recognized him from the news. The tragedy of losing Angie was compounded by the burden of suspicion that seemed to follow him like a shadow.

He looked up at the skyline he'd once dreamed of reaching, realizing how much those dreams had been altered in the span of one harrowing ordeal. With determination in his heart, tempered by the somber reality of his circumstances, Chris knew he had to find the truth, not just for Angie, but for himself. The fight for justice was far from over, and he would face it head-on, even if the journey might cast him further into the abyss.

Chapter 2

Chris sat alone, the only light in his living room coming from a single lamp that cast long shadows across the walls. His gaze was fixed upon a framed picture on the coffee table: him and Angie, caught mid-laughter under the bright sun of a day that now seemed a lifetime ago. Sorrow carved deep lines into his youthful face, a stark contrast to the carefree grins they both wore in the photograph.

His hands, usually steady and sure, trembled as he reached for the frame. The glass felt cool against his fingertips, the edges sharp—sharp enough to cut through the haze of memories that flooded his mind. He could almost hear Angie's laughter, a sound that used to fill rooms and lift hearts. They had shared so many dreams, painting their futures with bold strokes of ambition and the bright colors of hope. Now, all that remained were echoes of their past, each one a reminder of what had been stolen from him.

Clutching the picture close, Chris felt the rush of those days return—the days when every door seemed open, and justice wasn't just a distant concept, but something he believed he could touch, shape, even uphold. It was a time before the flaws of the world had shown themselves, before the unforgiving gears of the criminal justice system had ensnared him in their cold grasp.

The frame slipped from Chris's grasp as the silence of the room was pierced by the creak of a door. Jenny stepped inside, her presence like a steady beacon in the murky haze that enveloped him. She moved closer, her footsteps soft against the worn carpet. There was no need for words; her face said it all. Her brows drew together, a silent testament to the worry that gripped her heart.

With a grace born of countless times she'd been there before, Jenny laid her hand on Chris's shoulder. It was a simple gesture, but in that touch lay an entire history of shared struggles and unspoken promises.

Her fingers were warm—a stark contrast to the chill that had settled deep within him.

Chris turned his head, his eyes lifting from the shards of memory that lay scattered like broken glass at his feet. The room swam into focus, centering on Jenny's face. His gaze locked with hers, two pools of tear-filled sorrow meeting across an expanse of shared pain. In her eyes, he saw the reflection of his own torment, but there was something else too—strength, unwavering and fierce.

He tried to speak, to give voice to the whirlwind of loss that spiraled through him, but words failed. They clung to the back of his throat, unformed and heavy. Instead, what passed between them was an understanding that transcended language—a shared recognition of the injustice that had upended their world, the resolve to right a wrong that gnawed at the very fabric of their beings.

"Chris," Jenny whispered, her voice a lifeline in the gathering darkness. "I'm here."

His lips parted, a breath shuddering free, though no sound followed. Gratitude flickered across his features, mingling with the raw edges of his grief. It was a silent thank you, a nod to the ally standing steadfast beside him, ready to face the storm ahead, whatever it might bring.

Jenny's voice, soft as the light from the streetlamp filtering through the curtains, broke the silence. "You're not alone in this," she said gently, her hand steady on his shoulder. "We'll find our way through it—together."

Chris's breath caught, a tangle of sorrow and relief at her words. He looked up at her, the tremble in his hands slowly stilling. "Angie," he began, the name a whisper of anguish, "she was always there, you know? With a laugh that could chase away the darkest cloud." His eyes, glazed with unshed tears, searched the room as if the past might materialize from the shadows.

"Remember how she'd light up a party just by walking in?" Chris's voice cracked, the memories spilling out like water from a breached dam. "She made me believe in better days, dream bigger dreams. And now..." His throat tightened, squeezing the words into choked sobs.

Jenny squeezed his shoulder, a silent vow cast in the simple gesture. Chris drew in a ragged breath, finding solace in her presence—the quiet anchor in his tempest-tossed world.

Jenny's gaze never wavered from Chris's face, her eyes pools of compassion. She leaned forward slightly, the curve of her lips offering a silent comfort as he stumbled through his narrative. Her presence was a warm blanket, wrapping around him with an understanding that words alone could not convey.

"Chris," she said, her voice a soothing balm, "whatever darkness you're walking through, I'm here. You've always fought for what's right. Now it's time to fight for yourself."

It was as if her words ignited something within him—a spark in the bleakness. His jaw set, and a fierce light kindled behind his eyes. The lines of despair that had etched themselves into his features were now underlined by a steely resolve.

"Jenny," Chris replied, his tone threaded with a conviction that belied his shattered state, "they can say what they want. But I know—I know I didn't do this. Angie deserved better, and I won't rest until the truth comes out."

That spark flared brighter, casting away some of the shadows that clung to him. Jenny nodded, her own spirit reinforcing his. She saw the determination etched into his expression, a testament to the resilience that had always defined him.

"Let's start digging, then," she affirmed, her words cutting through the heaviness that filled the room. "The real story is out there, and we'll find it, piece by piece."

Jenny's nod was slow, deliberate. "Chris," she started, her voice steady and infused with a firmness that seemed to tether him to reality,

"I'm with you on this—all the way through." Her gaze locked onto his, unwavering. "We'll clear your name together."

Her promise hung in the air like a lifeline, an unspoken oath between two souls bound by shared history and now, a common purpose. The trust that had burgeoned over years of friendship was their foundation, and it was stronger than the concrete walls that surrounded them.

Chris drew in a deep breath, the kind that seemed to reach down into the depths of his despair and scoop out a measure of strength. He felt his hands steadying as he carefully set down the picture frame, the glass cool against his fingers. With a swipe of his sleeve, he cleared the remnants of tears from his cheeks. His grief was still there, raw and aching, but it was now laced with something fiercer: resolve.

"Thanks, Jenny," Chris's voice was rough with emotion, yet the quiver that had once been there had faded. "Angie... she believed in justice. I owe it to her to find it." His words were a whisper, yet they carried the weight of his newfound determination.

He rose from the couch, feeling the familiar comfort of action replacing the numbness of sorrow. There was work to be done, a truth to unearth, and for Angie's sake, he would dig until his hands were raw if that's what it took.

Jenny rose from her seat, the fabric of the couch whispering as she moved. Her hand lingered on Chris's shoulder, a silent testament to her steadfast presence. "Let's start sorting through what we have," she suggested, her voice a gentle nudge against the inertia of his grief.

"Any documents, pictures, anything that could point us in the right direction. We build our case from the ground up, piece by piece." Her words were uncomplicated, but they carved a path through the haze of Chris's sorrow.

He looked up at her, and it was as if someone had lifted the blinds just a crack, allowing a sliver of light to seep into the dim room. The earnestness in Jenny's eyes sparked something within him, a tiny flare of hope that he clung to desperately.

"Jenny," Chris found his voice, steadier now, colored with gratitude. "I can't thank you enough. With you here... I think I can actually do this." His lips twitched into a half-smile, a pale echo of his usual optimism but significant all the same.

"Angie deserves justice," he continued, the strength in his words building like the crescendo of a song he'd long forgotten. "And I'm not about to let her down. Not now, not ever." It was a promise, spoken aloud not just for Jenny or himself but for the very essence of Angie that seemed to linger in the air between them.

"Then let's get to it," Jenny said, her tone imbued with a resolve that matched his own. She didn't move her hand from his shoulder, instead giving it a reassuring squeeze, as if to physically impart the courage he needed to face the path ahead.

Together, they stood, two friends united by purpose, ready to step into the fray. Their journey had just begun, and though the road would be fraught with shadows and doubt, the first glimmer of dawn was on their horizon.

Chris rose first, his spine straightening as if each vertebra were infused with the steel of his resolve. Jenny's presence beside him was like a beacon, guiding him out of the shadows that had settled in the corners of the dimly lit living room. They didn't glance back at the memories enveloping the space; their focus was on the here and now—the immediate quest for truth lay ahead.

They crossed the threshold into the hallway, their footsteps in unison, echoing lightly against the bare walls. The door to Chris's bedroom loomed ahead, an unassuming barrier to the trove of documents and mementos that could very well hold the key to unraveling Angie's untimely demise.

"Okay," Chris said as he pushed open the door with more force than necessary, "we need to find anything that... that someone might have missed." His voice was firm, almost clinical, as if he were a detective scouring the scene for the first time.

Jenny nodded, her eyes scanning the room with analytical precision. "Receipts, photos, emails—anything unusual could be a lead. We know Angie, her habits. If something feels off, it's because it probably is."

"Right." Chris moved toward his desk, cluttered with papers and various gadgets. He began sifting through the pile methodically. "What about her friends? I mean, aside from us. Anyone who might have noticed something... someone acting strange around her?"

"Could be worth talking to them," Jenny agreed, pulling open drawers and peering inside. Her hands were steady, her movements deliberate. "We'll make a list. Get statements if we can. People remember more than they think they do."

"Especially when something doesn't sit right," Chris added, thumbing through a stack of mail. "Angie was... she was good at reading people. If someone made her uneasy..."

"Then she would've told someone," Jenny finished, her tone soft but edged with certainty. "We just have to hope they'll speak up now."

Chris looked over at Jenny, his eyes conveying a silent thanks. Their partnership in this search was not just practical—it was a lifeline in a sea of questions and doubt.

"Hey," Jenny said, breaking into his thoughts, "we're doing the right thing. Following this through, no matter where it leads." She spoke with a kind of gentle fierceness, an undercurrent of passion beneath the calm surface.

"Yeah," Chris replied, his voice barely above a whisper, yet laden with newfound determination. "For Angie."

The room, once stagnant with the weight of Chris's mourning, now buzzed with the kinetic energy of two friends on a mission. They filled it with their purpose, their shared conviction that justice was within grasp—if only they dared to reach for it.

Chris turned the key, locking the door behind them with a decisive click that seemed to echo down the narrow hallway of the apartment complex. The dim light from the overhead bulbs cast a wan glow over their determined faces as they strode toward the exit. In the pockets of his worn jacket, Chris clutched the crumpled list of names and places, each one a thread in the tangled web of Angie's last days.

"Alright," Jenny said, her voice a low hum against the buzz of the city that awaited them outside. "First stop, Angie's workplace. Someone there must've noticed if things were off."

"Agreed." Chris's reply was terse, his mind already racing ahead to the conversations they would need to have, the careful dance around suspicions and memories.

The building's front door creaked open, surrendering them to the cacophony of the city's heartbeat—the distant wail of sirens, the rhythmic thumping of bass from a passing car, the melodic chatter of people on the move. It all blended into a symphony of life that Angie would never be a part of again.

Chris paused for just a moment, looking back at the sturdy brick facade of the place he had called home. It felt like stepping off a ledge, leaving the sanctuary of grief for the raw exposure of action. But he knew there was no turning back. Not when the truth lay hidden, obscured by shadows that only their dogged pursuit could dispel.

"Come on," Jenny urged, reading his hesitation but mistaking none of it for doubt. She reached out, her fingers brushing against his arm—a touch that grounded him, reminded him why they were doing this.

"Right." A deep breath filled his lungs, and as he let it out, it carried away the last remnants of his uncertainty.

They walked shoulder to shoulder, their shadows merging and stretching before them as the sun began its slow descent. The city, with its towering silhouettes and endless possibilities, loomed large. Yet, within it, there existed the answers they sought; Chris could feel it like an electric current under his skin.

"Justice for Angie," Jenny murmured, almost as if she had read his thoughts. Her eyes were two fierce points of resolve in her steady face.

"Justice for Angie," Chris echoed, the words solidifying his resolve. They crossed the threshold where the shaded interior of the building gave way to the golden hour's amber flood.

Chapter 3

Detective Marco Ramirez leaned over his desk, the lamp casting a pool of light over the scattered case files that told the tragic story of Angie Thompson's untimely demise. A mosaic of photos, scribbled notes, and timeworn witness statements sprawled before him like puzzle pieces waiting to be placed. His fingers paused on a crumpled page, the statement of a bystander who claimed to have seen Chris Matthews near the scene. With a furrowed brow, he adjusted his glasses, his eyes scanning for a detail he might've missed before.

The room was silent except for the rhythmic ticking of the wall clock, each second punctuating the gravity of the task at hand. The air felt heavy with the residue of caffeine and cold pizza from countless nights spent in search of elusive answers. Detective Ramirez exhaled slowly, his breath mingling with the dust motes dancing in the beam of the desk light.

He reached for the phone records with a deliberate motion, tracing the incoming and outgoing calls that painted a digital trail leading up to the night Angie was murdered. Each number was a potential clue, each timestamp a piece of the narrative he was desperate to understand. Chris's resilience and hope, traits well-known throughout the precinct, now stood in stark contrast with the evidence mounting against him.

"Come on, Ramirez," he muttered to himself, "there's got to be something here."

Shifting his focus, Detective Ramirez stood and approached the whiteboard that dominated one wall of his office. It was a canvas of facts and theories, a testament to his relentless pursuit of justice. He uncapped a marker with a decisive pop, its scent a familiar comfort amidst the chaos of the unsolved. Link by link, he began to draw lines that connected Chris's phone records to the locations of the witnesses, their testimonies forming a web of interactions that held the potential for revelation.

"Angles, Marco, find the angles," he coached himself, his voice barely above a whisper.

Each note he added to the board was a step toward deciphering the puzzle. Potential alibis, discrepancies in timelines, and snippets of conversations laid out in a visual representation of his thought process. Occasionally, he would step back, tilting his head as if viewing the scene from a different perspective could reveal a hidden truth.

Detective Ramirez knew his reputation hinged on cases like this – high-profile and fraught with public outcry. Yet, it was not the accolades that drove him; it was the solemn vow to seek justice for Angie and her family, and perhaps even for Chris if he were indeed innocent. His methods were unyielding, but the shadows of doubt sometimes crept in, urging him to look deeper, question more.

"Could Chris really have done this?" he pondered, tapping the marker against his chin. "Or is there more to this story?"

His gaze returned to the whiteboard, to the constellation of evidence that sprawled across its expanse. In the crosshairs of lines and scribbles, Detective Ramirez glimpsed the glimmers of a theory, fragile yet formidable in its infancy. With every connection made, the silhouette of the crime grew sharper, and his resolve to uncover the truth grew stronger.

Detective Ramirez clicked his pen, signaling the start of their ad-hoc summit. The room filled with the rustle of fabric as his colleagues took their seats around the cramped quarters, each carrying the burden of open files and furrowed brows.

"Alright, let's hear it," he said, cutting through the tension like a sharp blade. His eyes met each detective's in turn, urging them to dig deeper into the case that had already stolen too many nights from their lives.

One by one, they presented their fragments of the puzzle. A sighting here, an inconsistency there. Each piece was scrutinized under the collective gaze of the room, weighed for its worth in the balance of truth and speculation.

"Her phone records don't align with her last known whereabouts," Detective Lopez pointed out, tapping on the highlighted lines of a document. "There's a gap we can't fill."

"Then we find something to fill it with," Ramirez countered, his voice a low growl of determination. He strode to the whiteboard, marker in hand, and drew a circle around the time stamp in question. "We keep digging until the earth gives up its secrets."

The room nodded in agreement, some scribbling notes while others whispered theories amongst themselves. Ramirez watched the machine of minds at work, each cog turning over evidence, trying to find the path that would lead them to Angie's killer.

"Johnson, I want you back at the crime scene. Anything could have been missed. Take Simmons with you," Ramirez ordered, dispatching his detectives with firm precision. "Lopez, cross-reference those phone records again. Look for any towers that might've been pinged out of order."

"Got it, boss," Lopez replied, already flipping through pages to revisit the data.

"Martinez, you're with me. We're going to comb through every frame of that surveillance footage again." Ramirez knew the devil lay in the details, and he'd be damned if he let it slip through their fingers.

"Understood," Martinez responded, a steely edge to her voice that mirrored Ramirez's own resolve.

"Remember," Detective Ramirez continued, his eyes sweeping across the faces of his team, "every second counts. Chris's alibi hinges on minute details, and so does our case."

"Sure thing, Ramirez," Johnson piped up, his youthful energy a stark contrast to the grizzled tenacity of his superior. "Detail is the name of the game."

"Exactly. And remember, we're not just looking for evidence against Chris," Ramirez added, his tone taking on the weight of his experience. "We're looking for the truth, no matter where it leads us."

With tasks assigned and motivation clear, the detectives dispersed, a renewed sense of purpose propelling them forward. The air in the room felt charged now, buzzing with potential leads and the silent promise of justice that hung in the balance.

Ramirez watched them go, each step a march toward redemption or revelation. They were close, he could feel it in his bones. But in this search for clarity, he knew the waters of truth would be muddied by the flaws inherent in their system—the flaws he fought against every day.

As the door closed behind the last detective, Ramirez turned back to the whiteboard, his steady hand adding another line, another connection. This was more than a case; it was a testament to their resolve, a challenge to their skill, and a quest for a peace that seemed ever elusive.

Detective Ramirez hunched over the phone, his finger tracing down a list of names as he dialed each number with methodical precision. The clock on the wall ticked away the seconds, but time seemed to stand still in the cramped office, swallowed by the gravity of Angie's murder case.

"Hello, this is Detective Ramirez from the 5th precinct," he intoned into the receiver, voice steady and professional. "I'm calling about the Angie Thompson case. Your name came up as someone who might have valuable information."

His pen danced across a notepad as he spoke, bullet points of questions lined up like soldiers ready for battle. Each query was crafted to peel back layers of alibis and dig for the hidden truths that lay beneath casual encounters and offhand remarks. He knew the devil was in the details, and he was determined to find it.

"Can you come in tomorrow at 10 AM? We need to talk face-to-face," Ramirez said, softening his tone to encourage cooperation. He listened intently to the responses, an occasional "Mhm" or "Understood" punctuating the conversation. By the end of the hour, he had filled his schedule with interviews.

He hung up the phone and stood, stretching out the stiffness that clung to his muscles from hours of sitting. Turning to the whiteboard that dominated one wall of his office, he uncapped a marker and began to write. Names in black ink, times in red, all organized in neat columns that reflected the inner workings of his mind. Angie Thompson at the top, her name underscored twice—a stark reminder of why they were all here.

"Let's see if any of you can lead us to Chris," he muttered, stepping back to survey his work. There was a rhythm to the chaos now, a sense of purpose that turned random facts into the potential for revelation.

With each name added, the picture became clearer, yet more complex. He could almost hear the witnesses speaking, their voices weaving together to form the narrative he sought so desperately to understand. For Angie. For justice. And in a way, for himself—to prove that despite the system's imperfections, perseverance could still uncover the truth.

Ramirez took a final moment to review his handiwork, then nodded once, satisfied. It was time to prepare for the interviews, to harness the threads of evidence and weave them into a tapestry of conviction. He'd start fresh in the morning, with a clear head and relentless resolve, because every detail mattered. Every witness could be the key.

"Tomorrow," he whispered to the silent room, a solemn vow hanging in the air. "Tomorrow we get closer."

Detective Marco Ramirez sat motionless in the dim glow of the monitor, the flickering images casting ghostly shadows across his determined face. Hours had morphed into what seemed like days as he combed through the grainy surveillance footage. There, in a corner of the frame, something caught his eye—a figure that moved with furtive urgency. He leaned closer, squinting, and reached for the control to rewind.

"Come on," he urged under his breath, his finger hovering over the pause button. "Show me your face."

The footage stuttered back to life, and Ramirez's heart raced as the figure approached the area where Angie's body was found. But just as the person came into clearer view, they glanced away, their features obscured by a hood. His gut clenched with frustration—so close to a breakthrough, yet still veiled in mystery.

"Dammit!" he slammed his fist against the desk, sending a pen skittering across the cluttered surface.

Withdrawing from the screen, Ramirez rubbed his weary eyes, feeling the weight of every unsolved case pressing down on him. In the silence of the room, he let his thoughts drift to Angie, her vibrant life cut short, her laughter silenced. She had been so full of life, a beacon to those who knew her. Now all that remained were echoes in the memories of her loved ones and the haunting questions left unanswered.

"Angie," he whispered, his voice tinged with a mix of resolve and remorse. "I'm going to find out who did this to you."

As he stood up to stretch his legs, his gaze fell upon the whiteboard filled with witness names—each a lifeline, a chance to dive deeper into the abyss and emerge with the truth. The thought of Angie's family, their grief a silent plea for closure, ignited a flame within him.

"Justice," he said, pulling on the threadbare edges of his determination. It wasn't just about solving a case; it was about restoring balance, about giving a voice to the silenced. He straightened his shoulders, feeling the mantle of his duty wrap tightly around him.

"Every piece matters," he reminded himself, glancing back at the frozen image on the screen. "Every moment captured here is a step toward the truth."

He settled back into his chair, the resolve in his veins blending with the caffeine that kept him anchored to the task. With a steady hand, he resumed the painstaking process of examining the footage, each frame a potential key to unlocking the shadowed past and bringing Angie's killer into the light.

The ring of the phone shattered the silence in Detective Ramirez's office. He snatched it up on the third ring, his heart hammering against his ribcage.

"Ramirez," he barked into the receiver, his voice bristling with impatience.

"Detective, it's Dr. Chen from forensics." The voice on the other end was measured, even, but Ramirez could detect a note of urgency that hadn't been there before.

"Talk to me, Doc. What do you have?"

"We've made some headway on the DNA analysis. There's a potential match. It's preliminary, but—"

"Potential?" Ramirez interrupted, his pulse quickening. The word hung in the air like a charged promise, and he leaned forward, elbows on the desk, gripping the phone like a lifeline.

"Yes, I need you to be cautious with this information, but it's promising. We're running it through CODIS now for confirmation."

"Keep me posted," Ramirez said, the gears in his mind already turning. "I don't have to tell you how big this is."

"Understood, Detective. You'll be the first to know once we confirm."

Ramirez ended the call and stood up so swiftly his chair rolled back and hit the wall with a thud. The fluorescent lights above glared down at him as he paced the cramped confines of his office. This was the breakthrough they needed, the flicker of light in the dark they'd been searching for. He stopped pacing, his gaze falling on the whiteboard. Angie's face flashed in his mind, her story urging him on.

Without wasting another second, he grabbed his jacket and headed for the district attorney's office. His shoes echoed in the empty hallway, each step a drumbeat of determination. When he arrived, he didn't bother with pleasantries.

"Chris might be our guy," Ramirez stated flatly, laying out the evidence in front of the district attorney—a woman as stern as she was sharp-minded.

"DNA match?" she asked, her eyebrows arching in professional curiosity.

"Potentially. We need to move fast, get a search warrant for his place. If he's our perp, who knows what else he's capable of?"

"Bring me something solid, Ramirez, and I'll push it through."

"Solid is my middle name," he replied, though his insides churned with the familiar frustration of bureaucracy. He knew every second counted, yet the law demanded its due process.

"Your dedication is your best and worst trait," the DA remarked with a wry smile. "Just remember, we need more than just dedication to convict someone."

"Trust me," Ramirez said, his eyes reflecting a mix of steely resolve and the weight of countless cases past. "I've got more than enough fire in me to turn over every rock until justice is served."

"Then go," she urged, her tone laced with the gravity of their shared mission. "Get that warrant. And Ramirez? Make damn sure we nail this bastard to the wall."

"Count on it," he said and turned on his heel, already mentally preparing for the next phase of the hunt. Angie deserved that much, and he would stop at nothing to deliver it.

The first light of dawn crept over the horizon as Detective Ramirez checked his watch, a sense of urgency quickening his pulse. He stood in the muted glow of the streetlights, surrounded by the hushed tones and shuffling footsteps of his assembled team. They were a tableau of determination, faces set with purpose beneath the brims of their caps.

"Alright, listen up," Ramirez whispered, his voice low but carrying. "We've got one shot at this. We get in, we search, we find what we're looking for. Remember, it's not just about evidence—it's about giving Angie's family some peace."

He eyed each officer and detective, their faces illuminated by the soft blue light of predawn. They nodded, their expressions mirroring his own resolve. Each one grasped the gravity of the task ahead, the silent promise they made to Angie and themselves.

"Gear up," he instructed, motioning towards the unmarked vans parked discreetly down the block. They complied with practiced efficiency, pulling on gloves and checking flashlights, each movement precise and deliberate.

Ramirez himself felt the familiar weight of the bulletproof vest as he secured it around his torso. The Kevlar hugged his frame—a shield against danger, a reminder of the risks. His fingers brushed over the service pistol at his hip, a testament to the grim possibilities of their profession.

"Time to move," he said, his tone leaving no room for hesitation. He led the way, his steps confident despite the flutter of anticipation in his stomach. The team followed in silence, a shadow moving in unison towards the suspect's nondescript residence.

The door loomed before them, an ordinary barrier that held the potential for extraordinary revelations. Ramirez gave the signal, and without a sound, the lock yielded to their practiced entry. Inside, the house was still and dark, the air thick with the scent of stale cigarettes and neglect.

"Split up. Document everything," Ramirez ordered, his eyes scanning the dim interior. The team dispersed, their movements synchronized and methodical as they combed through each room.

Ramirez's gaze was sharp, dissecting the space around him. He moved through the living room, running gloved fingers along dusty surfaces, looking for anything out of place. His instincts, honed by years on the force, buzzed softly at the back of his mind.

In the bedroom, he paused, noting a stack of papers on a nightstand. Carefully, he flipped through them, seeking a hint, a clue—anything that might connect the dots they'd so painstakingly laid out. His heart thumped louder in his chest with each page turned.

"Detective," called a voice from the other room, steady yet laced with the tension that gripped them all. "You might want to see this."

Ramirez's boots left muffled thuds on the carpet as he crossed the threshold into the adjacent room. There, a junior detective held up a small, clear evidence bag containing an item too familiar to be coincidental. It was a piece of jewelry, delicate and glinting under the beam of a flashlight—a necklace that Angie had often worn, a signature piece that had been missing since the night she was taken from them.

"Good work," Ramirez murmured, his words barely audible as a surge of vindication washed over him. This was it—the breakthrough they needed. The room seemed to contract around them, every breath, every heartbeat amplified in the newfound significance of their discovery.

The team continued to scour the residence, each new piece of evidence cataloged with meticulous care. Ramirez watched, his mind already racing ahead to the implications, to the courtroom where justice would play its hand.

As the sun climbed higher, casting long shadows across the floorboards, the house gave up its secrets, one by one. And with each revelation, Angie's voice seemed to echo through the halls, urging them closer to the truth, to the moment when the gavel would fall and her story would finally be told.

Detective Ramirez stood in the center of a room that felt charged with silent accusations. The air hung heavy, pregnant with the scent of dust and old secrets. He watched as his team moved through the suspect's residence like ghosts searching for a haunting truth. They sifted through drawers, lifted couch cushions, and examined every nook with thorough eyes, their gloves whispering against surfaces.

"Check behind those paintings," Ramirez instructed, pointing to a cluster of frames on the wall. His voice was calm but carried an undercurrent of urgency. Each officer nodded, understanding the gravity of their task. There was a collective sense of purpose that bound them together—a silent vow to unearth the reality of Angie's final night.

The sound of paper rustling drew Ramirez's attention to an officer holding a stack of old photographs. "Sir, there's a whole box of these," the officer said, indicating a cardboard container tucked away beneath a side table. "Looks like they go back years."

"Any with Angie?" Ramirez asked, stepping closer.

"Several, yeah." The officer handed him a photo where a younger Angie laughed, her eyes reflecting a spark that seemed eternal. Ramirez's heart clenched at the sight, the vibrant life in her expression now just a ghostly imprint on glossy paper.

"Keep them," he said, handing the photo back. "They could show a pattern."

As the search continued, each piece of potential evidence was sealed and tagged, their futures as courtroom exhibits already imagined by the meticulous minds gathering them. Detective Ramirez took a moment to glance out the window, noting how the neighborhood looked normal, undisturbed, oblivious to the shattered lives within its midst.

A murmur from another room pulled him back, an officer calling out, "Detective, you need to see this."

He entered to find a small USB drive being slipped into another bag, the data it held now a silent witness awaiting its turn to speak. Ramirez nodded acknowledgment, his mind already constructing the narrative it might reveal.

Finally, after what seemed like hours of methodical collection and cataloging, the house fell quiet. The officers gathered in the living room, their faces etched with fatigue but eyes still burning with resolve.

"Good work, everyone," Ramirez said, his voice steady, though his insides churned with anticipation. "Let's get everything back to the lab. We've got a long night ahead."

The officers began to file out, each carrying pieces of a puzzle they hoped would soon be complete. Detective Ramirez lingered for a moment longer, taking in the scene. Then, with a slow exhale, he turned off the lights and closed the door behind him.

Outside, he paused on the sidewalk, his gaze lifting to the sky where the first stars of evening were beginning to twinkle. For Angie, he thought, for justice—this is only the beginning.

"Ramirez, we ready to roll out?" an officer asked, approaching with the last of the equipment.

"Let's move," he replied, stepping toward the fleet of vehicles waiting to take them back to the precinct. As he settled into the front seat of his car, Detective Ramirez allowed himself a small smile. One step closer, he mused. One step closer to justice for Angie Thompson.

Chapter 4

The metallic click of the handcuffs echoed off the bare walls as Chris Matthews was ushered into the stark, windowless interrogation room. Detective Marco Ramirez's grip on Chris's arm was firm but not harsh, a silent reminder that escape wasn't an option. The door shut behind them with a definitive thud, severing Chris from the outside world and enveloping him in a cloak of tension.

"Have a seat," Ramirez said, his voice a low rumble that filled the small space.

Chris obliged, the chair's cold, unyielding surface pressing against his back. He watched as Ramirez moved to the opposite side of the table. The detective embodied the very essence of authority, his broad shoulders squared and his stance solid. His gray hair, though sparse, seemed to underscore his experience rather than hint at weakness.

Ramirez leaned forward, elbows resting on the table, fingers laced together. His eyes, sharp and discerning, fixed on Chris, studying him like a puzzle to be solved. The overhead light cast shadows over Ramirez's furrowed brow, deepening the stern expression etched on his face.

Chris felt the weight of those eyes and fought to keep his own steady. He knew his innocence, yet the detective's authoritative presence stirred a flicker of doubt within him. It was as if Ramirez could see through to every thought, every fear that Chris harbored.

"Chris Matthews," Ramirez began, his tone even but loaded with an unspoken promise of the grilling to come, "you know why you're here."

Chris's hands tensed on his lap, his heart pounding a rhythm of anxiety. This was it—the moment his resilience would be tested against the seasoned detective's resolve.

"Would you like some water, Chris?" Detective Ramirez's voice was unexpectedly soft, almost friendly, as he pushed a plastic cup across the table.

"Sure," Chris replied, his throat feeling parched all of a sudden. He reached for the cup, grateful for the momentary distraction from the tension that had been building since he entered the room. There was a strange comfort in the mundane act of sipping water.

"Long day, huh?" Ramirez continued, his tone casual, as if they were just two acquaintances catching up. "I get it. These fluorescent lights don't do anyone any favors."

Chris managed a half-smile, taking another sip. The detective's demeanor disarmed him, and for a fleeting second, Chris let himself believe that maybe this wouldn't be as harrowing as he had feared.

Then something changed.

Ramirez's face hardened, his once warm eyes turning into scrutinizing slits. "It's interesting, though, how these 'long days' seem to coincide with nights when certain events unfold. Like the night Angie died."

"Angie?" Chris echoed, confusion lacing his words. He tried to maintain his composure, but the mention of her name sent a jolt through him.

"Angie Collins," Ramirez clarified, his voice no longer carrying that friendly lilt. "Young girl, full of life—until someone decided to end it."

"I—I don't know what you're talking about," Chris stammered, the false sense of security shattering around him.

"Really?" The detective leaned in closer, his gaze unwavering. "Because we found your fingerprints in her apartment. And neighbors say they saw someone matching your description in the area that night."

"But I was at work," Chris protested. His heart raced as he realized the gravity of the implication. "You can check with my boss. I didn't even know Angie."

"Yet somehow, your prints are there." Ramirez tapped the file in front of him, the sound echoing ominously. "It's circumstantial, sure. But it's compelling."

Chris's mind raced, his innocence fighting against the web of accusations that Ramirez spun. He knew his hands had never touched the walls of Angie's home, yet here he was, cornered by evidence he couldn't explain.

"Look, I don't know why my prints would be there," Chris insisted, his voice betraying a tremor of uncertainty. "But I didn't hurt anyone. I swear."

"Swear all you like," Ramirez said, his tone now sharp as broken glass. "But someone took Angie's future away. And right now, Chris, all signs point to you."

The room felt colder, the air thinner. Chris's hope was being suffocated by the pressure of an accusation that seemed to grow heavier with each word the detective spoke.

The steel chair scraped against the linoleum as Chris shifted, a cacophony in the sterile silence of the interrogation room. Detective Ramirez loomed across the table, his presence like a storm cloud ready to burst.

"Chris, think about it," Ramirez coaxed, his voice a low rumble. "A young woman's gone, and you're caught up in this mess. I know it's hard, but we can sort this out quickly."

"I've told you everything," Chris replied, his throat tight, the words barely squeezing out. Confusion swirled within him, dark and disorienting. How had his life tangled so suddenly with Angie's death?

"Let's not dance around, huh?" Ramirez leaned in, elbows on the table, his eyes intent on Chris. "You give me something solid, something to go on, and maybe things get easier for you."

"Immunity?" Chris asked, the word foreign on his tongue.

"Cooperate, show remorse—it goes a long way," the detective offered, his voice a siren song promising a way out. The fluorescent lights hummed above, casting harsh shadows on Ramirez's face, deepening the lines etched by years of interrogations.

"Remorse for something I didn't do?" Chris's heart pounded against his ribcage, the sound threatening to drown out reason. "That doesn't seem right."

"Right or not, it's how the game is played," Ramirez said, pushing forward a folder thick with implications. "And right now, you're the one in the hot seat."

"Game?" Chris echoed, the word bitter. His palms felt clammy, his fingers clenching into fists. This was no game to him; it was his life spiraling out of control.

"Chris," Ramirez continued, relentless. "I'm trying to help you here, but you need to meet me halfway. Give me something to work with, and I can make the rest go away."

"Make the rest go away?" Chris's voice cracked, and he hated himself for it. He searched Ramirez's face for some sign of compassion, some hint that this nightmare could be just a terrible mistake.

"Listen to me, son," Ramirez said, his tone shifting, a note of urgency threading through the firmness. "Confess, and we can end this today. You'll see the outside again, breathe fresh air. That's more than Angie can say."

"End this today?" Chris repeated, the walls feeling closer, the air thicker. "But ending it isn't the same as clearing my name. I want the truth, not an easy out."

"Truth is a luxury," Ramirez countered, his eyes never wavering. "In here, it's about survival. Your choice, Chris."

Survival versus truth—a choice no innocent man should have to make. Chris swallowed hard, his resolve the only thing keeping him anchored in the sea of doubt that Ramirez had unleashed upon him.

Chris's shoulders hunched as if he could shield himself from the barrage of accusations. His mind raced, each thought a frantic sprinter in a maze with no exit. Ramirez's words echoed in his head: "Survival" and "truth" seemed to morph into abstract concepts rather than tangible paths he could choose between.

A bead of sweat trailed down Chris's temple, despite the chill in the room. He felt the weight of Detective Ramirez's gaze, heavy like a hand pressing down on his chest. His own heart thumped, a traitorous drumbeat that seemed all too willing to surrender to the rhythm set by Ramirez's persistent questioning.

"Think, Chris," Ramirez prodded, leaning back now, watching Chris squirm. "You're a smart kid. You know how this works. Help yourself."

Chris's thoughts tangled further. If he just said the words, just let out what Ramirez wanted to hear... would it really be an end to this madness? Would the whispered promises of freedom and immunity hold any water once they left Ramirez's lips?

He blinked rapidly, the fluorescent light above casting a harsh glare on everything it touched. The urge to confess, to blurt out a lie just to stop the relentless pursuit, clawed at him. It promised relief, a momentary cessation of this torment. But at what cost? A lifetime knowing he had buckled, that he had stained his own hands with falsehood when his heart knew he was innocent?

"Isn't a false confession better than a real sentence?" he pondered silently, the idea creeping up like a shadow at dusk. Yet, those same shadows whispered of deceit and injustice—of a life lived behind bars constructed not of iron but of lies.

Ramirez leaned forward again, his eyes searching. "It's your call, Chris. Only you can decide how long this goes on for."

Chris's breath hitched. Glimpses of his old life flickered in his mind—laughter, dreams, the feeling of being untethered to such grim realities. Could he trade his truth for a shot at reclaiming that past? Or would the lie consume whatever remained of the young man who still believed in justice?

"Is there even a place for truth here?" he wondered, his resolve wavering like a flame in the wind. Ramirez's unyielding stare bore into him, expecting, demanding.

"Time's ticking." The detective's voice cut through the silence, a reminder of the urgency of the choice laid before him.

Chris drew in a shuddering breath, his internal conflict raging as fiercely as a storm against his spirit. To confess or to cling to the truth—he stood at the crossroads of his destiny, every option fraught with its own peril.

Chris straightened his back, the coolness of the metal chair against his skin grounding him to the reality of the interrogation room. Detective Ramirez's gaze was like a weight, heavy with expectation. The clock on the wall ticked steadily, marking time as if each second were a step closer to an inevitable fall.

"I didn't do it," Chris said, his voice steady despite the turmoil within. "I've told you everything I know. Angie was my friend."

Ramirez's jaw clenched at the denial, his patience thinning like ice under a relentless sun. He leaned in, the distance between them shrinking until Chris could count the creases etched into the detective's weather-worn face.

"Friends don't lie for each other when one of them ends up dead, Chris." The words were deliberate, edged with accusation.

"Nor do they make up stories to imprison the innocent," Chris retorted, the resilience that wove through his being pulling taut, refusing to snap under pressure.

A muscle twitched in Ramirez's cheek, signaling the escalation of his frustration. He slapped a photograph onto the table, the image of Angie smiling up at them both—a haunting reminder of what was lost.

"Explain this!" Ramirez demanded, pointing to a figure in the background. "Isn't that you at the party where she was last seen alive?"

Chris leaned forward, eyes flicking over the photo. It was him, alright, but it meant nothing sinister. "Yes, and there were dozens of us there. Being somewhere doesn't mean I'm involved in what happened after."

"Convenient," Ramirez grunted, his voice laced with skepticism. He pushed back from the table, his chair scraping loudly against the floor. Standing, he towered over Chris, casting a shadow that felt as though it sought to engulf the truth itself.

"Every piece of circumstantial evidence adds up, kid. The sooner you come clean, the easier it'll be for everyone."

"Except for me," Chris shot back, unwilling to bend. "And the real perpetrator who's still out there. I won't confess to something I didn't do."

For a moment, the room stilled, the only sound the relentless ticking. Then Ramirez loomed closer, his breath hot with impatience. "Think hard about your next move, Chris. This is your life we're talking about."

Chris met the detective's gaze, neither defiance nor fear in his eyes—only the clear certainty of his innocence. "Then let's make sure we get it right. Because I'm not the one you're looking for."

Detective Ramirez, faced with unwavering determination, felt the edges of his control fray. He slammed his palms down on the table, causing Chris to flinch, but he did not look away.

"Your stubbornness isn't going to save you," Ramirez growled.

"Neither will a false confession," Chris replied, the weight of justice holding his words firm. "I want the truth, even if it's harder to find."

Hours had trickled by, each minute stretching out like a thread fraying at the edges. The room felt both claustrophobic and impossibly vast, walls closing in yet echoing back every word as if mocking Chris's steadfastness. His body slouched forward, the sharp lines of resilience that once defined his posture now softened into curves of exhaustion. Sweat beaded on his brow, his hands clenched and unclenched beneath the table, seeking a comfort they couldn't find.

"Chris," Detective Ramirez began again, his voice a grating loop of insinuation, "we can keep going around in circles, or you can end this now."

The interrogation had drained Chris's spirit, siphoning away the bright optimism that once fueled his resolve. The flicker in his eye had dimmed, not extinguished but shadowed by the relentless onslaught of accusations. His responses, once delivered with the clear ring of truth, now stumbled from his lips, heavy and uncertain. He could feel the fabric of his reality tearing, threads of doubt weaving into his thoughts.

"Look at you," Ramirez continued, leaning in closer, his eyes unyielding. "You're a wreck, kid. How much longer do you think you can hold out?"

Chris's head pounded with a rhythm that matched the ticking clock on the wall—a metronome to his faltering heart. His dreams, the wide city skylines of his ambition, seemed like distant memories, obscured by the oppressive cloud of the present. He thought of his family, their faces contorted with worry, and the crushing weight of what his silence would mean for them.

Ramirez saw the change, the momentary lapses in Chris's armor. The detective pounced with the finesse of a seasoned interrogator, words laced with false promise. "Confess, and all this goes away. It's your word against a mountain of evidence that's only going to grow. Make it easier on yourself."

And there it was—the fulcrum upon which Chris's fate teetered. To confess would be to betray everything he stood for, every principle he believed in. Yet the allure of an end to this torment was a siren's call, tempting in its sweet poison. Desperation clawed at him, a beast with unforgiving talons.

"I... I don't..." Chris's voice trailed off, his throat tight, a noose of words left unsaid.

"Say it, Chris," Ramirez urged, his tone almost gentle now, coaxing the lie from the depths of Chris's shattered resolve.

A tear escaped, tracing a path down Chris's cheek as he surrendered to the inescapable pressure, his voice trembling with uncertainty and regret. "I did it. I killed Angie." The words fell into the stale air of the interrogation room, each syllable a betrayal to his soul.

Detective Ramirez's expression hardened, victory and disappointment mingling in his eyes. He pushed back from the table, his chair scraping once more against the floor as he stood up to leave the room.

"Finally," he said, though the triumph in his voice was hollow.

Chris sagged against the cold, hard surface of the table, his confession hanging between them—an ugly tapestry woven from the threads of coercion. The reader was left with a sense of injustice, the weight of the situation pressing down like the final page of a story that should have read differently, a narrative hijacked by the flaws of a system that should have protected the innocent.

Chapter 5

Chris Matthews sat rigid on the wooden bench, a stark contrast to the fluid sea of dark robes and hushed conversations that surrounded him in the courtroom. His fingers tapped an anxious rhythm against his thigh, the only outward sign of the turmoil churning within him. The room's stale air seemed thick with anticipation, and despite the coolness, beads of sweat gathered at the base of his neck.

He had always believed in justice, in fairness—concepts now hanging in the balance, waiting to be tipped by the scales of law. His eyes, a window to the resilience he carried like a shield, darted across the room, seeking something familiar, something grounding amidst the foreign territory of legalese and judgment.

Laura Simmons rose from her seat beside him, a pillar of determination clad in the armor of a tailored suit. She approached the podium with purpose, her red hair a flame of defiance against the sterility of the courtroom. Chris watched as she squared her shoulders, ready to face the sea of skepticism that awaited her words.

"Your Honor, ladies and gentlemen of the jury," Laura began, her voice steady and clear. "Today we are here to discuss the case against Chris Matthews, a case built on a foundation as insubstantial as shadows at dusk."

She paused, allowing her statement to linger in the minds of those present, her blue eyes briefly locking with each juror as if imparting a sliver of unspoken understanding. "The prosecution would have you believe that Mr. Matthews is guilty beyond a reasonable doubt," she continued, "yet as we will demonstrate, the evidence—or rather, the lack thereof—tells a different story."

Chris felt a flicker of hope spark within him as Laura spoke, her words painting a picture of truth amid the murkiness of accusation. She moved with conviction, highlighting not what was present but what was missing—a concrete link to tie Chris to the crime he stood accused of.

"Throughout this trial, I urge you to remember that justice is not served by filling gaps with conjecture or by accepting questionable testimony as fact," Laura implored, her gaze unwavering, her voice imbued with the weight of every wrongfully accused soul she'd ever defended. "We must demand more; we owe it to the very principles upon which our legal system stands."

Chris watched her, his heart still racing, but now with a thread of optimism weaving through the anxiety. Laura's belief in him, in the truth, was palpable—a beacon in a storm that threatened to engulf his very future. And for a brief moment, in the hush that fell upon the courtroom after Laura's final words, Chris allowed himself to believe that maybe, just maybe, justice might prevail.

The prosecutor, a man with a hawkish nose and eyes that seemed to miss nothing, rose from his seat like a specter of doom. His voice filled the room, cold and calculating as he began to weave a damning narrative around Chris. "Ladies and gentlemen of the jury," he intoned, "the evidence will show that Chris Matthews confessed to the crime."

Chris's hands clenched under the table, knuckles white. The so-called confession was nothing more than words wrenched from a frightened young man after hours of relentless questioning. It hung in the air between them, a ghostly accusation that whispered of guilt.

"Detective Harrison," the prosecutor called, beckoning the first witness with a practiced flick of his wrist.

The detective took the stand, his testimony a well-rehearsed script of certainty. He recounted the night of the interrogation, asserting the validity of the confession obtained. The prosecution painted a picture of a case closed, but the canvas was marred by the smudges of coercion.

Laura Simmons stood then, her posture rigid with purpose. She approached Detective Harrison with a predator's grace, ready to dismantle the illusion piece by piece. "Detective, you claim Mr.

Matthews willingly confessed after a brief conversation?" Her voice dripped skepticism, a clear challenge to the story spun before the jury.

"Yes, ma'am," the detective replied, though his eyes darted away for just an instant.

"Can you tell us exactly how long this 'brief conversation' lasted?" Laura's question was a scalpel, making the first incision into the heart of the prosecution's case.

"Nearly four hours," he admitted, and the courtroom stirred, the number hanging heavy in the air.

"Four hours," Laura echoed, letting it resonate. "And during this time, was my client provided with food, water, or breaks?"

"Standard procedure was followed," the detective hedged, but his confidence seemed to fray at the edges.

"Standard procedure," she repeated, turning to the jury with raised eyebrows. "No food, no water, isolated in a room, peppered with questions and accusations for hours on end. Is this what we call a willing confession, ladies and gentlemen? Or does it bear the mark of desperation?"

She paced slowly, giving the jury time to digest her words, to see the image of Chris not as a criminal, but as a victim of circumstance. Her gaze then snapped back to the detective. "Did Mr. Matthews ever ask for a lawyer during this interrogation?"

The detective shifted uncomfortably. "He... may have mentioned it."

"May have mentioned it," Laura pounced on the ambiguity. "Yet, somehow, in those four long hours, no legal counsel was provided. Interesting."

With each question, Laura chipped away at the foundation of the prosecution's case, revealing the cracks and inconsistencies hidden beneath their veneer of certainty. She returned to her seat, leaving behind a trail of doubt as palpable as the tension that now gripped the courtroom.

Chris watched as the jury absorbed Laura's words, their expressions clouded with thought. Hope flickered within him again, fanned by Laura's fiery defense. In that moment, the battle lines were drawn not just between guilt and innocence, but between truth and the shadows that sought to obscure it.

The courtroom's heavy air seemed to press down on Chris, who sat rigid in his seat, hands clasped together as if in silent prayer. His gaze occasionally flitted toward the gallery where Jenny Mitchell was perched on the edge of her seat, her knuckles white as she gripped the wooden bench. Alongside her were Chris's family and friends, their faces a mosaic of hope clashing with creeping fear. Each time the door creaked open or a lawyer shuffled their papers, their heads snapped up, eyes searching for some sign, any indication of which way the scales of justice would tip.

Jenny's foot tapped an anxious rhythm on the floor, a metronome to the beat of Chris's heart. She caught Chris's eye, offering him a tight smile that carried the weight of their shared past, a silent promise that she stood with him, come what may.

In contrast to the strained atmosphere surrounding Chris's supporters, the other side of the gallery buzzed like a hive disturbed. Curious onlookers craned their necks to whisper among themselves, speculating with the fervor of those unburdened by personal stakes. Reporters hunched over their notebooks, pens darting across paper, eager to capture every dramatic twist and turn. Their eyes gleamed with the prospect of a headline-grabbing story, indifferent to the human drama unfolding before them.

"Order in the court," boomed the bailiff's voice, cutting through the murmurs and bringing a sudden stillness to the room.

Chris swallowed hard, bracing himself for what was to come. He fixed his eyes ahead, his unwavering determination masking the whirlwind of emotions within. Jenny leaned forward, her resolve steeling her features as she prepared to witness the battle for Chris's future. The courtroom, once abuzz with anticipation, now awaited the next act in rapt silence.

The courtroom's heavy doors swung open as Laura Simmons stood, her posture erect with the confidence of a seasoned warrior entering battle. Her heels clicked against the wooden floor, commanding attention. "Your Honor," she began, her voice reverberating through the hushed chamber, "I call Mr. Alan Green to the stand."

Alan, a middle-aged man with kind eyes shadowed by the gravity of the occasion, took his place in the witness box. His hands were steady as he swore to tell the truth, but there was a tremor in his voice that spoke to the solemnity of his oath.

"Mr. Green," Laura addressed him, her tone even, "please recount for the court where you and Chris Matthews were on the evening of the murder."

"Chris and I were volunteering at the community center," Alan testified, his words painting a picture of a different scene—a place filled with laughter and camaraderie, far from any hint of crime. "We were setting up beds for the homeless shelter event. He didn't leave my sight the whole night."

Laura nodded, turning to face the jury, letting the implication of his statement sink in. "No further questions, Your Honor."

As Laura sat down, Judge Collins leaned forward slightly, his gaze moving between the witness and the jury, ensuring every word spoken was considered with due gravity. The lines on his face spoke of years spent weighing the scales of justice, his eyes sharp and discerning beneath the silver thatch of his hair.

"Does the prosecution wish to cross-examine?" Judge Collins asked, his voice neutral yet firm, embodying the impartiality expected of his position.

The prosecutor rose, their questions like barbs aimed at poking holes in Alan's testimony. But under Laura's watchful eye, Alan's account remained unshaken, a steadfast alibi in a sea of doubt.

"Thank you, Mr. Green. You may step down," the judge finally said after the cross-examination yielded no cracks in the defense's presentation.

"Your Honor," Laura continued, her next words carefully chosen, "I would like to present Exhibit A, time-stamped surveillance footage from the community center on the night in question."

The courtroom's air tightened as the video played, the grainy images showing Chris's figure, unmistakable even in the low resolution, engaged in the act of service, his back to the camera, his movements sure and purposeful.

"Let the record show Chris Matthews was not at the scene of the crime," Laura stated, her voice a beacon cutting through fog, guiding the jury toward the light of truth.

Judge Collins watched the footage intently, giving no sign of his thoughts as he observed the evidence, aware that each piece could tip the balance of a man's fate. He instructed the jury to consider the new evidence with the same focus he himself demonstrated.

"Is there anything further from the defense?" Judge Collins inquired once the video concluded, looking over to Laura with an expression that offered no clues to his own conclusions.

"Nothing further at this time, Your Honor," Laura replied, confident that her case had been made, her client's innocence underscored by the alibis and evidence she had laid bare before the court.

The judge gave a curt nod, indicating the proceedings would continue, and the courtroom exhaled a collective breath it hadn't realized it was holding. Chris looked on, hope mingling with the fear in his heart, as the wheels of justice slowly turned.

The courtroom was a silent battleground as Laura Simmons rose, the heels of her shoes clicking on the polished floor like the ticking of a clock counting down the final moments of deliberation. She squared her shoulders and locked eyes with the jury, twelve citizens upon whose judgement Chris's future teetered.

"Ladies and gentlemen of the jury," she began, her voice steady but laced with urgency. "You have seen the evidence presented before you. Or rather," she paused for emphasis, "the lack thereof."

Chris's heart hammered against his ribs, each beat a drum of hope as he watched Laura command the room. She moved with purpose, circling like a guardian around the core of her argument.

"Chris Matthews' innocence rests not just on what we have shown, but also on what the prosecution has failed to show. There is no fingerprint, no DNA, no unquestionable proof that ties Chris to this terrible act." Laura's hand swept through the air, dismissing the flimsy threads the prosecution had attempted to weave into a rope strong enough to hang.

"Remember, doubt is not a whisper; it is a shout," she continued, her voice rising. "And when justice calls, we must listen closely. We cannot convict a man on whispers. We must demand the roar of certainty."

As Laura took her seat, the prosecution stood, their stance rigid and faces set in stone. The lead prosecutor, Mr. Harlan, cleared his throat, his eyes sweeping across the jury like a lighthouse beam cutting through darkness.

"Make no mistake," Harlan's voice boomed, "a young life was brutally taken, and Chris Matthews confessed to being at that crime scene."

Chris felt a cold shiver run down his spine. Laura leaned forward, her blue eyes never leaving the jury, reminding them silently of the truth they'd been shown.

"Confessions can be... complicated," Harlan conceded, pacing slowly. "But we ask you to look at the context, the totality of evidence. It's easy to get caught up in technicalities, yet we must not lose sight of justice for the victim."

He stopped and turned to face them squarely, his hands resting on the railing, "Do not let clever words cloud your judgment. Remember the pain, the loss, the void left behind. Chris Matthews must be held accountable."

The tension in the room was palpable as Harlan concluded, his final words hanging heavy in the air. The spectators, the family, and friends—all were still, as if afraid to disturb the gravity of the moment.

Chris sat motionless, his fate now resting in the hands of others. He looked to Laura, her composed presence a silent fortress against the storm of accusations. In her gaze, Chris found a reflection of his own resilience, an unspoken vow that no matter the outcome, the fight for truth would persist.

The heavy door to the jury room closed with a definitive click, echoing in the cavernous courtroom. Chris's eyes followed the twelve men and women who held his future in their hands. He watched as they sat around the long table, stoic and silent, their brows furrowed in thought. They exchanged glances that spoke to the gravity of their task, their faces etched with the responsibility of deciding another person's fate. The clattering of the outside world faded into an oppressive hush, punctuated only by the occasional shuffle of paper as jurors reviewed notes from the trial.

Chris felt the wooden bench beneath him, hard and unyielding, much like the situation he found himself in. His fingers gripped the edge, knuckles whitening, as he attempted to still the tremor in his hands. He focused on taking deep breaths, each inhale a silent plea for calm, each exhale a release of mounting tension. Chris's dark hair fell slightly over his forehead, a stark contrast to the pallor of his skin that betrayed his inner turmoil.

Laura Simmons, his defense attorney, sat beside him, her posture straight but not rigid. She placed a reassuring hand on his shoulder, her touch grounding. "Remember, Chris, we've done everything we can," she said quietly, her voice a gentle anchor in the storm of uncertainty.

Chris nodded, swallowing the lump in his throat. "I know," he replied, his voice barely above a whisper. "It's just—waiting like this, it's..." Words failed him, lost in the sea of emotions that threatened to capsize his composure.

"Hope is not lost," Laura said firmly, her conviction a testament to her belief in his innocence. "You have to hold onto that."

He looked up at her, finding solace in her steady gaze. Her presence was a reminder of the fight they had fought together, a battle for truth amidst a maze of conjecture and doubt.

Outside the jury room, time seemed to slow, each tick of the clock stretching longer than the last. Chris could see Jenny Mitchell among his family and friends in the gallery, her fingers clasped tightly together, her expression a mirror of his own hope and fear. Their eyes met, and she offered a small, encouraging smile, a silent message of solidarity.

The jury room remained a fortress of deliberation, its occupants hidden from view, yet their presence loomed large in the mind of everyone within the courtroom. The air was thick with anticipation, and whispers rippled through the rows of seats as spectators and reporters alike speculated on the outcome.

Chris closed his eyes, allowing the sounds of the courtroom to wash over him. Each murmur, each creak of a chair, felt amplified in the silence of waiting. He pictured the skyline of the city where he grew up, the place where dreams were as numerous as the stars. He envisioned himself free once more, walking those familiar streets with a renewed purpose.

"Stay strong, Chris," Laura whispered, her words a lifeline in the momentary darkness. "Justice will find its way."

With his heart pounding a relentless rhythm, Chris opened his eyes and braced himself for the return of the jury, for the words that would either grant him freedom or steal it away. His future, once vast and unwritten, now hung in the balance, a story awaiting its final chapter.

The jury door creaked open. Every head in the courtroom turned, eyes tracing each juror as they entered, their steps slow and deliberate. The weight of what they carried was written plainly on their faces—a burden of responsibility that had etched lines of care into their brows.

Chris felt his breath catch in his throat. He watched them, trying to read their expressions, searching for a clue, a hint of mercy or condemnation. His heart raced, each beat a drum echoing against the walls of his chest.

Laura Simmons, her blue eyes revealing none of the turmoil she must have felt, placed a steady hand on Chris's shoulder. It was a silent message, an anchor in the storm of uncertainty.

"Will the foreperson please stand?" the judge's voice sliced through the room like a knife, crisp and authoritative. In those few words, the murmurs hushed, and the air grew dense with expectation.

A woman rose from the jury bench, her features set in a mask of solemn duty. She held a single piece of paper, which trembled ever so slightly in her grasp.

"Has the jury reached a verdict?" the judge asked, his tone neutral yet carrying the gravity of the moment.

"We have, Your Honor," came the foreperson's reply, her voice steady despite the visible shaking of her hands.

"Please read the verdict."

The foreperson's lips parted, and the courtroom leaned in collectively, holding its breath. "We find the defendant..."

Chris closed his eyes for just a second, a silent prayer escaping into the stillness.

"Guilty."

The word fell upon the room, reverberating off the walls, and for a moment, time seemed to freeze. Chris's hands unclasped, falling limp at his sides. The simple utterance of guilt, a mere syllable really, threatened to unravel the very fabric of his future.

Laura's grip tightened on Chris's shoulder, her presence a reminder that this battle was not fought alone. Though the word 'guilty' hung in the air like a specter, it was not the end. Not if she had anything to say about it.

From the gallery, Carol Thompson's resolve did not waver, though pain flashed across her eyes. Samuel Bennett, standing tall amidst the sea of spectators, allowed no change in his somber expression, but the clenching of his jaw spoke volumes.

In the oppressive silence that followed, the courtroom filled with the sound of hearts breaking and dreams deferred. Yet amidst the despair, a flicker of defiance remained—hope was down, perhaps, but not extinguished. The fight for justice, for truth, would go on.

The courtroom erupted, a cascade of gasps and cries as the word "guilty" echoed off the walls. Jenny Mitchell clutched her chest, tears streaming down her cheeks. She looked to Chris for something—reassurance, perhaps, or defiance—but he sat motionless, his face a mask of shock.

"Chris," she whispered, but her voice was lost in the clamor. The gallery was a storm of emotion; disbelief and sorrow mingled in the air like a bitter perfume. Family and friends held each other, their sobs punctuating the heavy silence that had settled over Chris.

His mother's face crumpled with grief, her hands covering her mouth as if to stifle the truth from spilling into reality. Her son, the boy who once chased dreams through city streets, now stood at the mercy of a flawed system, his spirit encased in the guilty verdict.

"Order!" The judge's voice sliced through the chaos, but it did little to stem the tide of despair that had washed over Chris's loved ones. Laura Simmons faced them, her eyes solemn. There was no victory in this room, only the residue of a fight yet to be finished.

Chris finally turned his head, his gaze drifting across the sea of faces. Each one mirrored the torment he felt inside—a shared agony, a collective injustice. The spark that once lit his eyes seemed dimmer now, but not extinguished. He had learned long ago that resilience was not just about standing tall but also about enduring when all else told you to break.

"Chris," a voice said again, firmer this time. He looked up to see Laura leaning toward him, her eyes searching his. "We'll appeal," she promised, her conviction a lifeline in the turbulent waters of his thoughts.

He nodded slowly, letting her words anchor him. For a moment, the courtroom, with its wood-paneled walls and stoic judge, faded away. It was just Chris, his family, friends, and the unyielding belief that the final chapter of his story remained unwritten. They would fight on, together, against the imperfections of a system that had failed them today.

"Justice," Chris murmured to himself, the word bitter on his tongue yet essential to his soul. It was a distant beacon now, but it was there, waiting to be reclaimed.

Chapter 6

The heavy steel door clanged shut behind Chris Matthews, its finality resonating through his bones. He shuffled forward in line, his hands cold and cuffed in front of him. Fear prickled at the back of his neck, a stark contrast to the resolve that steeled his jaw. As he stepped into the processing area, his heart hammered with the kind of uncertainty that comes when life tilts on an unfamiliar axis.

"Matthews," a guard barked, signaling him forward. The man's eyes, impassive and cool, skimmed over Chris as if he were just another number, another day's work. Chris's personal items—a wallet, a set of keys, a photo of his family—were swept away into a plastic bin with a dismissiveness that stung. They were replaced by a rough fabric uniform, the color of ash and indifference.

"Put these on," the guard instructed, his voice echoing off the high, unforgiving walls. Chris dressed quickly, the fabric scratching against his skin, the uniform hanging loosely from his average-built frame.

He emerged from the changing room into the belly of the prison. Here, the air was thick with the scent of bleach and despair. Fluorescent lights flickered overhead, casting a pallid glow on the concrete floors. The constant cacophony of metal doors slamming, guards shouting commands, and the undercurrent of inmates' murmurs created a symphony of intimidation.

Chris's breath misted in the chill of the sterile atmosphere. He could feel the weight of the guards' gazes upon him, their scrutiny as sharp as the barbed wire that crowned the prison walls. Every step he took echoed in the hollow space, a testament to the isolation that now enveloped him.

He paused for a moment, letting the scene etch itself into his memory—the coldness seeping into his very marrow, the way hope seemed to falter beneath the relentless noise. But Chris Matthews was not one to be easily broken. His eyes, dark and resolute, held onto the spark that had always driven him, the undying ember of optimism and justice that no prison could extinguish.

"Keep moving," a guard nudged him, and Chris obliged, his footsteps steady. Though everything familiar had been stripped away, leaving him exposed to the harsh reality of his new existence, his spirit remained unyielding. This was but the beginning of a journey—a test he was determined to endure, a truth he was bound to uncover.

Chris shuffled forward, the freshly issued rubber soles of his standard-issue shoes squeaking against the polished floor. The echo of his footsteps mingled with the distant clamor of inmates, a dissonant reminder that this concrete maze was now his reality. He passed rows of cell doors, each clanging shut with a finality that made his heart lurch. Eyes peered out from behind bars, sizing him up, some with indifference, others with a predatory calculation that sent shivers down his spine.

He swallowed hard, wrestling with the instinct to appear unfazed while his mind raced with strategies for survival. Chris knew he had to stay sharp, keep his wits about him, but nothing in his life before had prepared him for this. His youth spent in the city's bustle seemed a world away; here, there were new rules to learn, and the cost of ignorance could be dire.

"Step lively, Matthews," a gruff voice barked from behind him. One of the guards ushered him along, his baton tapping rhythmically against his thigh. Chris nodded, though the guard couldn't see the determination set in his jaw, the silent promise that he would not let this place break him.

As he turned a corner, a sudden commotion erupted—a flurry of shouts and curses as two inmates clashed. Muscle and sinew collided with a violence that was both shocking and banal in its setting. Guards swarmed in, shouting orders, their batons rising and falling with a practiced ease that spoke of routine. Chris felt a tightness in his chest, a mix of fear and anger at the injustice of it all. He forced himself to look away, to focus on the sliver of sky visible through a high window, reminding himself of the world beyond these walls.

The prison's daily rhythms were monotonous yet jarring. Every scheduled activity, from meals eaten in tense silence to the brief respite of yard time, was punctuated by the omnipresent guards' commands. "Lights out" was announced with the same authoritative tone as "Line up" or "Back to your cell." Privacy was an alien concept—every movement watched, every word overheard. Even in his bunk at night, Chris could feel the collective breaths of a hundred men, the stifling closeness of shared confinement.

Despite it all, Chris clung to his sense of self, his belief in his innocence. He'd replay the events leading to his conviction, finding holes in the narrative that was spun around him, fueling his resolve to fight. In the moments when despair threatened to take hold, he'd think of the skyline of his childhood city, the promise of tomorrow, and the truth that needed to come to light. He wasn't just serving time; he was biding it, waiting for the moment when justice would finally tip in his favor.

Chris shuffled into the prison yard, the crunch of gravel underfoot mingling with the cacophony of voices and the distant clatter of weights. He kept his gaze low, acutely aware of the predatory stares that traced his every step. The open sky above offered little solace; it was merely a reminder of the freedom he yearned for.

"Hey, kid." The voice cut through the noise, warm but edged with authority. Chris looked up to see a muscular man leaning against the wall, his arms crossed. "You're Matthews, ain't ya?"

Chris nodded, tensing as the man pushed off from the wall and approached him. This was Frank Turner, a name whispered throughout the cellblocks. Despite the scars and tattoos that marked his time here, his eyes held a flicker of something unexpected—kindness, perhaps?

"First days are the toughest," Frank said, falling into step beside Chris as they walked along the perimeter of the yard. "But you look like you got some fight in ya."

"Trying to," Chris admitted, the words feeling brittle in his throat.

"Listen," Frank continued, his voice dropping. "Stick close during mess and rec. Don't make debts, don't take favors. Keep your head down and your back covered."

"Thanks," Chris replied, his gratitude genuine but heavy with the weight of his new reality.

Over the following weeks, the two formed an unlikely camaraderie. They shared stories between the clang of iron bars and the piercing whistles signaling the end of yard time. Frank spoke of years spent within these walls, of regrets and lessons learned. Chris, in turn, talked about the life he'd left behind, the dreams that still burned bright despite the dampening effect of cold steel and concrete.

"Got a sister out there," Chris said one afternoon, passing Frank the basketball they'd been tossing back and forth. "She believes in me—believes I'll get out."

"Family's good," Frank grunted, taking a shot at the hoop. The ball bounced off the rim, and he caught it on the rebound. "Don't lose that hope."

In moments of quiet, they'd sit side by side on the metal benches, watching birds dart past the razor wire, sharing pieces of smuggled fruit or the rare luxury of a magazine article. It was in these small acts—a shared nod, a knowing look—that their friendship took root, growing stronger amid the harshness that surrounded them.

"Being in here... changes a man," Frank said one day, his eyes tracking a guard's baton as it tapped rhythmically against a railing. "But don't let it change what matters. You keep fighting for that truth."

"I will," Chris vowed, the resolve in his heart echoed in his voice. "I have to."

As days melted into weeks, and weeks into months, the bond between Chris and Frank deepened. They became fixtures to each other in a place where uncertainty ruled, a mutual understanding forming that was as solid as the bars that held them. Together, they faced the unrelenting tides of prison life, each buoyed by the other's strength, both clinging to the hopes of a future where justice would prevail.

Chris shuffled toward the chow hall, his feet dragging against the concrete like lead weights. The clatter of trays and the sharp scent of disinfectant met him at the door, mingling with the low murmur of inmates trading stories over a meal that tasted of resignation. The fluorescent lights flickered overhead, casting an unforgiving glow on the worn tables and benches.

"Keep your head up, Matthews," Frank murmured from beside him, his voice low and edged with the wisdom of years spent within these walls. "And keep your eyes on your plate. Easiest way to avoid trouble here is minding your own."

Chris nodded, picking at the starchy potatoes with a plastic fork. "I just can't shake the feeling that each day here is a day stolen from my life," he confessed, the words spilling out with the weight of his longing for freedom.

"Can't argue with that," Frank conceded, his lips curling into a rueful smile as he scooped up a forkful of beans. "But you gotta play the long game. Keep your hope, sure. But don't let it blind you to the reality of this place."

"Hope's all I've got," Chris countered, his brow furrowed. "It's what keeps me going—believing that one day, I'll walk out of here a free man."

"Believe that, by all means," Frank said, leaning closer, his tattoos shifting with the movement. "But temper it with steel, 'cause you're gonna need both in here." His eyes, hard as flint, held a glimmer of something akin to respect.

The clang of metal doors signaled the end of the mealtime, and they stood up, trays in hand. As they joined the line returning their dishes, Chris felt the grinding routine of prison life trying to erode his resolve. Standing in line, waiting for orders, moving as a unit—it gnawed at his sense of individuality.

"Feels like being part of some twisted machine," Chris muttered under his breath, aware of the guards' watchful eyes tracking their every move.

"Yep," Frank grunted in agreement, sliding his tray onto the stack with a clatter. "You're a cog now. Best learn how to turn smoothly unless you want to get crushed."

"Doesn't mean I have to like it," Chris replied, a stubborn set to his jaw. He followed the flow of prisoners back to their cells, the monotony of the march punctuated by the occasional shout or burst of coarse laughter from other inmates.

"Nobody says you have to," Frank said as they reached their cellblock. "Just remember, in here, it's adapt or suffer."

"Then I'll adapt," Chris vowed, stepping into the cramped space that was now his world. His fingers closed around the cold bars for a moment before he turned to face Frank. "But I won't give up. Not on the outside, not on justice."

Frank's expression softened, just for a moment, before the mask of the seasoned inmate slid back into place. "That's the spirit, kid. Just make sure you survive long enough to see it happen."

As Frank ambled away, Chris lay back on his bunk, staring at the ceiling where the shadows played a silent movie no one cared to watch. Despite the foreboding steel and stone, the distant echoes of despair, Chris held on to the one thing they couldn't take away—hope. It burned in his chest, a defiant flame in the suffocating darkness.

Chris shuffled along the corridor, his feet dragging against the smooth concrete floor. The sounds of the prison were a constant cacophony; keys clinking, doors slamming shut, voices raised in anger or despair. He was a boat adrift on a turbulent sea, every wave threatening to capsize him.

"Hey, Matthews," Frank called out, falling into step beside Chris as they headed towards the yard. "Keep your head up and your eyes open. You don't want to seem weak, but don't stare too long either."

"Feels like I'm walking a tightrope," Chris murmured, his gaze flickering across the faces of other inmates who sized him up with indifferent or predatory stares.

"More like navigating a minefield," Frank replied, his voice gravelly with experience. "Stick close, and watch how I move. There's an art to this dance."

As they traversed the yard, Frank's advice was a lifeline. He pointed out the cliques and loners, the troublemakers and the peacemakers. "See that big fella by the weights? Steer clear of him. And that group over there, they're okay as long as you respect their space."

"Feels like everyone's got a short fuse around here," Chris said, his throat tight.

"Short fuse, long memories," Frank nodded. "But remember, most guys just want to do their time without extra drama. Keep your nose clean, and you'll manage."

"Thanks, Frank," Chris said genuinely, feeling a shard of confidence pierce the gloom.

"Anytime, kid."

Later, in the relative quiet of the library, Chris found an unexpected sanctuary. The musty smell of old paper was a welcome reprieve from the sterile sting of disinfectant that permeated the rest of the facility. Rows of worn spines offered a promise of distant places and thoughts unchained.

He selected a book at random, the pages softened from countless thumbings. As he read, the words blossomed into vivid scenes that lifted him from the grey reality of incarceration. Each sentence was a step on a path leading away from the bars and barbed wire, towards landscapes of the mind where he could roam free.

"Books are lifelines," Frank's voice echoed in his memory. "They remind you there's a world beyond these walls that's worth fighting for."

Chris clung to that thought, letting the tales of triumphs and tribulations fuel his resolve. Within these stories lay the wisdom of ages, the struggles of heroes and heroines who faced their own battles against injustice.

"Knowledge is power," he whispered to himself, the words a silent oath. "And one day, it'll help me reclaim my life."

In the margins of the pages, Chris scribbled notes, questions, reflections. He wasn't just reading; he was preparing, arming himself with insights that transcended the confines of his present reality. With each turn of the page, he was not just passing time, he was shaping it, molding his future with the strength of his convictions.

"Find something good?" Frank asked later, as they walked back to their cells.

"More than good," Chris replied, a spark of determination lighting his eyes. "It's hope in printed form."

Chris's hands worked nimbly, threading the needle with a steady hand that belied the tremor of nerves he had felt upon his arrival. As he mended another inmate's torn shirt, a small crowd gathered around, their expressions a blend of curiosity and tentative respect. In this place where trust was a rare commodity, Chris's willingness to extend a helping hand was slowly chipping away at the walls between him and the others.

"Thanks, man," grunted the shirt's owner, a burly man named Hector with a scar tracing his jawline. "Didn't think I'd find a tailor in here."

"It's no big deal," Chris replied, handing back the mended garment. "Just trying to keep busy."

"Keeping busy" became Chris's mantra. He volunteered to help in the kitchen, shared book recommendations with fellow readers, and listened when others needed to talk. These small acts were like ripples on the surface of water, spreading further than he could see.

"Never thought I'd say this about a newbie," mused an older inmate named Luis as they walked the yard one afternoon, "but you're alright, Matthews."

Chris's resilience was born not just from his own determination but also from the connections he was forging. Despite the heavy shadows that loomed over them all, there was still room for humanity here. And it was in these moments of connection that Chris found strength.

As the days turned into weeks, whispers of "Matthews can help" wove through the cell blocks. His reputation grew—a reputation built not on might but on kindness and a readiness to stand by his principles. Slowly, he became more than just another number; he became a beacon of solidarity in a world starved for justice.

As the sun dipped below the horizon, casting long shadows across the prison yard, Chris sat on a bench, his thoughts turning inward. The cold metal of the seat bit through his uniform, yet it was a discomfort he scarcely noticed anymore. In the quiet solitude, he allowed himself a moment to reflect.

He thought of the person he used to be before the handcuffs clicked shut around his wrists, before his life was reduced to the confines of these walls. But dwelling on the past was a luxury he could not afford—not if he wanted to forge a path forward. He had adapted, yes, but he had not surrendered. The fight for his innocence was far from over.

"Got your head in the clouds again?" Frank's voice interrupted, pulling Chris back to the present.

"More like focused on the road ahead," Chris replied, the corners of his mouth lifting in a half-smile.

Frank settled beside him, nodding slowly. "You've come a long way, kid. Just remember, it's a marathon, not a sprint."

"I know," Chris said, his gaze firm and unwavering. "And I'm in it for the long haul."

The sky darkened, stars peeking through the veil of night, symbols of distant hopes and dreams. Chris closed his eyes, absorbing the weight of his journey. It was true that adversity had tested him, shaped him in ways he never expected, but it hadn't broken him. With each passing day, his will to reclaim his life from the clutches of this mistaken identity grew stronger.

He stood up, feeling the resolve solidify within him like steel. Tomorrow, he would wake up in his cell, the bars would still stand cold and unyielding, but his spirit, much like the dawn that followed the darkest nights, would rise again, relentless and bright.

"Justice may be blind," Chris murmured to the stars, "but my eyes are wide open. And one day, they'll see the truth set me free."

Chapter 7

The door to The Innocence Project's office swung open with a quiet determination, much like the man who pushed through it. Samuel Bennett stepped inside, his piercing blue eyes scanning the room that buzzed with the low hum of hushed conversations and clicking keyboards. The energy was palpable, but so too was the weight of the responsibility they all shouldered. Samuel's presence, as always, served as a silent beacon, rallying the spirits of everyone present. His salt-and-pepper hair seemed to shimmer under the fluorescent lights, lending him an air of gravitas.

"Alright, team, let's gather around," Samuel called out, his voice steady and authoritative, yet tinged with an unmistakable warmth. The clatter of activity ceased almost immediately, as if his words were the tide pulling back the sea, revealing the shore beneath. Researchers and lawyers, each a dedicated soldier in the fight against injustice, abandoned their posts and formed a semicircle around Samuel.

"We're here for Chris Matthews," he began, locking eyes with each member of his team in turn. "A young man who's carrying a burden no innocent person should bear. Time is not our ally, friends. With every tick of the clock, Chris's hope fades just a little more."

He reached into the satchel slung over his shoulder, pulling out a file thick with the scars of legal warfare—dog-eared pages and color-coded tabs spilling from its sides. "Chris is resilient, optimistic even behind bars, but that's not enough to right this wrong. It's on us to unearth the truth, to shine a light where shadows have fallen."

The team leaned in closer, hanging on every word as if drawing strength from his conviction. "We've got leads that need chasing, evidence that needs reexamining, and witnesses whose memories might just hold the key to freeing an innocent man," Samuel continued, his hands gesturing emphatically, mirroring the urgency of his message.

"Every file revisited, every interview conducted is a step towards justice—not just for Chris, but for those who'll follow in his footsteps if we don't act now." The room was rife with nods of agreement, faces set in grim resolve.

"Are we clear on why this matters?" Samuel asked, though it was less a question and more a call to arms. A chorus of 'yes' echoed back at him, each one charged with purpose.

"Then let's get to work." Samuel's command cut through the tension, releasing them back to their mission. As the team dispersed, their movements were swift, their intent clear. They were more than just workers; they were guardians of a cause greater than themselves, warriors in a battle where the line between defeat and victory was drawn with the ink of perseverance and hope.

Samuel strode across the room, his piercing blue eyes scanning over the faces of his team. Each member was a beacon of hope for those lost in the cracks of a flawed system, and today, their resolve would be tested once more.

"Alright, let's divide and conquer," he announced with a voice that commanded attention yet carried the warmth of camaraderie. "Linda, I need you on case files. Dig through every page; we're looking for discrepancies, anything overlooked."

Linda nodded sharply, her fingers already itching to flip through the reams of paper that could vindicate an innocent life. She settled at her desk, a fortress of documents rising around her as she began the meticulous task of combing through the maze of legalese and evidence logs.

"Tom, you're on interviews. Talk to anyone and everyone connected to the case. We need fresh perspectives, maybe someone saw something they didn't realize was important." Tom's nod was curt, his jaw set in determination as he reached for his recorder and notepad, tools of the trade for a man who knew how to listen between the lines.

"Marie, hit the streets. See what leads you can scrounge up from old contacts. Sometimes the truth hides in plain sight among those who've got no reason to guard it." Marie's eyes glinted with the thrill of the hunt, her past as an investigative journalist a perfect match for the task at hand.

The rest of the team received their assignments with equal measures of gravity and passion. The office buzzed with activity as computers fired up, phones rang with urgency, and strategy huddled into focused whispers.

As Samuel watched them work, he felt the familiar surge of pride and responsibility. They were not just a team; they were a lifeline to the forgotten. Every keystroke, every call made, every door knocked on was laced with the potential to rewrite a life's story.

Linda paused, her finger tracing a line in a transcript that didn't add up. Tom leaned forward during a phone call, catching a break in a witness's voice. Marie's sneakers padded against the pavement, her senses alert for any clue that might lead to redemption.

They worked as if time itself was against them, aware that with each passing second, Chris's hope hung by a thread. But here, within these walls, they wove new threads, stronger and more resolute, spun from justice and the unyielding belief that the truth would prevail.

The cold metal handle of The Innocence Project's door felt strangely grounding in Carol Thompson's grasp, its chill seeping into her palm like a stark reminder of the reason she stood there. She pushed it open, stepping through the threshold with a posture that bore both the weight of loss and the backbone of resolve. Her gaze swept across the room, taking in the hive of activity where every individual seemed to be a vital part of a larger organism fighting for justice.

"Mrs. Thompson?" Samuel approached, his voice tinged with both respect and an understanding of the heavy burden she carried.

"Yes," Carol replied, tugging at the hem of her jacket—a subconscious shield against the chill of uncertainty. "I'm here because I need to see... I need to understand."

Samuel nodded, motioning her toward a quieter corner of the bustling office. The walls embraced them with the muted echoes of tireless work, of lives hanging in the balance.

"I've read the reports, seen what the media has churned out," Carol began, her words hesitant yet firm. "It's hard to look past all that noise, to believe that maybe—just maybe—the system got it wrong with Chris."

Her fingers curled and uncurled at her side, as if grappling with the invisible threads of doubt and hope that intertwined within her. Carol's eyes, darkened by sorrow but alight with a flicker of inquisitiveness, met Samuel's earnest gaze.

"Can you tell me—straight and true—do you think my daughter's real killer is out there while... while an innocent man sits in prison?"

Samuel's response was measured, his tone carrying the gravity of their shared quest for truth. "That's exactly what we're working to find out, Mrs. Thompson. We leave no stone unturned, question everything, and chase down every possible lead."

A silent breath escaped Carol's lips, a release of some tightly held fear. Her head tilted slightly, acknowledging the sincerity in Samuel's voice. It was this sincerity that coaxed the tendrils of curiosity from their defensive coil.

"Then show me," Carol said, her voice stronger now, the determination to seek answers for Angie—and perhaps for Chris—rising within her like dawn after a long, dark night. "Show me how you're going to find the truth."

Samuel led Carol to a quiet corner of the bustling office, away from the hum of computers and hushed conversations that filled the room. The walls here were adorned with letters of gratitude and photos of those they'd helped—faces of relief and joy that seemed to watch over them.

"Mrs. Thompson," Samuel began, his voice a soft echo in the secluded space, "I know this is hard. You're carrying a burden no mother should bear."

Carol folded her arms, a protective barrier around herself. She scanned the faces on the wall, each one a story of hope restored. She nodded for Samuel to continue, her posture stiff but attentive.

"Chris's case," he continued, "is fraught with inconsistencies. Witnesses whose stories wavered under pressure, evidence not strong enough to stand on its own, and an alibi overlooked by eager prosecutors." Samuel's hands moved as he spoke, punctuating the air with his passion for justice.

"An alibi?" Carol's voice quivered slightly, betraying her intrigue.

Samuel nodded, "Yes. A credible one that we believe was dismissed too quickly." He leaned forward, his blue eyes earnest and unwavering. "We've seen it before—how the rush for closure can trample the truth. We're here to right those wrongs."

Carol's gaze returned to the smiling faces on the wall. She pictured Angie among them, her vibrant spirit dimmed only by the injustice of her untimely death. The thought of an innocent man paying for a crime he didn't commit added a chilling layer to her grief.

"Tell me more about this... alibi," she said, the fortress around her heart showing the first signs of wear.

Samuel detailed the timeline they'd reconstructed, the witnesses they intended to revisit, the threads of Chris's life that night that were left unexplored. With each word, Carol felt the rigid walls of skepticism begin to crack, light seeping through the fissures.

"Your team believes in him that much?" she asked, her voice less guarded now, a note of wonder threading through her words.

"More than believe," Samuel replied, his tone steady and sure, "we're driven by the evidence, and it points to a different narrative than the one presented in court."

Carol considered his words, feeling the taut strings of doubt loosen. A glimmer of something new shone in her eyes—a hesitant hope. She thought of Angie again, her laughter like a warm embrace, her quest for fairness as fierce as Carol's own. If there was even a sliver of chance that the wrong person was behind bars, then Angie would have wanted the truth uncovered.

"Okay," Carol sighed, her decision carrying the weight of both her love for her daughter and her burgeoning trust in the man before her. "Let's find the truth together."

Samuel offered a small, reassuring smile, one that held the promise of unwavering support. Together, they turned back toward the office—their steps in sync, their purpose united.

The Innocence Project's office was a hive of activity, but the buzz quieted as Chris Matthews stepped into the center of the room. His eyes, dark and intense, swept over the faces of the team members who were his lifeline to the outside world.

"Thank you all for being here," Chris began, his voice carrying the weight of gratitude and resolve. "I know it's not easy, sifting through the rubble of that night, looking for something we might have missed."

Samuel leaned forward attentively from where he sat at the head of the table, his gaze never leaving Chris. The others mirrored his focus, pens poised over notepads, ready to document every word.

"I keep going back to the alley," Chris continued, his fingertips grazing the tabletop as if he could feel the cold concrete of that fateful place. "There was a guy there, arguing with Angie. He had a tattoo on his neck, like a snake coiling around a dagger. I've never seen him before, or since."

"Did anyone else see him?" Samuel probed, his question slicing through the silence.

"Maybe," Chris replied, uncertainty clouding his features for a moment. "But no one's come forward."

"Then we'll find them," Samuel declared with determination. The team nodded in agreement, their shared mission fueling a palpable energy in the room.

The researchers divided into pairs, some pulling up maps of the city to canvas the area anew, while others combed through witness statements with fresh eyes. Lawyers poured over forensic reports, questioning every detail, every test that had been run. They sought discrepancies, any cracks in the foundation of the case against Chris.

"Look at this," one researcher called out, pointing to a grainy surveillance photo on her laptop screen. "Could this be our mystery man?"

"Hard to tell," another admitted, leaning in close. "But it's worth tracking down the original footage."

The office became a symphony of low murmurs and clicking keyboards. Time blurred as they dug deeper, chasing leads, unraveling threads, piecing together a puzzle that had been left incomplete by the criminal justice system's hasty assembly.

"Chris," Samuel said, motioning for him to come closer to where he was examining a set of interview transcripts. "These inconsistencies in the witness accounts—they don't add up."

"Because they're not telling the whole story," Chris affirmed, his conviction unshaken. "Angie knew something... something important. We just need to figure out what it was."

"Then we keep digging until we unearth it," Samuel concluded, his words a vow.

The team rallied around the promise of uncovering the truth, each member driven by a deep-seated belief in justice. Chris watched them work, their dedication mirroring his own, and in their tireless pursuit, he found an ember of hope that refused to be extinguished.

Samuel Bennett leaned over a cluttered desk, frustration etching deep lines into his forehead as he pored over the latest batch of interview transcripts. The room buzzed with the sound of fervent activity; each member of his team was engrossed in their tasks, yet progress seemed stubbornly out of reach.

"Another dead end," muttered Rachel, one of the researchers, pushing away from her computer with a sigh. Her fingers had been flying across the keys for hours, chasing the ghost of an alibi that now appeared to be nothing more than a mirage.

"Keep at it," Samuel urged, his voice steady despite the sinking feeling in his gut. "It's there. We just haven't found it yet."

The Innocence Project's office was a hive of shared resolve, but doubt cast long shadows across the room. They hit walls of silence where witnesses once spoke, tangled in contradictions that muddied the waters of Chris's case. Each lead seemed to fray, pulling them further from the truth they sought.

"Samuel," came a hesitant voice from the corner. Carol Thompson, her eyes usually a well of skepticism, now flickered with something else. "What if we're wrong?"

"We're not," Samuel replied without hesitation. He met her gaze squarely, his own eyes reflecting the unwavering flame of conviction. "There's a crack in this case wide enough to shatter it. We just need to find it."

As night crept closer, so did exhaustion, but no one entertained the thought of surrender. They were the last line of defense for people like Chris, those ensnared by a system that sometimes valued finality over truth.

And then, in the midst of mounting tension, a shout cut through the air like a lifeline.

"Got something!" It was Jason, another lawyer, who practically vibrated with adrenaline as he held up a paper. His hands shook slightly—a blend of excitement and the weight of potential discovery.

"Talk to us, Jason," Samuel said, crowding around with the rest of the team.

"It's an old lab report," Jason explained rapidly, "but look here. The timestamp on this evidence log—it doesn't match the security logs from that night. This evidence... it could have been tampered with."

Silence fell, thick with implication. All eyes turned to the document, to the glaring inconsistency spelled out in black and white. If the evidence was compromised, it meant the bedrock of the prosecution's case against Chris might crumble away.

"Could this be it?" breathed Carol, the edges of her doubt eroded by the promise of this new lead.

"Let's find out," Samuel said, heart racing. There was work to do—phones to ring, experts to consult, angles to consider—but in that moment, the possibility of justice rekindled their determination.

"Chris," Samuel called out, waiting for him to join the circle of hope that had formed around Jason's discovery. "We're not done yet."

Chris moved forward, the light of optimism never quite leaving his eyes even amid the storm of setbacks. He looked down at the report, and for the first time in what felt like forever, the spark of hope seemed to burn a little brighter, fueled by the tenacity of those who fought in his name.

Samuel leaned against the edge of his desk, a fortress of papers and legal books surrounding him. He watched Carol pace the room, her strides measured, her expression a canvas of worry and wonder. The dim light from the overhead lamp cast shadows that seemed to dance with her every movement, animating the weight of their task.

"Samuel," she said, pausing mid-step, "do you ever get scared? Scared that we might not..." Her voice trailed off, leaving the question hanging like a noose in the air.

"Every day," he replied without hesitation, his blue eyes locking onto hers. "But fear isn't the end of the story—it's just a part of it. It's what we do with that fear that defines us." He pushed off from the desk and walked over to her, a hand extended in silent solidarity.

Carol took his hand, her fingers gripping firmly. "Angie needs this. Chris deserves this," she whispered, the usual tremble in her voice replaced by a steel thread of resolve.

They stood there, two warriors in a battle for truth, their shared determination pulsing like a heartbeat. Samuel's smile was small but fierce. "We'll find the way, Carol. For Angie, for Chris, for all the others who rely on us."

The clock on the wall ticked loudly, marking the seconds as they slipped into minutes. Each tick was a reminder that time was both an enemy and an ally, that it could bring salvation or condemnation depending on what they made of it.

"Let's go through everything again," Samuel suggested, releasing Carol's hand and gesturing toward the table littered with evidence. "Piece by piece, witness by witness. We leave no stone unturned."

Carol nodded, her short brown hair catching the light as she moved to join him at the table. They bent over the documents, their heads close, voices hushed as they discussed each shred of evidence with painstaking attention.

As the night deepened, the office grew quiet, save for the soft rustling of paper and the occasional creak of a chair. The world outside continued on, oblivious to the hope being kindled within these four walls.

Suddenly, Samuel's finger stabbed down on a page, halting Carol's speech. "Here," he said, a triumphant note creeping into his voice. "This interview—didn't Chris say he saw someone that night? Someone the police never followed up with?"

Carol's eyes widened as she read the passage, her breath catching in her throat. "Yes, I remember. He mentioned a man with a red baseball cap, loitering around the scene."

"Exactly," Samuel confirmed, a sense of urgency electrifying the air. "If we can track this man down, if he's the one..."

The sentence hung unfinished, the implications too vast to articulate. They shared a look that conveyed volumes—the thrill of a lead, the terror of another dead-end, the inexorable push forward.

"Let's find him," Carol said, her voice now a command.

"First thing in the morning," Samuel agreed. "We'll start with the neighborhood, see if anyone remembers anything about that night. It's a long shot, but..."

"But it's a shot we've got to take," Carol finished for him, her eyes brightening with a flame of tenacity.

"Exactly," Samuel echoed. They exchanged a nod, a silent pact forged in the dwindling hours of a long night.

The chapter closed with the two of them standing side by side, their profiles etched against the windowpane. The city lights were distant stars, witnesses to the solemn vow taken in the quiet of The Innocence Project's office—a vow to fight until the very end.

And somewhere out there, under the same blanket of darkness that shrouded the city, was a man with a red baseball cap. A man who might hold the key to Chris's freedom—or the weight to sink their hopes forever.

Chapter 8

Carol Thompson sat hunched over her kitchen table, a fortress of newspaper clippings and case files spread before her like a map of the battlefield she was navigating. The early morning light spilled across the documents, casting long shadows that seemed to stretch towards justice just beyond reach. She traced a finger over a photo of Chris, his dark eyes holding a spark despite the weight of his wrongful conviction. In those eyes, Carol saw an echo of Angie's spirit, the vivacity she once carried before the world demanded its cruel toll.

She reached for the phone, its cord coiled like a lifeline, and dialed the familiar numbers with practiced ease. Her voice, when she spoke, was a blend of warmth and resolve, the kind that could only come from years of being a mother and now, a crusader for truth.

"Hi, June, it's Carol," she began, her words carrying the weight of something greater than a simple conversation. "I'm calling about Chris Matthews... Yes, Angie's friend. He's been wronged by a system we trusted to protect the innocent."

June's response was a murmur of acknowledgment, soft but clear in the quiet of Carol's kitchen. Carol listened intently, nodding even though June couldn't see. It was important to make them feel heard, to build the bridge before you crossed it together.

"Look, I've known Chris since he was a boy," Carol continued, her tone painting a picture of Chris's character as vivid as the one clipped to the file in front of her. "He's been caught in a nightmare, and I can't stand by while an innocent young man loses years of his life."

There was a pause, the silence punctuated by the ticking of the wall clock, each second a reminder of time slipping away from Chris.

"Can I count on you to help? Maybe write a letter or come to the next meeting?" Carol asked, her plea wrapped in the gentle persuasion of someone who believed down to their bones in the cause they championed.

"Of course, Carol. You know you always have my support," came June's eventual reply, a note of admiration threading through her words. Carol's ability to draw out the best in people was a testament to her character, one that held fast even when the waves of adversity crashed against her resolve.

"Thank you, June. Every voice matters," Carol said, a smile touching her lips. She imagined Angie smiling too, somewhere beyond the pain, proud of her mother's unyielding spirit.

The calls continued, a rhythm of outreach and empathy, Carol weaving a tapestry of community around Chris's cause. With each conversation, she laid another stone in the foundation of their shared fight for justice, her narrative resonating with the hearts of those she reached.

"Justice is not just a word, Tom," she insisted on another call, her voice firm yet lined with compassion. "It's a living thing we must nurture and defend, especially when it's threatened. We owe it to Chris, to Angie, and to ourselves."

Tom hesitated, skepticism a shadow in his voice. "But what if there's nothing we can do?"

"Then we do it anyway," Carol replied, her determination a lighthouse in the fog of doubt. "We do it because it's right, and because giving up is not a choice we can live with."

As the morning waned, Carol hung up the phone, her list of supporters growing with each name she scribbled down. Her kitchen had become a command center, the heart of a movement fueled by the courage to challenge the flaws of a broken system. And at the core of it all was Carol, a beacon of hope in the search for redemption, her belief in Chris's innocence unwavering as the rising sun.

Carol Thompson stood at the front of the crowded community hall, her hands uncharacteristically trembling as she arranged her notes on the podium. The room buzzed with the low murmur of neighbors and friends, a patchwork of concerned faces turning towards her. As she looked out over the gathering, Carol drew in a deep breath, feeling the weight of every word she was about to deliver.

"Good evening," she began, her voice steady despite the nerves that danced beneath her skin. "I'm here tonight because we're at a crossroads. A young man's life hangs in the balance—Chris Matthews, whom many of you know." She paused, letting Chris's name settle in the air like a somber melody.

"Chris sits in a cell for a crime he did not commit. And while the real perpetrator remains free, justice remains chained." Her eyes scanned the room, connecting with those of her audience, imploring them to understand. "But," she continued, a fire igniting in her words, "we have the power to help right this wrong."

Carol recounted the inconsistencies in the evidence, the hasty trial, and the ignored testimony that pointed away from Chris's guilt. She spoke of Angie, her daughter, whose spirit had always been a beacon of hope and fairness. "Angie believed in a world where truth mattered," she said, her voice quivering momentarily. "We owe it to her memory—and to Chris—to fight for that truth."

As she concluded her appeal, the room erupted into applause. Heads nodded in agreement, and eyes that once held doubt now shone with resolve. Carol had woven her conviction into their hearts, and together they formed a collective force ready to champion Chris's cause.

Later, under the somber sky of the early evening, Carol found herself standing by Angie's grave. The marble headstone was cold to the touch, a stark contrast to the warmth of the memories that flooded back. Kneeling down, she brushed away some fallen leaves, her fingers tracing the engraved name of her beloved daughter.

"Angie," she whispered, the cool breeze carrying her words, "I feel so lost without you. But when I think of what's happening to Chris, I can almost hear your voice urging me on."

She placed a single white rose upon the grave, its petals soft and pure—a symbol of the innocence she fought to protect. "I promise you, Angie, I won't let fear stop me. Chris didn't take you from us, and I'll do everything in my power to prove it."

In that quiet cemetery, surrounded by whispers of the past and dreams of a just future, Carol Thompson made a vow. She would be steadfast, a relentless seeker of truth in a world that too often turned its back on justice. For Angie. For Chris. For all those silenced by wrongful convictions. With renewed determination, she stood up, her silhouette etched against the fading light, ready to face whatever battles lay ahead.

Carol Thompson had transformed her living room into a hub of quiet activity. The coffee table, usually adorned with family photographs and magazines, was now stacked with pamphlets and legal documents, each one carefully highlighted and annotated. A warm aroma of freshly brewed coffee mingled with the scent of cinnamon from a plate of homemade cookies, an inviting atmosphere for the guests trickling into her home.

"Thank you for coming," Carol greeted each arrival with a hug or a firm handshake, her brown eyes locking onto theirs with earnest gratitude. The gentle hum of conversation filled the space as neighbors and friends settled in, some perched on couches while others leaned against walls lined with photos that told stories of happier times.

"Everyone, please, find a seat," Carol announced, her voice steady and sure. She cleared her throat, standing before the small assembly like a conductor at the head of an orchestra. "I know many of you have questions about Chris Matthews—about the night we lost Angie, and the trial that followed."

A hush fell over the room as Carol unfolded a piece of paper, her hands betraying a slight tremor. "Chris is innocent," she stated plainly, the silence amplifying her conviction. "And I've gathered evidence that supports his claim, evidence ignored during the investigation."

"Come on, Carol," a voice interjected from the back. It was Bill Henderson, a longtime resident known for his skeptical nature. "You can't seriously believe that boy didn't do it. The jury found him guilty."

Carol met Bill's gaze, her expression composed, her heart pounding against her chest. "Bill, the jury wasn't given the whole story." She walked over to him, holding out a photograph. "Look at this. The timestamp on this security footage places Chris at a convenience store miles away when Angie... when it happened."

Bill squinted at the image, then up at Carol. "That could have been tampered with," he challenged, crossing his arms defensively.

"Forensic experts have verified its authenticity," Carol continued, her tone patient but unwavering. "And there's more—witness statements that contradict the prosecution's timeline, phone records, and" —she paused for emphasis— "a lack of any physical evidence connecting Chris to the crime scene."

The room fell silent again as Carol's words sank in. She could see the gears turning in Bill's mind, and in those of the others seated around him. Her ability to address concerns without judgment or hostility allowed a space for doubt to grow—a seed of skepticism not aimed at her, but at the verdict they had all accepted as truth.

"Justice isn't just about punishing the guilty, Bill," Carol added, her voice softening. "It's about protecting the innocent too. And if we've punished an innocent man, we continue to victimize him every day he remains behind bars."

Bill looked down, chewing on the inside of his cheek. Around him, heads nodded, whispers of agreement fluttering through the air like tentative birds taking flight. Carol sensed the shift in the room, the threads of solidarity weaving together as hearts and minds opened to the possibility of a grave injustice having occurred.

"Alright, Carol," Bill finally said, his skepticism not gone but tempered with a cautious curiosity. "What do you need us to do?"

A collective breath seemed to be exhaled, and Carol felt a surge of hope. "Help me get the word out. Talk to your friends, write to officials, attend rallies. We need to be Chris's voice until he can speak for himself again."

As the meeting drew to a close, Carol watched her living room slowly empty, the weight of responsibility now shared among a community united by a common cause. They left with more than just cookies and coffee stirring in their bellies—they carried a burning question that promised to ignite action.

"Thank you," Carol whispered to the empty room, her reflection in the window nodding back at her. She had done what she set out to do tonight: kindle a flame of advocacy in the hearts of her neighbors. Now, together, they would turn that flame into a wildfire of justice for Chris.

Carol's fingers were steady as she dialed the number for the local newspaper. The cold hum of the dial tone was soon replaced by a receptionist's disinterested greeting. With each ring, her resolve deepened; this was not just another call—this was an appeal for justice.

"Good morning, Daily Herald, how can I help you?" The voice on the other end sounded rushed, but Carol wasn't deterred.

"Hello, my name is Carol Thompson. I'm calling about Chris Matthews' case—the young man who was wrongfully convicted last year. I have some information that could shed new light on his situation. Could we possibly set up an interview?"

There was a brief pause, the kind that often preceded rejection. Carol tensed, ready to counter with all the determination of a lioness protecting her cub.

"Please hold for our editor," said the receptionist, unexpectedly relenting.

A flicker of triumph lit Carol's eyes as she waited, her heart beating a drumroll of anticipation. When the editor came on the line, Carol's voice was calm but insistent, her words painting the stark image of injustice that had been dealt to Chris.

"Chris Matthews isn't just a statistic or a headline—he's a living, breathing symbol of what's broken in our criminal justice system," Carol pressed, her tone threaded with urgency. "The public needs to hear his story. They need to know the truth."

"Alright, Mrs. Thompson," the editor replied, her tone reflecting a newfound interest. "We'll do an interview. Let's see where this leads."

Carol hung up, a small victory secured. She knew that the power of the press could turn the tide in their favor, bringing much-needed attention to Chris's plight.

Days later, Carol stood at the back of a packed town hall meeting, the buzz of community chatter a blanket over the room. Her gaze was fixed on the officials seated at the front, their expressions varying degrees of concern and indifference. As the floor opened for questions, Carol's hand shot up, unwavering.

"Mrs. Thompson, go ahead," the moderator gestured to her, recognizing the familiar face of steadfast advocacy.

"Thank you," Carol began, her voice carrying across the sea of heads. "I stand before you today not just as a grieving mother but as a citizen deeply troubled by the flaws in our legal system. Chris Matthews' conviction is riddled with doubts and discrepancies that cannot be ignored. We demand a thorough review of his case. We seek justice, not just for Chris, but for our community's faith in the law."

Murmurs rippled through the crowd, her plea hitting home for more than a few in attendance. Some nodded in agreement, while others exchanged skeptical glances, their complacency challenged by Carol's fervor.

"Mrs. Thompson, we understand your concerns," one official offered, his voice a blend of sympathy and formality. "Rest assured, we will take your request into consideration."

"Consideration isn't enough," Carol countered, her stance firm. "Action is needed. We won't rest until Chris Matthews gets the fair trial he deserves."

As Carol retook her seat, a murmur of admiration followed her. It was clear to everyone present that this woman would not be silenced. Her voice was more than a call for justice; it was a clarion bell, ringing out against the walls of bureaucracy, demanding to be heard.

Carol Thompson's fingers tapped a staccato rhythm on the polished surface of the conference table, betraying her impatience. Across from her sat a lawyer known for unraveling the knots in the toughest of wrongful conviction cases. His office was a sanctuary of order, every book and file meticulously placed—a stark contrast to the chaos of injustice Carol sought to remedy.

"Ms. Thompson," the lawyer began, adjusting his glasses as he pored over the files she had spread between them, "I've been through the case notes you provided. There are certainly avenues we can explore. An appeal based on new evidence, perhaps a push for a retrial."

"Whatever it takes," Carol said firmly, her hands clenching into determined fists. "Chris is innocent, and I'll move heaven and earth to prove it."

The lawyer nodded, his gaze meeting hers with an understanding that bordered on reverence. "It won't be easy or quick. And it will require significant resources." His words were a gentle warning, but Carol heard only a challenge to be met.

"I understand. That's why we're organizing a fundraiser. The community trusts me, they know I wouldn't fight this hard if there wasn't a shadow of a doubt about Chris's guilt."

"Good," he replied with a nod. "Keep me updated on your progress."

As the meeting concluded, Carol felt a renewed surge of purpose. She stepped out into the crisp afternoon, where autumn leaves danced along the sidewalk, mirroring the whirlwind of activity in her mind. Plans for the fundraising event occupied every thought as she made her way back home.

Days later, Carol's living room transformed into a command center. Neighbors and friends filled the space, their conversations humming with anticipation. Streamers adorned the walls, and tables groaned under the weight of homemade treats and auction items.

"Thank you all for coming," Carol addressed the gathered crowd, her voice steady and clear. "Every penny we raise tonight brings Chris one step closer to freedom—to the justice he has been denied. Your support means more than just funds; it's a beacon of hope, shining against the darkness of doubt."

Heads nodded, and smiles of encouragement lit up the room. The chatter resumed, now infused with a sense of mission as people opened their wallets and hearts.

"Remember, this isn't just for Chris," Carol continued, weaving through the clusters of supporters, her eyes alight with fervor. "It's a stand against a system that sometimes gets it wrong. We're here to fix that—one case at a time."

Auction items found eager bidders, laughter mingled with the clinking of glasses, and the tally of donations grew. Carol moved among her neighbors, her spirit buoyed by the swell of solidarity.

As the evening waned and the last guests departed, Carol sat alone, counting the stack of bills and checks. Each was a tangible testament to the trust her community placed in her cause—their shared belief in Chris's innocence and the right for justice to prevail. With a tired yet triumphant smile, Carol whispered into the quiet room, "We're getting there, Chris. We're getting there."

Carol Thompson sat across from her lifelong friend, June, in the cozy embrace of her kitchen. The walls, bathed in the soft glow of the morning sun, seemed to lean in, privy to the brewing storm of doubt and conviction.

"Carol, I just don't know," June said, her voice threaded with hesitation. Her fingers fidgeted with the ceramic mug before her, avoiding Carol's earnest gaze. "I mean, Chris... he's not the person we thought he was, right?"

Carol took a deep breath, her hands clasped around her own cup as if drawing strength from its warmth. "June, I understand your doubts. There was a time when I wrestled with them too," she began, her tone even, eyes reflecting the journey she'd taken from uncertainty to belief. "But the pieces don't fit. The evidence that condemned him—it's flimsy at best."

June looked up, her brow furrowed, searching Carol's face for assurance. "You really believe he's innocent?"

"With every fiber of my being," Carol replied, the conviction in her words unwavering. "The Chris I know is resilient, hopeful, and incapable of the crimes he's accused of. He's been wronged by a system that's supposed to protect us."

June sighed, the skepticism in her eyes slowly dissolving into contemplation. Carol reached out, placing a gentle hand over hers. "Trust me, there's more to this story. And I won't rest until the truth comes to light."

Later that week, Carol stood at the podium in the city council chambers, her posture confident, her resolve palpable. The room was filled with the hum of anticipation as community members lined the seats, their expressions a mix of curiosity and support.

"Members of the council," Carol addressed the panel of officials seated before her, "I stand before you today not just as a grieving mother, but as a citizen who believes in the power of justice." She held up a thick stack of papers—petitions scrawled with hundreds of signatures. "These are the voices of our community, echoing a single, urgent plea: review Chris Matthews's case."

A murmur swept through the room as council members leaned forward, their interest piqued. Carol's eyes scanned the faces before her, each one a potential ally in her quest.

"Chris's conviction was a miscarriage of justice," she continued, her voice steady and persuasive. "New evidence has come to light, and it begs for examination. How can we stand idly by when an innocent man's life hangs in the balance?"

A councilwoman cleared her throat, adjusting her glasses as she regarded Carol. "Mrs. Thompson, while we understand your concerns, the council isn't in the business of—"

"Overturning wrongful convictions might not be your business," Carol interjected, her fervor rising, "but ensuring that justice prevails within our community certainly is." She leaned in, her expression imploring. "You have the power to make this right. Please, I urge you to consider what's at stake."

The room fell silent, the weight of Carol's words settling heavy on the hearts of those present. After a long pause, the councilman at the center of the table nodded solemnly. "We will take your request under advisement, Mrs. Thompson. Thank you for bringing this matter to our attention."

As Carol stepped away from the podium, a whisper of hope fluttered within her. It was a small victory, perhaps, but it was progress—a sign that the tides were turning in Chris's favor. And for Carol, that was enough to keep the flames of her determination burning bright.

Carol's cellphone vibrated against the kitchen table, jolting her from the reverie of her thoughts. She glanced at the screen, recognizing the number immediately—it belonged to a prominent community leader who had been reticent about joining Chris's cause until now. With a mix of apprehension and hope, she answered.

"Carol Thompson speaking."

"Carol, it's James," came the firm yet warm voice on the other end. "I've been doing some thinking about Chris Matthews' case. It's time I take a stand with you."

A surge of gratitude rushed through Carol, and she clutched the phone tighter. "James, that means the world to us. Your voice carries weight in this town. People listen when you speak."

James's chuckle was dry but not without warmth. "Then let's make sure they hear us loud and clear, shall we? I'll be at the courthouse tomorrow, and I'll bring others. It's time for justice to prevail."

"Thank you," Carol said, feeling as though a strong wind had filled her sails after a long calm. "See you there."

After hanging up, Carol stood by the window, looking out at the neatly lined houses that made up her neighborhood. She could feel the momentum building, like gathering clouds before a storm. This was a fight she intended to win.

The next morning, under a sky that promised rain but held back its tears, Carol stood outside the courthouse, a banner in her hand that read 'Justice for Chris Matthews'. Around her, a sea of faces—a mixture of determination and empathy—echoed the sentiment, their signs creating a patchwork of support.

"Today, we stand together, not just for Chris, but for every soul that has been wrongfully trapped behind bars!" Carol's voice rang out clear and strong, amplified by a handheld megaphone. She looked into the eyes of those gathered, seeing their resolve mirror her own.

"Chris is a beacon of hope," she continued, "a reminder that resilience can thrive even in the darkest of times. But hope alone isn't enough—we need action, we need voices, we need justice!"

The crowd responded, a chorus of agreement rising up, harmonizing with the rhythm of passing cars and the distant murmur of the city. Their message was simple: They demanded a review, a second look at a conviction that reeked of doubt.

"Let our presence here today send a message," Carol declared, her heart pounding with the fervor of her words. "We are watching, and we will not rest until the truth has its day in court!"

The protest was peaceful, but its energy was palpable, a living thing that fed off the passion of its participants. And at the center of it all, Carol stood as a pillar of unwavering strength, her voice the rallying cry for a cause that grew stronger with each passing moment.

Carol's hands trembled slightly as she sifted through the day's mail, a mixture of bills and leaflets until her fingers brushed against an envelope thicker than the rest. It carried weight, both physically and with the potential it held within its sealed edges. Her heart quickened as she recognized the embossed logo in the corner—an image of a scale, balanced yet in motion. The Innocence Project.

With urgency, but a reverence reserved for moments that might change one's life, Carol carefully tore open the envelope. The letter inside was neatly typed, each word meticulously chosen, a stark contrast to the haphazard scrawl of her own notes that littered the kitchen table.

"Dear Mrs. Thompson," it began, the words blurring a little as Carol's eyes filled with unbidden tears. She blinked them away, reading on about how the Innocence Project had reviewed Chris's case and found several concerning discrepancies warranting their full attention. They were offering their assistance, their resources, and most importantly, their belief in Chris's innocence.

A sob caught in Carol's throat. This letter was more than just paper; it was a lifeline, a beacon of hope amidst the years of battling shadows and doubts. It was validation that her fight, her refusal to let Chris's plight be buried under red tape and indifference, was not only necessary but righteous.

"Chris," she whispered to the empty room, "we've got a chance now. A real chance." The warmth of hope kindled in her chest, spreading like sunlight through chilled limbs. For so long, she'd been the solitary rock against which the relentless waves of bureaucracy crashed. But now, the tides were turning.

She envisioned Chris's face, his optimism that never waned even when faced with steel bars and cold, indifferent walls. Carol knew that this news would ignite that spark in his eyes, the same way it set fire to her resolve.

"Mom?" a voice called from the doorway, and Carol turned to see her son, concern etched in his furrowed brow. "Everything okay?"

"Better than okay," Carol said, her voice steady despite the emotion that danced at the edge of each word. "The Innocence Project is taking on Chris's case."

For a moment, they stood in silence, letting the gravity of those words sink in. Then, together, they let out a breath neither realized they'd been holding—a shared exhalation that seemed to expel years of pent-up fear and frustration.

"Mom, that's amazing!" His voice cracked with hope, mirroring her own feelings.

"Yes, it is." Carol folded the letter, a precious document she would file alongside all the evidence she had gathered over the years. She placed it on top, a symbol of a new chapter in their arduous journey.

"Let's tell Chris," her son suggested, already reaching for the phone.

Carol nodded, the gesture full of newfound conviction. They had a powerful ally now, and with the Innocence Project by their side, the path to justice seemed clearer, less fraught with insurmountable obstacles.

"Today, we celebrate," she said, her voice firm with determination. "Tomorrow, we fight on."

And in the privacy of her kitchen, surrounded by the detritus of her tireless advocacy, Carol allowed herself to believe, perhaps for the first time in a long while, that the fight could truly be won.

Chapter 9

Chris Matthews sat rigid in the sterile chill of the Innocence Project's office, his gaze locked on the silent phone on the desk. Each tick of the clock was a drumbeat to his racing heart—a symphony of hope and dread playing out in real time. The room, usually a haven for him and Samuel Bennett, now felt like a holding cell for their collective breath.

"Any moment now," Samuel murmured, his voice a steady anchor in the storm of anticipation swirling around them. His fingers tapped an impatient rhythm on the tabletop, betraying his composed exterior.

"Feels like forever," Chris replied, his words edged with a decade of waiting in shadows. He glanced at Samuel, finding solace in his mentor's unwavering presence. Despite the weight of what hung in the balance, Chris clung to the resilience that had become his second skin—hope was a fire he refused to let die.

Meanwhile, miles away but worlds apart, forensic scientists clad in white lab coats hovered over advanced machinery in the crime lab. Their faces, obscured by masks and goggles, were portraits of concentration as they pipetted, scanned, and recorded with meticulous precision. The air hummed with the sterile scent of cleanliness and the quiet buzz of technology dissecting truth from tiny strands of genetic material.

The crisp snap of latex gloves punctuated the silence, each movement deliberate and methodical. Within this temple of science, every detail mattered—every protocol was scripture. The gravity of their task was etched into each scientist's furrowed brow; their work could be the key to freedom or continued captivity.

As the machines whirred and blinked, digital readouts inching toward a verdict, the tension became palpable, a living thing that filled the spaces between the scientists. It flowed through cables and circuits, an electric current of possibility that held more than just data—it held lives in the balance.

Back in the office, Samuel caught Chris's eye, offering a nod that spoke volumes. "Remember, whatever happens, we've come a long way," he said, his voice the embodiment of conviction. "Justice doesn't sleep, and neither will we."

Chris drew strength from Samuel's unwavering dedication, his own convictions mirrored in the resolve of the man who had championed his cause without falter. Together, they waited, teetering on the edge of a future undefined but for the contents of a computer screen in a distant lab, where fact met fate in the quest for truth.

Chris couldn't sit still. His legs carried him back and forth across the small confines of the room, each step a silent plea for news that might never come. The worn carpet beneath his shoes felt like the rough terrain of the years he'd been climbing, seeking a peak that seemed always just out of reach. The clock on the wall ticked in rhythm with his racing heart, marking time as if each second were a weight added to the scale of his fate.

"Chris," Samuel's voice was a tether, pulling him back from the precipice of his own thoughts. "You need to breathe, man."

He knew Samuel was right. But how could he stand still when every fiber of his being vibrated with the tension of waiting—waiting for the words that could unravel the knots that injustice had tied around his life? His hands clenched and unclenched at his sides, a physical manifestation of the turmoil within.

"Alright, I'll try," Chris conceded, forcing his feet to halt their relentless march. He took in a deep breath, the air feeling too thin to satisfy his lungs.

As if on cue, the phone rang. The shrill tone cut through the silence like a verdict being read aloud. Samuel reached for it, his hand steady despite the uncertainty that hovered over them like a storm cloud.

"Hello?" Samuel's voice was calm, but Chris could see the faint pulse throbbing at the base of his lawyer's neck.

Chris watched, suspended between hope and dread. His eyes locked on Samuel's face, searching for a sign, any indication of the future that awaited him. He felt as if he were standing on the edge of a chasm, the ground ready to crumble beneath him.

"Understood," Samuel spoke into the receiver, his brow creasing slightly. He hung up without another word and turned to face Chris.

The moment stretched taut between them, filled with unsaid questions and unshed tears. Chris's throat felt tight, his voice lost somewhere between his chest and his mouth.

"Well?" The word was barely audible, a whisper torn from his lips by the sheer force of his need to know.

Samuel's eyes met his, and in them, Chris saw an echo of the resilience that had kept him going all these years. "The DNA," Samuel paused, letting the silence swell before he continued, "it's not yours, Chris."

In that instant, the world seemed to realign. The crushing weight of uncertainty lifted, replaced by a fragile filament of hope that dared to shine through the cracks in Chris's carefully guarded heart. It wasn't over, not yet—but it was the beginning of something. Something like freedom.

Chris's knees buckled, and he grasped the back of a chair to steady himself. A laugh, startled and disbelieving, bubbled up from his chest as relief coursed through him like a wave washing away years of grime from a forgotten statue. He drew in a deep breath, the air tasting sweeter than he remembered.

"Are you sure?" It was a question tethered to a thousand others, but it was the only one that managed to escape his lips.

"Absolutely," Samuel replied, his voice firm with the weight of evidence now tipping the scales in their favor. "The DNA doesn't lie, Chris."

Around them, the Innocence Project's office seemed to pulse with new life. The stacks of papers, the buzzing fluorescents, even the scuffed linoleum floor—all bore witness to this pivotal moment. And Chris felt it all, the gritty texture of reality mingling with a hope so long deferred it felt foreign in his hands.

"Thank you," Chris said, finally finding his voice amidst the shock. With those words, something unclenched within him—a knot of fear and doubt that had been a constant companion.

Samuel clapped a hand on Chris's shoulder, grounding him in the present. "This is just the beginning, my friend. We've got work to do." His eyes blazed with a fire that could ignite the darkest corners of despair. Samuel Bennett was more than a lawyer; he was a crusader for the wronged, and his next battle loomed large.

"Let's take this to the district attorney," Samuel declared, gathering the sheaf of documents that held Chris's future within their crisp edges. "They can't ignore this. It's irrefutable."

Chris watched as Samuel readied himself, straightening his tie with a determination that rivaled the steadfastness of mountains. He knew the road ahead would be fraught with bureaucracy and resistance, but seeing Samuel's fervor, his belief in justice, solidified Chris's resolve.

"Today, we're making things right," Samuel said, his voice a blend of promise and conviction. It wasn't just Chris's fight anymore; it was theirs, and Samuel wouldn't rest until the scales of justice had been balanced.

"Let's go," Chris agreed, steeling himself for the next chapter. With each step they took towards the door, the heavy chains of the past loosened, and the light of possibility grew stronger. Today marked not an end, but the heralding of a dawn that Chris had almost ceased to dream of.

Samuel Bennett strode into the district attorney's office with the confidence of a man holding truth in his hands. The tightness in his jaw belied a readiness for battle, and his piercing blue eyes locked onto the district attorney who sat behind a desk cluttered with legal briefs and case files.

"Good morning," Samuel began, extending a hand that seemed to carry the weight of justice within its grasp. The district attorney accepted it with a firm grip but a wary gaze, as if the handshake were a contract he wasn't sure he wanted to sign.

"Mr. Bennett, I've heard you have something urgent to discuss regarding the Matthews case?" The skepticism in the district attorney's voice was as clear as the glass that separated him from the bustling city outside his window.

"Indeed, I do," Samuel responded, setting a slim folder on the mahogany surface. "What I have here is new evidence—DNA testing results that conclusively prove Chris Matthews's innocence."

"Conclusive is a strong word, Mr. Bennett." The district attorney leaned back, his fingers tenting in front of him. "We both know DNA evidence can be... tricky."

"Tricky, yes, but not in this case," Samuel countered, opening the folder to reveal several pages of scientific data. "The DNA collected at the crime scene does not match Chris's. Not even remotely."

He pointed to a series of charts and graphs that painted an irrefutable picture. "See here? The genetic markers—they don't lie. And they tell a story quite different from the one that put Chris behind bars."

For a moment, there was only the sound of the city's heartbeat through the walls, punctuated by the soft shuffle of papers as the district attorney reviewed the documents. Samuel watched, patient but unyielding, as facts and figures challenged doubt and reluctance.

"Every strand of DNA is unique, like a personal signature written into our cells," Samuel continued, guiding the district attorney through the labyrinth of nucleotides and alleles. "This signature," he tapped the paper, "is not Chris Matthews's."

"Mr. Bennett, your dedication to your client is admirable," the district attorney replied, finally looking up. "But you understand, overturning a conviction isn't a simple matter."

"Which is precisely why I'm here," Samuel insisted. "To ensure that the simplicity of the truth isn't lost in a web of complications. This new evidence doesn't just cast doubt—it screams innocence."

The air felt charged with the resonance of Samuel's words, and for a second, it seemed as though the very foundations of the room were shifting. This was more than just a meeting; it was a pivotal turning point, hinging on the balance between skepticism and science, between the past's shadows and the light of exoneration.

"Let's go over these details together," Samuel offered, his tone a blend of professionalism and passion. "Chris has been waiting long enough for justice, and every day we delay is another mark against the system we both serve."

As the sun traced its arc outside, casting elongated shadows across the room, the two men delved into the heart of the evidence. It was a dance of logic and law, each step carefully measured, each turn scrutinizing the path to redemption. And as the dialogue unfolded, the scent of change lingered in the air, potent and promising, like rain after a long drought.

The silence in the district attorney's office was palpable, broken only by the soft ticking of a clock and the faint hum of the city outside. The district attorney sat behind the desk, fingers steepled, eyes narrowed in concentration on the file before them—an echo of the lives hanging in the balance.

"Look, Samuel," the district attorney began, their voice tinged with the weight of responsibility, "I took an oath to seek justice, not just to prosecute. If we got it wrong..." They let the sentence hang, unfinished but understood.

Samuel Bennett leaned forward, his own commitment mirrored in his steady gaze. "And if you did, wouldn't seeking justice mean setting it right?"

A sigh escaped the district attorney, a sound heavy like the closing of old books, full of dust and shadows. They were a gatekeeper of order, yet here they stood at the precipice of disorder, staring down the possibility that their pursuit of justice had ensnared an innocent man. It was a sobering reckoning with the system they upheld, a system that now demanded humility and courage in equal measure.

"Reducing Chris's sentence... it implies doubt. It implies we made a mistake," the district attorney said slowly, each word measured against the scales of justice in their mind.

"Isn't the implication of innocence more important?" Samuel countered, his voice firm, yet respectful. "Especially when it's backed by irrefutable evidence?"

The district attorney picked up the report once more, the pages filled with graphs and figures that painted a stark picture—one that could not be ignored. They scanned the evidence, each line a thread unraveling the tapestry of guilt once ascribed to Chris Matthews. It wasn't just about acknowledging a single error; it was about confronting a potential flaw in the fabric of justice itself.

"Time served," they finally spoke, the words resonating with the gravity of their decision. "It's clear that this new evidence cannot be overlooked. Chris Matthews' sentence will be reduced to time served."

Samuel exhaled, a release of tension he hadn't realized he'd been holding. This was a monumental shift, a crack in the wall of a decade-long confinement. It was a declaration that the truth still held power, even after years of silence.

"Thank you," Samuel said, extending his hand across the desk. The district attorney accepted it, their handshake a silent testament to the complex machinery of justice—imperfect, but capable of rectification.

As the meeting concluded, and Samuel left the office with the promise of a new chapter for Chris Matthews, the district attorney remained seated, contemplating the turning tides of fate and law. In the end, it was about balancing the scales, and today, the weight of truth had tipped the balance.

The phone rang with the kind of urgency that bends time, each ring a chime counting down to Chris Matthews' fate. Seated in a hard plastic chair that mirrored the rigidity of his tension-filled body, Chris lunged for the receiver, his hand a little unsteady but quick. Samuel Bennett watched, his eyes reflecting the gravity of the moment.

"Hello?" Chris's voice was a tightrope of hope and fear.

"Chris, it's Samuel," came the reply, warm yet laced with the magnitude of the news he bore. "The district attorney has agreed. Time served, Chris. They're acknowledging the new evidence."

For a second, the world seemed to pause, the hum of fluorescent lights above now a distant echo as Chris absorbed the words. Then, a wave of relief crashed over him, so intense it almost buckled his knees. He gripped the edge of the desk to steady himself, his other hand clutching the phone like a lifeline.

"Really?" The word tumbled out, half question, half exclamation. The walls of the sterile office faded away as years of pent-up emotions surged forward. His heart hammered a victory beat, the rhythm of a man whose innocence could finally breathe freely after being held captive by cold bars of injustice.

"Really," Samuel confirmed, the smile evident in his voice. "You're coming home, Chris."

"Thank you," Chris whispered, a mantra of gratitude that carried the weight of a thousand sleepless nights. Tears welled in his eyes, not of sorrow but of salvation—a cleansing flood washing away the grime of doubt and despair.

"Justice," Chris said aloud, savoring the taste of the word, "it's been served at last."

Samuel's chuckle on the other end was a soft note of celebration. "Yes, it has. We'll start the paperwork immediately. It won't be long now."

Chris hung up and took a deep breath, the air filling his lungs like a promise of freedom. Around him, the office buzzed with the mundane sounds of work, oblivious to the seismic shift that had just occurred in one man's life. But within him, everything had changed.

He leaned back, allowing the chair to take his weight as he closed his eyes, envisioning the world beyond these walls—a world that held possibility, a future untainted by the shadow of a cell. There were dreams he had packed away, dreams that could now see daylight once more.

"Exoneration," he murmured to himself, the word a new chapter waiting to be written. With the clarity of dawn breaking, Chris realized that this was just the beginning. The road ahead would be long; reclaiming his life, his name, his identity would take time. But for the first time in what felt like eternity, the path was his to walk.

A sense of hope swelled within him, its warmth radiating through every fiber of his being. He stood up, no longer confined by the expectations of a system that had failed him. Chris Matthews was ready to step into the light, into a life reclaimed, with the resilience and optimism that had sustained him now paving the way for a journey toward exoneration and beyond.

Chapter 10

Chris Matthews stood at the prison gates, his heart a drumbeat of anticipation in his chest. The cold metal bars had kept him from the world for so long, and now, on the brink of freedom, they seemed almost surreal. His dark hair fluttered slightly in the breeze, a physical reminder that there was life beyond these walls—a life he was about to reclaim.

With each second ticking by, the nervous energy within him grew. This was the moment he had envisioned through the darkest nights, the beacon that had sustained his hope. Chris's eyes, which had seen too much yet somehow retained their spark, were fixed on the space just beyond the gate. He could almost taste the sweetness of the air that waited there.

Then, with a mechanical clank that echoed off the concrete and barbed wire, the gates began to swing open. For an instant, time paused, the sound carving a memory deep into Chris's mind. And as the gap widened, inviting him to step through, it was as if the world itself held its breath.

He hesitated for the barest of moments, the gravity of the situation anchoring his feet to the ground. This threshold was more than just metal and movement—it was the line between his past and everything that was yet to come. Excitement coursed through him, mingled with a trepidation that tugged at the edges of his newfound freedom.

But resilience had been Chris's unwavering companion, and it lent strength to his legs now. With a deep breath that filled his lungs with promise, he stepped forward, crossing from confinement into the wide expanse of possibility. The sunlight hit his face, warm and bright, like a gentle affirmation of his release.

"Here goes nothing," Chris murmured to himself, a small smile playing on his lips as he embraced the uncertainty ahead. Each step felt like a declaration, an assertion of his presence in a world that hadn't waited for him but was now forced to acknowledge his return. He was no longer a number, a case, a file—he was Chris Matthews, and his story was far from over.

Chris squinted as the world outside the prison gates came into sharp focus. The city sprawled before him, alive and pulsating with energy that was foreign to the stillness of his cell. A cacophony of sounds assaulted his ears—the distant honking of cars, the rhythmic thumping of construction work, and the fragmented melodies of street performers all coalescing into a symphony of freedom.

He inhaled deeply, and the smells overwhelmed him: exhaust mixed with the tantalizing aroma of street food, an undercurrent of fresh paint from nearby graffiti art, and the faintest hint of jasmine from someone's passing perfume. It was disorienting, this sensory overload, after years of inhaling nothing but the sterile, recycled air of incarceration.

"Chris!" The familiar voice cut through the urban hum, grounding him.

Turning toward the sound, Chris's eyes landed on a small group clustered near the curb. Their faces lit up like beacons of hope in a sea of indifference. His mother's smile stretched wide across her face, etched with lines of worry that had deepened in his absence. His father stood beside her, his posture stiff with barely contained emotion, while his sister bounced on the balls of her feet as if she might leap forward at any second.

"Mom, Dad, Sarah," Chris breathed their names like a mantra.

The moment he crossed the invisible line separating him from them, they surged forward. His mother's arms wrapped around him first, her embrace fierce as if she intended to shield him from any further harm. His father's hand clapped firmly on his back—a silent message of support—while his sister squeezed between them, tears glistening in her eyes as she laughed through sobs.

"Look at you, Chris," his mom whispered, pulling back just enough to see his face. "We've got you now, son."

"Welcome home, boy," his father added, voice thick with emotions he generally kept tucked away.

"Missed you so much, big bro," Sarah sniffed, her words muffled against his chest.

As their arms encased him, the tension that had been coiled tight within him since he'd heard the cell door lock for the last time began to unwind. Here, with the city's chaos at his back and his family's warmth surrounding him, Chris felt the first true glimmer of something he'd only dared to dream of—home.

Chris turned, his gaze sweeping over the group of loved ones who had gathered to usher him back into the world. And then he saw her—Jenny. She stood slightly apart from the rest, a solitary figure brimming with quiet strength. Her eyes met his, and in that instant, Chris felt as though no time had passed at all.

"Jenny," he said, his voice catching on her name.

"Chris." Her reply was a whisper, but it carried the weight of years.

They moved towards each other, almost hesitantly, as if afraid this moment might shatter under its own significance. When they finally embraced, it was a collision of past laughter and present tears—a silent conversation of shared pain and enduring loyalty. Jenny's arms clung to him tightly, and Chris could feel the tremor of her breath against his neck.

"It's really over," she murmured, pulling away just enough to search his face for the boy she once knew.

"Thanks to you," Chris replied, acknowledging the fight she had waged on his behalf.

"Always," she promised, and there was a fierceness in her tone that spoke of battles fought and won.

Their reunion was a blend of joy and sorrow, laughter spilling over the edges of their relief as they exchanged stories and apologies. There was a depth to their connection that needed no words, an unspoken understanding that had endured despite the chasm of time and hardship between them.

As the initial rush of emotions subsided, Sarah pulled out her phone, her fingers flying over the screen with practiced ease. "Let's get a photo, everyone!" she called, rallying the family once more.

"Wait, what's that?" Chris asked, squinting at the device in his sister's hand.

"Oh, Chris, this is a smartphone," Jenny explained gently, taking the phone from Sarah and holding it up for him to see.

"Smartphone..." Chris echoed, turning the word over in his mind like a pebble made smooth by the river of progress that had swept past him while he was behind bars.

"Here, let me show you," Jenny said, guiding his fingers to swipe across the screen. Images flicked by in a blur, snippets of life that had gone on without him. "This is social media. It's how we stay connected now."

"Connected," he repeated, the concept both foreign and familiar.

"Everyone's on here," Jenny continued, pointing to icons and feeds filled with faces and names. "It can be overwhelming, but you'll catch up. We'll help you."

Chris nodded, his eyes wide with a mixture of curiosity and apprehension. A world of information at his fingertips—another freedom to acclimate to. He watched as Jenny navigated through photos and messages, demonstrating the power of this pocket-sized window to the world.

"Seems like I've missed a lot," Chris said, a half-smile tugging at his lips as he contemplated the digital landscape stretching out before him.

"Yeah, but don't worry," Jenny assured him, squeezing his hand. "We've got time to fill in the blanks. Together."

"Starting with a selfie," Sarah chimed in, flashing a bright smile as she held up the phone.

"Selfie?" Chris asked, the word strange on his tongue.

"Picture of ourselves, by ourselves," Jenny laughed, pulling him close.

With a click, their smiles were frozen in time, a snapshot of new beginnings. And Chris, standing there between the concrete memories of incarceration and the boundless possibilities of the future, felt the warmth of hope kindling anew within his chest.

Chris hesitated outside the café, his hand resting on the cool metal of the door. The buzz of conversation from within seeped through the glass, an echo of a life he'd been forced to leave behind. He drew in a deep breath and pushed the door open.

"Chris? Is that really you?" A voice tinged with disbelief cut through the hum of voices. It belonged to Mark, an old friend who had shared many late nights discussing dreams over cups of coffee.

"Hey, Mark." Chris's voice wavered slightly, betraying his nerves. "Yeah, it's me."

Mark stood up, his chair scraping against the floor, and walked over with an awkward gait. They embraced briefly, a stilted connection that spoke volumes of the years lost and the uncertainty of their reunion.

"Man... I—We heard what happened, but..." Mark trailed off, struggling to find the right words. "I'm sorry, Chris."

"Thanks," Chris managed to say, searching Mark's face for signs of the old camaraderie they once shared.

Some friends, like Mark, offered hesitant smiles and well-meaning apologies. Others averted their eyes, uncomfortable and unsure how to bridge the chasm of Chris's absence. Each interaction was a reminder of the time that was stolen, of friendships left to wither in the shadow of doubt and suspicion.

Leaving the café with a heart heavier than when he entered, Chris turned towards home—a place untouched by the skepticism of the world around him.

As he approached the house, the sight of the weathered red bricks and the familiar creak of the front gate flooded him with a sense of belonging. His mother was there, waiting on the porch with arms wide open.

"Welcome home, my boy," she said, her voice thick with emotion as she wrapped him in an embrace that seemed to piece back together parts of him that had been chipped away by cold prison walls.

"Mom," Chris whispered, allowing himself to sink into the warmth of her love, letting it chase away the chill of isolation.

Inside, the scent of fresh paint mingled with the aroma of his favorite childhood meal simmering on the stove. The walls were adorned with framed memories, each one a testament to a life put on pause. His father clapped him on the shoulder, a silent message of support that needed no words.

"Your room's just how you left it," his sister Sarah said with a smile, leading him down the hallway. "Though I did sneak in sometimes when I missed you."

"Wouldn't expect anything less," he replied, the corners of his mouth lifting in genuine amusement.

Stepping into his room, he was enveloped by the tangible presence of his past—the baseball trophies lining the shelf, posters of his favorite bands still clinging to the walls, and the bedspread rumpled just as he'd left it that fateful morning years ago.

"Feels like another lifetime," Chris murmured, running his fingers over the coarse fabric of the quilt his grandmother had made.

"Let's make this one better," Sarah said, squeezing his hand.

"Better," he echoed, determination lighting his eyes. Here, among the relics of his youth, Chris found a foundation strong enough to rebuild upon. With the love of his family as his cornerstone, he felt ready to face whatever lay ahead.

The clatter of dishes and the warm, inviting scent of roasted chicken filled the air as Chris took a seat at the head of the dinner table. His mother, with her practiced hands, set down a steaming bowl of mashed potatoes, her apron dusted with flour from the rolls she'd baked earlier. The kitchen was alive with energy, his family bustling about to bring the celebratory meal together.

"Pass the gravy, will you?" his brother Tom asked, reaching across the table and giving Chris a wink. Their glasses clicked in a toast, the sound mingling with the chatter of shared stories—the ones Chris had missed all those years.

"Remember how you used to eat peanut butter straight out of the jar?" Sarah teased, eliciting a chorus of laughter from around the table. Chris smiled, feeling the warmth of belonging envelop him like a cloak.

Yet, beneath the comfort of family and the familiarity of home-cooked food, an undercurrent of uncertainty tugged at Chris's heart. He listened to his nephew's excitement over his new coding project at school, a world so foreign to what Chris knew. The conversation drifted to advancements and jobs that had emerged while he had been away, a stark reminder of the gap in his life that needed bridging.

"Everything's so different now," Chris said softly, more to himself than to anyone else, his fingers tracing the rim of his glass. "I'm going to have to start from scratch, aren't I?"

His father met his gaze, the lines on his face etched with empathy. "You've always been a quick learner, son. You'll find your way."

Chris nodded, taking solace in his father's unwavering faith in him, yet he couldn't shake the feeling of being a stranger in this rapidly evolving world. The challenge of finding employment loomed large in his mind. He wasn't the same ambitious twenty-year-old who left all those years ago; he was starting anew, with a tarnished record and a decade long gap in his resume.

"Hey, I heard the garage down the street is hiring," Tom offered, breaking into his thoughts. "Might not be your dream job, but it's a start, right?"

"Right," Chris agreed, trying on the idea like a new coat, testing its fit. A start was all he needed. He pushed aside the lingering doubts, focusing instead on the present moment—the laughter, the love, and the simple joy of being together again.

"Here's to new beginnings," Chris toasted, raising his glass. The table echoed his sentiment, their voices blending into a harmony that promised support through every step of his journey back into the world he once knew.

Chris stood at the threshold of his old room, the familiar scent of cedar and worn pages from a stack of dog-eared novels greeting him like an old friend. His mother's gentle hand rested on his shoulder, her touch grounding him in the reality of this long-awaited moment.

"Everything is just as you left it," she said, her voice a soft melody of reassurance. "Take all the time you need to settle back in."

The walls, once plastered with posters of rock bands and movie stars, now held only shadows of the past. Chris traced his fingers over the faded marks, each one a reminder of dreams paused but not forgotten. He sat gingerly on the bed, the springs creaking under his weight—a subtle nod to the passage of time.

His sister, Emma, perched beside him, her smile a beacon in the sea of change. "You know, there's a community center nearby that offers computer classes. Could be useful, right? Help you get up to speed with all the tech stuff."

"Good idea," Chris said, the corners of his mouth lifting in gratitude. Her practical suggestions were a lifeline thrown into the waters of uncertainty that he found himself navigating.

"Everyone understands, Chris. You've been dealt a bad hand, but we're all here for you," Uncle Joe chimed in, leaning against the doorframe with arms crossed. "I'm talking about friends, too. We've got your back."

"Thanks, Uncle Joe. It means more than you know," Chris replied, his voice steady despite the emotion welling up inside him.

As night fell, the hum of the city outside melded with the quiet of the house. Lying in his childhood bed, Chris let his eyes wander over the relics of his youth—the baseball glove on the shelf, awards from science fairs, the telescope pointed toward the window, once his portal to the stars. Each object whispered tales of who he was and who he might still become.

He closed his eyes, allowing the memories to wash over him: the joy of hitting a home run, the pride of a blue ribbon, the wonder of gazing up at the expansive night sky. But interwoven with the joy were threads of pain—the sting of handcuffs on his wrists, the echo of a cell door slamming shut.

Opening his eyes to the darkness, Chris felt the weight of his journey. There was so much to rebuild, so many wrongs he couldn't right. Yet amidst it all, there was a spark of something undefinable—hope, perhaps, or determination. Maybe it was simply the warmth of being surrounded by those who believed in him.

Tomorrow, he would wake up in his own bed, in his own home, no longer bound by bars or the judgments of others. With every sunrise, he'd have the chance to write a new chapter—one where justice wasn't just a dream glimpsed through the bars of a prison window, but a reality he could help shape.

"Whatever comes next, I'm not facing it alone," he whispered into the silence, drawing comfort from the presence of his family just beyond the bedroom door. As sleep finally claimed him, Chris Matthews clung to the promise of a new day.

Chris stood in the middle of the community center's bustling lobby, his gaze fixed on the colorful array of flyers pinned to the corkboard. Each one represented a cause, a plea for volunteers, a chance to make a difference. He reached out, fingers brushing against a flyer that called for criminal justice reform advocates.

"Hey," Jenny said, approaching him with two steaming cups of coffee from the nearby stand. "Thought you could use a pick-me-up."

"Thanks," he replied, accepting the cup with a grateful nod. The warm scent wafted up, grounding him in the moment.

"Planning your next move?" she asked, following his line of sight to the bulletin board.

"Something like that," Chris said, turning to face her. "I've been thinking about all the guys I left behind—innocent and stuck in there. I want to help change the system that failed us." His words carried the weight of conviction, an unshakeable resolve shining through.

Jenny's eyes sparkled with admiration. "That's the Chris Matthews I know—always looking out for others. Count me in."

They wandered outside, finding their way to the park where they'd spent countless hours dreaming of the future. They settled onto a bench, the same old oak tree casting dappled shadows over them.

"Remember when we used to sit here, planning our world tours and grand adventures?" Jenny chuckled, a nostalgic glint in her eye.

"Feels like a lifetime ago," Chris said. But as he looked at her, he felt the threads of their past weaving together with the present.

"Maybe we can still have adventures," Jenny suggested, "just a different kind. We can travel, talk to people, share our story... Your story."

"Could be our story," Chris corrected gently. "You've been with me every step of the way."

"True," she conceded, bumping her shoulder against his playfully. "So, where do we start?"

"Local community meetings, getting the word out, maybe set up a blog or something. Gotta admit, though, I'm still trying to get a handle on this whole digital world."

"Leave that to me," Jenny said with confidence. "I'll be your tech guru."

"Deal," Chris agreed, his heart lighter than it had been in years.

As the sun dipped lower in the sky, painting it with strokes of orange and pink, they spoke of dreams both old and new—their conversation a delicate dance between the life they once imagined and the reality they now embraced.

"Whatever happens," Chris mused, "we're going to make a difference. Not just for me, but for anyone who's ever been wronged by a system meant to protect them."

"Here's to second chances," Jenny raised her empty coffee cup in a toast.

"Second chances," Chris echoed, a sense of purpose surging within him. Together, they watched the sunset, their shared vision for the future as bright as the fading light.

Chris tossed on his bed, the once-familiar blanket of darkness now a canvas for his thoughts. The quiet of his childhood room enveloped him, so different from the cacophony of prison life—the clanging bars and the low murmur of desperate voices that had been his nightly lullaby for far too long. He exhaled slowly, trying to let go of the day's whirlwind of emotions.

The mattress felt softer than he remembered, cradling his average-built frame as if promising a comfort he wasn't sure he deserved yet. He closed his eyes and saw Jenny's smile, the curve of it like a beacon in the night. Her laughter, a melody that seemed to fill the empty spaces left by years of silence. They had sat side by side, their dreams weaving together into a tapestry of hope, vivid and real.

But as the elation of freedom gave way to the stillness of the night, Chris's mind raced with uncertainties. There was a world outside these four walls that had moved on without him—a world full of smartphones and hashtags, where time had sprinted ahead, leaving him to play catch-up.

He thought about his friends, some who had met his return with open arms and others whose eyes held questions they couldn't voice. The city had changed, too; it bustled with a rhythm that seemed faster, louder, and he felt like an outsider trying to learn a dance everyone else knew by heart.

"Tomorrow," he whispered to the dark, "I'll start fresh." But the words felt heavy, burdened by the knowledge of the challenges that lay sprawled like a road map with no clear destination. Finding a job, rekindling old relationships, building new ones—each task loomed like a mountain in the distance.

Yet amidst the tangle of fears and doubts, a steady undercurrent of gratitude pulsed within him. Gratitude for the warmth of his family's embrace, for the sustenance of their shared meal, for the unwavering support that had never waned even when the truth seemed lost in a labyrinth of lies.

Above all, he clung to the resolve that had sparked earlier that day—a determination to turn his ordeal into a force for change. It shimmered within him, a fledgling flame kindled by injustice but fueled by the desire to ensure no one else suffered a similar fate.

"Justice reform," he murmured, the words shaping the silhouette of a purpose that stretched beyond himself, reaching out to touch the lives of unseen others caught in the unforgiving gears of a flawed system.

Chris turned to his side, the soft pillow accepting the weight of his head. His breathing steadied, syncing with the gentle rise and fall of shadows cast by the moonlight peeking through the curtains. His past, with its sharp edges and cold corners, was a chapter closed; the future, though uncertain, beckoned with the promise of a story yet to be written.

"Second chances," he thought, allowing the corners of his mouth to lift slightly, despite the turmoil within. A silent vow settled in his chest—to fight, to speak, to stand for those who had fallen or might fall. And with that, the first day of his newfound freedom drew quietly to an end, a single step on the long road to redemption that lay ahead.

Chapter 11

Chris Matthews paced the sterile hallway of the courthouse, his footsteps echoing against the marble floors. Short, dark hair neatly combed, he looked every bit the man who had weathered a storm but refused to be defined by it. His eyes, a deep brown and alive with purpose, scanned the corridor for his attorney, Laura Simmons.

"Chris," Laura called out as she approached him. Her red hair was a stark contrast against the sea of grey suits, her blue eyes sharp and focused. She extended a folder thick with papers toward him. "Everything's ready for filing the lawsuit."

"Good," Chris replied, taking it from her. They found an empty bench, the leather cool beneath their touch. The folder crinkled as he opened it, the sound oddly comforting in the cavernous space filled with hushed voices and the occasional gavel's rap.

"Here we've outlined the evidence we've gathered over the past months," Laura said, tapping on the documents. "Witness statements, DNA reports, expert testimonies - it's all here."

Chris nodded, his gaze fixed on the pages. He could see years of his life spelled out in legal terms, each word a step closer to reclaiming his truth. "And the witnesses?" he asked.

"Ready and prepped," Laura assured him. "We've got people who believe in you, Chris. They're committed to setting this right."

"Thank you, Laura." Chris's voice held a raw edge, a mix of gratitude and the weight of what was yet to come. "This isn't just for me. It's for everyone who's been trapped in this flawed system."

Laura regarded him with a blend of warmth and admiration. "Your story has power, Chris. You're going to make a difference with it."

"Once I get restitution," Chris added, closing the folder with a sense of finality. "I'm putting it towards justice reform. Lectures, campaigns, whatever it takes."

"Restitution is only part of the journey," Laura said, standing up as they prepared to face the court. "But it's a start. And I'll be with you every step of the way."

Chris stood beside her, his determination palpable. "Let's do this," he said, his words not just a statement, but a vow. Together, they walked into the courtroom, ready to turn the page on a painful chapter and write a new narrative of redemption and change.

As the heavy wooden doors of the courtroom creaked open, a hush fell over the gallery. The judge, draped in the solemn black robes of authority, took their place with an air that seemed to squeeze the room tighter. Chris Matthews felt a knot tightening in his stomach, a physical embodiment of the tension that filled the space like thick smoke. He shifted in the hard, wooden chair, feeling the grain press against his palms as he gripped the edge of the table.

Beside him, Laura Simmons sat with her back straight as a steel rod, a binder of documents opened before her, her blue eyes scanning the pages with practiced focus. Chris caught a glimpse of the jury filing in, their faces a mosaic of curiosity and duty, and for a moment, he saw his fate resting in their hands.

"Order in the court!" the bailiff's voice boomed, and the murmurings subsided to silence.

Across from them stood the opposing counsel, James Carlton, a man whose reputation preceded him. His suit was impeccably tailored, the gray fabric contrasting sharply with his stern demeanor. As he arranged his papers on the lectern, his movements were deliberate, each action calculated for maximum impact.

Laura leaned toward Chris, her voice a low whisper. "Keep your focus. We've prepared for this." Her words were a lifeline, grounding him amidst the waves of anxiety.

Carlton began his opening statement, his voice echoing off the high ceilings. "Ladies and gentlemen of the jury, we are here today to uphold the integrity of our justice system..." His words were smooth and polished, each one delivered with the precision of a seasoned orator. He painted a picture of a state wronged, urging the jury to consider the gravity of overturning a conviction.

When it was Laura's turn, she rose with a grace that belied her fierce spirit. "The true measure of our justice system isn't how it punishes but how it corrects its mistakes," she began, her tone infused with earnestness that resonated in the wood-paneled room. She laid out the evidence methodically, each piece a building block in the fortress of Chris's innocence. Her strategy was not just about persuasion but about illumination – shedding light on the truth that had been obscured for so long.

Chris watched as the jurors leaned in, their expressions shifting with the ebb and flow of the arguments. In Laura's careful narration of events and the presentation of exculpatory evidence, there was a beacon of hope, and Chris found himself clinging to it.

The trial would be long, the road to redemption winding and uncertain. But as the opening salvos were exchanged in that venerable court, Chris felt the stirrings of something powerful within him – a resilience that had carried him this far and would carry him through whatever lay ahead.

Chris's heart thumped loudly, echoing the solemn cadence of the courtroom clock. Each tick was a reminder of the time he had lost, each tock a step toward the justice he sought. He sat, his hands folded neatly on the table, feeling the coarse texture of the wood beneath his fingertips—a stark contrast to the smoothness of the handcuffs he'd once worn.

"Stay focused," Laura whispered, her voice steady, a lifeline in the tumultuous sea of Chris's emotions. She passed him a reassuring glance before turning her attention back to the witness stand.

The state's witness, a former detective, recounted the night of the crime with a confidence that seemed unshakeable. Chris listened, his jaw set firm, his eyes betraying none of the turmoil that churned within him. The detective's words twisted the knife of injustice deeper, painting a picture that was all too familiar yet wholly untrue.

Laura rose, her movements precise and deliberate. "May I remind the court," she began, countering the testimony with hard evidence, "that my client's whereabouts were confirmed by not one, but three independent sources that night?" Her blue eyes swept across the jury, connecting with them, urging them to see beyond the badge to the fallibility it concealed.

Chris watched as Laura navigated the treacherous waters of legal combat. She wielded objections like a sword, parrying the state's thrusts with swift precision. When a crucial piece of evidence was called into question, she pounced, revealing its inconsistencies with the skill of a chess grandmaster. It was this meticulous dismantling of the prosecution's case that kept Chris's hope alive, even as the weight of each testimony tried to crush it.

"Your honor, the evidence before us is clear," Laura asserted, her voice rising with controlled passion. "My client has been the victim of a grave miscarriage of justice."

As the trial wore on, Chris felt the strain of maintaining his composure. The room seemed to shrink, the air growing thick with tension. He could almost hear the whispers of doubt creeping through the minds of the jurors. But he held onto the belief that truth would prevail, that the years spent behind bars would not be in vain.

"Justice will be served," he murmured under his breath, more a prayer than a promise.

Laura concluded her argument with a final, emphatic statement that resonated in the now hushed courtroom. "We ask not for sympathy, but for justice. We ask you to right the wrong that has been done to Chris Matthews."

Chris closed his eyes for a moment, allowing himself to envision the life that awaited him beyond these walls—a life where he could use his voice to champion change, to ensure that no other innocent soul would endure the nightmare he had faced.

When he opened his eyes again, the jury was filing out to deliberate, and Laura was gathering her notes, her expression unreadable. They had laid bare the truth; now, it was in the hands of those twelve strangers.

"Thank you," Chris whispered to Laura, his voice laced with gratitude for her unwavering defense. She gave him a nod, her eyes reflecting the fierce battle they had fought—and the battles still to come.

"Let's hope the jury sees the truth as clearly as we do," she replied, her gaze returning to the door through which the jury had disappeared. The wait would be agonizing, but together, they stood on the precipice of vindication.

Chris sat in the modest living room of his small, sunlit apartment, the worn-out couch groaning under his weight as he leaned forward, clutching his cell phone like a lifeline. The early morning light spilled across the room, casting long shadows on the walls that seemed to hold their breath along with him. His heart pounded in his ears, a cacophony of hope and trepidation as the seconds stretched into an eternity.

"Mr. Matthews," came the static-laden voice of his attorney, Laura Simmons, from the other end of the line. "The jury has reached a decision on the settlement."

Chris' throat felt like sandpaper, every ounce of moisture deserting him as he awaited the numbers that would either anchor him to his past or launch him into a future he had scarcely allowed himself to dream of.

"Eleven point seven million dollars," Laura announced, her voice a mixture of triumph and disbelief.

For a moment, Chris couldn't breathe; the walls seemed to sway, the floor beneath him unsteady. It was as if all the years of anguish and wrongful accusation had crystallized into this one figure—a number both surreal and life-altering.

"Chris, are you there?" Laura's voice pierced through his shock.

He found his voice, a mere whisper, laced with the weight of what had just been lifted from his shoulders. "Yes... I'm here. I just... Thank you, Laura. Thank you."

As the call ended, the emotions Chris had kept dammed up for so long broke free. Relief washed over him, followed swiftly by waves of vindication and then a surge of purpose. This wasn't just a settlement; it was a mandate to change the very system that had stolen years from his life.

Later that day, Chris's tiny kitchen buzzed with a warmth that had nothing to do with the summer heat outside. His family and closest friends huddled around the formica table, cups of coffee in hand, as they discussed the future—one now bright with possibility.

"Think about what this means, Chris!" his sister exclaimed, her eyes alight with pride and excitement. "You've got the power to make a real difference now."

"Exactly," said his best friend, Mark, clapping him on the back. "We could start setting up speaking engagements at colleges, town halls... anywhere they'll listen."

"Imagine the lives you can touch," his mother added, her voice soft but resolute. "You can help ensure no one else goes through what you did."

Chris listened to them, the passion in their voices feeding the flame that Laura's announcement had kindled within him. They threw out ideas, each one a spark flying towards a grander vision—workshops, partnerships with justice reform groups, even a nonprofit organization bearing his name.

"Guys," Chris finally interjected, his voice steady with newfound authority. "This is more than just a speaking tour. This is a crusade for truth, for fairness—for a system that sees people, not just cases."

Nods of agreement circled the table, each face reflecting the fire of shared conviction.

"Then let's do it," Mark said, determination etched into his features. "Let's shake the foundations of justice until they remember what they're supposed to support."

Chris looked around at the eager faces of those who had stood by him, who had believed in him when the world turned its back. He felt the surge of their collective energy, the promise of battles won together.

"Alright," he said, his resolve hardening into certainty. "Let's get to work."

Chris sat at his desk, a fortress of papers stacked around him, each one a stepping stone on the path he was carving out for himself. The glow from the laptop screen bathed his face in a soft light as he penned email after email, his fingers tapping out invitations and requests with a rhythm that matched the beating heart of his mission.

"Dear Mr. Johnson," he began another message, addressing the head of a local community center, "I am writing to you not only as a survivor of wrongful conviction but as a voice for those still lost in the shadows of injustice."

His phone buzzed intermittently, affirmations of venues locked down and partnerships formed. With every confirmation, Chris felt a twinge in his chest, a mixture of excitement and gravity—the weight of the words he would soon impart to eager ears.

"Another one confirmed," Laura said, peering over his shoulder with a proud smile. "The University of Chicago's law school is on board."

"Excellent," Chris replied, the corners of his eyes crinkling with satisfaction. "Every ear we reach is a step closer to change."

Days blurred into nights as Chris delved into crafting speeches that would resonate with the souls of strangers. He wove his narrative with a precision that betrayed his meticulous nature, ensuring his story wasn't just heard, but felt. It had to be more than statistics and legal jargon; it had to throb with the pulse of lived experience, of pain and triumph.

***

The day of the first speech arrived, and Chris stood backstage, the murmur of the assembling crowd a distant roar in his ears. He closed his eyes, inhaling deeply, grounding himself in the moment before stepping into the spotlight.

"Ladies and gentlemen," the host announced, "please welcome a man of remarkable courage and conviction—Chris Matthews."

Applause erupted like a thunderous wave as Chris emerged, his gait steady, his dark hair neatly combed, his eyes glinting with a purpose that silenced the room.

"Thank you," he began, his voice clear and commanding, yet tinged with an undeniable warmth. "My name is Chris Matthews, and I spent five years of my life locked away for a crime I didn't commit."

He paused, letting the weight of the statement hang in the air.

"I stand before you today, not seeking sympathy, but advocating for justice reform—a system that recognizes its flaws and strives to protect the innocent."

The audience leaned forward, hanging on to his every word, their faces a tapestry of emotions—anger, sorrow, resolve.

"Imagine the fear," Chris continued, his hands gesturing to emphasize his points, "of being ripped from your life, labeled as something you're not, and thrust into a nightmare that seems to have no end."

Whispers of agreement fluttered through the crowd, a communal bond forming in shared outrage.

"But I'm one of the lucky ones," he admitted, his voice softening. "I'm here with you today. Others are not so fortunate. Together, we can be their voice. Together, we can steer the course of justice back to its true north."

A hush settled over the room. In that silence, Chris's call to action echoed, reverberating off the walls and into hearts.

"Join me in this crusade," he implored. "For truth, for fairness, for a future where justice serves all."

As he concluded, the audience rose, a standing ovation that resonated with more than applause—it thrummed with the beginnings of change, a promise to take up the torch Chris had ignited. His story had transcended mere words; it became a clarion call, rallying them to the cause he held so dear.

Chris stepped off the stage, his spirit buoyant with hope. This was just the beginning, he knew, but it was a powerful one. And with each step, each speech, he'd chip away at the monolith of injustice until it crumbled into a fairer tomorrow.

A surge of energy coursed through the crowd as Chris descended from the stage, shaking hands that reached out to him eagerly. The warmth in their clasp matched the encouragement glowing in their eyes—a reflection of the fire he'd stoked with his words.

"Your story, it's incredible," a woman said, her voice laced with admiration. "How can we help?"

"Truth needs allies," Chris replied, maintaining eye contact. "Talk about it, spread the word, demand change."

They nodded fervently, ready to become foot soldiers in his campaign for justice reform. It was a mosaic of faces, each bearing its own story, yet united by a common thread of resolve. They wanted to be part of something larger than themselves, and Chris, with his unwavering optimism, had shown them the way.

"Count me in," a young man declared, his determination palpable. "I want to be on the right side of history."

Chris's heart swelled at the sentiment, a tide of solidarity lifting him higher. He saw himself not just as a speaker but as a catalyst for a movement that was gathering momentum before his very eyes.

Each person who approached him, each pledge to join the cause, was a victory in itself.

As the last of the audience filed out, leaving behind a hum of inspired conversations, Chris found a quiet corner to gather his thoughts. The speaking tour, once a distant dream, had taken form, each speech another step on an arduous journey toward truth.

He thought of the countless hours spent hunched over his laptop, the meticulous planning of every detail, the relentless pursuit of justice that had consumed him. And now, here he stood, no longer alone in his fight.

The impact of his tour was tangible, measured in the sparks he'd ignited in the hearts of those who listened. With each stop, each story shared, he was chipping away at the indifference that often shrouded the flaws of the criminal justice system.

"Keep pushing forward," he whispered to himself, a personal mantra that had seen him through the darkest of times. Now it was a promise, not just to himself but to all those who had suffered injustice.

His renewed sense of purpose coursed through him, steeling his resolve. There would be setbacks, he knew, moments when the mountain of systemic change seemed insurmountable. But Chris Matthews would face them head-on, armed with the power of his experience and the support of a growing legion of advocates, all marching toward a horizon of accountability and redemption.

With a deep breath, Chris closed his eyes, envisioning the future they would build together—one where the scales of justice were balanced for everyone. He opened his eyes, the spark of hope in them brighter than ever, and prepared for the road ahead.

Chapter 12

The neon glow of Las Vegas bled into the night sky as Chris Matthews navigated through the throngs of Halloween partygoers. The pulsing beat of music throbbed in his ears, a rhythmic heartbeat to the chaos of costumes and laughter that surrounded him. A sea of witches, superheroes, and monsters danced under the flickering lights, their faces hidden behind masks and painted grins.

Chris's gaze swept across the room, searching for a familiar face amid the masquerade. He adjusted his faux detective badge, a small nod to the theme of justice he held dear, even on a night meant for escapism. His eyes settled on Stephanie Brown, standing alone by a table adorned with jack-o'-lanterns. Her costume was simple—a black cat, complete with ears and painted whiskers on her cheeks—reflecting her desire to blend rather than stand out.

Taking a deep breath, Chris mustered a smile and made his way through the crowd, each step a deliberate move toward the quiet teenager who seemed so out of place among the revelry. Stephanie's large, expressive eyes caught his approach, and she tucked a strand of brown hair behind her ear, her body language a mixture of curiosity and retreat.

"Hey, Stephanie!" Chris called out over the din, his voice carrying the warmth of genuine interest. "Great costume! Mind if I join you?"

Her lips curved into a tentative smile, a silent invitation that spurred Chris forward. As he closed the distance between them, the clamor of the party faded into the background, replaced by an anticipation of shared conversation and the simple pleasure of connection.

Chris reached out a hand, his gesture meant to bridge the gap between them. "I thought we could—"

"Are you serious?" Stephanie's voice spiked, her eyes widening in shock as she misread the intention behind his outstretched hand. She recoiled as if he had offered her a venomous snake instead of camaraderie. "You think I'm into... into that stuff?"

"Wait, no!" Chris's hand dropped back to his side, his brow furrowing in confusion. The pulsing music seemed to fall away, leaving only the tension between them. "Stephanie, I just wanted to talk, that's all."

"Talk?" Her words were edged with disbelief, her body tensed like a cornered animal. "With your hand out like you're dealing? Is that your idea of a conversation starter at these parties?"

"Dealing?" The false accusation stung, and Chris felt the weight of it settle heavily on his shoulders. "No, I swear. I wouldn't—I don't do that. I was just reaching to get your attention over the noise."

Her gaze held onto his, searching for the truth in his earnest face. The party raged around them, a whirlwind of costumes and laughter that felt miles away from the bubble of misunderstanding they found themselves in.

"Look, I'm here to enjoy the party, not to cause trouble," Chris continued, his voice steady yet laced with concern. "I just thought you might want some company. Halloween can be overwhelming when you're alone."

The defensiveness in Stephanie's stance wavered, her eyes softening slightly as she took in his genuine expression. The painted whiskers on her cheeks twitched with a frown, betraying the conflict within.

"Okay," she said finally, her voice quieter now, but still threaded with caution. "Maybe I jumped to conclusions. This whole scene is just... it's not really my thing."

The music in the room throbbed like a pulse as Chris tried to smooth things over with Stephanie, but before more words could be exchanged, a heavy hand landed on his shoulder. He turned to face the newcomer, heart sinking as he recognized the imposing figure of David Brown, Stephanie's stepfather.

"Is there a problem here?" David's voice boomed, cutting through the din of the party with the precision of a knife. His eyes, hard and unyielding, fixed on Chris as if pinning him against an invisible wall.

"Mr. Brown," Chris started, taken aback by the sudden intrusion. "I was just—" But his words were steamrolled by David's rising temper.

"Stay away from her!" David's accusation sliced through the air, barbed and raw. The protective veil that shrouded him seemed to tighten around his muscular frame, his wrestler's instincts ready for combat.

"Sir, you've got it all wrong," Chris stammered, trying to keep his own voice even despite the adrenaline spiking through his veins. "I wasn't doing anything wrong. I promise."

Chris's plea hung between them, a fragile bridge over a chasm of misunderstanding. He hoped his sincerity would shine through the chaos, reach this man driven by loyalty and fear for his stepdaughter's safety.

"Stephanie, tell him," Chris urged, looking at her for support. But Stephanie remained silent, her wide eyes darting between her stepfather and Chris, trapped in her own turmoil.

"Look, I know how it may have looked, but I was just trying to talk to her," Chris explained, his optimism, the beacon that had always guided him through darker times, flickering in the cold shadow of David's suspicion.

David's jaw clenched, his response coiled and ready to strike, but he paused, perhaps taking a moment to measure Chris's earnest demeanor. For a fleeting second, the possibility of peace glimmered.

"Nothing happened," Chris continued, his resilience refusing to bow under pressure. "I swear on my word. There was no danger, no threat—just a simple mistake."

The music swelled around them, oblivious to the tension that gripped the trio. Chris stood firm, his eyes pleading for understanding, hoping that truth and justice would prevail in the end.

David's eyes narrowed, the simmering anger in his gaze spilling over as he ignored Chris's words. With a swift, muscular movement that betrayed his wrestling past, David shoved Chris with such force that the younger man stumbled backward, his feet tangling with the legs of a nearby chair.

"Back off!" David barked, his voice booming above the Halloween festivities, each syllable a hammer striking iron.

Chris staggered, his balance wavering but not breaking—much like his spirit. His resilience had been tested before, but never in such an abrupt onslaught of hostility. Still, he refused to meet aggression with aggression. Chris raised his hands, palms open and facing forward, a clear sign of peace amidst the brewing storm.

"Mr. Brown, please," Chris implored, his voice steady but laced with urgency. "I'm not here to cause trouble. You've got it all wrong."

The plea hovered in the air, a fragile bubble of reason ready to burst. Chris's heart raced, yet he stood rooted to the spot, determined to bridge the gap with words rather than fists. The hope for understanding flickered within him, a lone candle against the darkness of accusation and fury.

"Listen to me," Chris continued, his eyes locked onto David's. "I respect Stephanie. I would never put her—or anyone—in danger."

Around them, the party's gaiety played on, a stark contrast to the tension that coiled tight between the two men.

David's patience had frayed to its final thread, snapping as he lunged with the precision of a man whose body remembered the ring even if his mind forgot its restraint. His hands, once tools for applause and autographs, now propelled him forward in a blur of motion aimed squarely at Chris.

"David, no!" Chris's admonishment was cut short as David's bulk collided with him, sending both men crashing to the ground. The impact jolted through Chris's frame, the cold, hard floor of reality meeting the heat of David's unbridled anger.

Pinned beneath David's muscular weight, Chris fought to protect himself, arms raised in defense. Each blow that David dealt was deflected by instinct more than skill, but each block was a small victory against the onslaught. Chris's hope for a peaceful resolution gave way to a primal need to survive as fists rained down upon him, the rhythm relentless as a metronome set to the tempo of fury.

"Stop this madness!" Chris gasped, his voice strangled under the pressure of David's assault. His words were punctuated by grunts of exertion, the physical toll evident in every breath. The scent of sweat mingled with the artificial fog lingering from the party's ambiance, a twisted perfume marking the struggle.

Chris could feel the bruises blooming like dark flowers across his skin, each strike a petal unfurling in pain. He maneuvered, attempting to shield his face, his eyes scanning desperately for an opening, any chance to escape the barrage. Despite the chaos, Chris's thoughts remained lucid—clinging to the belief that justice would prevail, that truth would outshine the lies clouding David's judgment.

"David, listen to me..." Chris tried again, his voice a thread weaving through the cacophony of shouts and music surrounding them. But David's ears were closed, sealed by the wax of wrath, his actions deaf to the pleas of reason.

The room spun around Chris, a carousel of costumes and concerned faces blurring into insignificance against the stark reality of David's rage. In this moment, Chris understood the true fight was not against the man on top of him but against the shadows of misunderstanding that turned fear into violence.

The Halloween party's jolly chaos turned to a horrifying spectacle. Ghouls and witches, once dancing, now stood frozen as David's wrath unfolded before their eyes. The music's beat was drowned out by the collective gasp of the crowd, their costumes a stark contrast to the grim reality playing out.

"Hey, break it up!" shouted a man dressed as a cowboy, his voice edged with panic as he and others surged forward in an effort to intervene.

"Stop, you're killing him!" screamed a woman clad as a vampire, her fake fangs forgotten as genuine fear twisted her features.

Chris, pinned beneath David's heavyweight, felt hands clawing at them both, trying to pry apart the battle that had erupted. His optimism waned, a dimming light against the darkening prospect of David's unyielding anger.

"David, please," Chris choked out, his resilience tested as he struggled for air, his fingers weakly grappling at the vice-like grip around his throat. His plea was lost in the cacophony of shouts, the voices of the bystanders blending into a desperate chorus.

But David's ears were immune to their cries. The former wrestler's hands tightened, his muscular arms constricting like pythons, squeezing with a deadly purpose. The tattoos on his forearms, symbols of his life's journey, now seemed to twist and dance with each pulse of his exertion.

"Get off of him!" someone yelled, body pressing against David's back, but the ex-wrestler was relentless, a statue of fury anchored by a misguided sense of protection.

Chris's vision blurred, the edges of his sight darkening as if night were falling within the crowded room. His thoughts of justice and truth, those guiding stars of his conscience, flickered as he fought against the encroaching shadows. He tried to speak, to reason, but the words were trapped behind the crushing force of David's grasp.

"David, he didn't do anything!" another bystander insisted, their voice tinged with urgency, but the accusation only fueled David's conviction, driving him deeper into the abyss of rage.

Chris's fight for breath became a silent battle, the struggle visible only in the quickening terror in his eyes and the futile flutter of his hands. The crowd's alarm crescendoed, a symphony of distress that reverberated through the gaudy decorations and strobe lights, casting long, distorted shadows across the scene of unfolding tragedy.

The crowd surged with a single purpose, their hands clawing at David Brown's iron grip. Panic painted every face as they pulled at his arms, the muscles bulging beneath tattooed skin. The strength of many began to overwhelm the one, their desperation fueled by the sight of Chris Matthews' struggle for air.

"Let go, David! You're killing him!" cried a man dressed as a sheriff, the irony of his costume lost in the grim reality unfolding before them.

David's jaw clenched, his loyalty morphing into a dangerous beast that refused to back down. But the collective will of the crowd was an unstoppable force, prying away his fingers that had become instruments of harm rather than protection. Finally, with a heave from several costumed heroes, David's hands snapped open, releasing Chris from his deadly embrace.

Chris gasped, gulping down the precious air like a diver surfacing from too long underwater. His body convulsed with the shock of sudden freedom, his resilience a flickering candle in the storm of the night's events.

"Move back! Give him space!" The command cut through the cacophony as medical professionals, signaled by the commotion, pushed their way through the throng. They knelt by Chris's side, their faces set in lines of focus as they assessed the damage.

"Stay with us, Chris," one EMT urged, her voice a blend of command and encouragement, while her partner prepared oxygen. "Can you hear me?"

Chris's eyelids fluttered, his mind grasping at the threads of consciousness. The medics worked with swift precision, a dance of urgency as they stabilized his neck, checked his vitals, and administered oxygen. Their hands moved deftly, guided by training and the hope that lingered against the odds.

"Keep fighting, kid," murmured the older medic, his eyes meeting Chris's for a moment, conveying a silent promise to do everything in his power to pull him back from the precipice.

Around them, the party's revelry had dimmed, the music now a haunting backdrop to the drama that had hijacked the evening. Whispers of justice and redemption wove through the murmurs of the crowd, reflecting on the flaws of a system that could escalate to such violence. And amidst it all, Chris lay, his life hanging in the balance, a testament to the razor's edge between celebration and catastrophe.

The air, once thick with festivity, now clung heavy with dread. Chris's pulse stuttered under the medic's fingertips, a faltering rhythm that fought valiantly against the silence threatening to consume it. The EMTs exchanged a glance, a wordless conversation of seasoned eyes that had seen too much and yet never enough.

"Stick with me," the female medic pressed, her voice threading through the chaos with focused calm. Her partner, hands steady as he worked the defibrillator, nodded at her cue. They stood poised on the precipice, ready to wage war against the shadow that crept over Chris's features.

A shock—a desperate plea for the heart to beat. The machine's whine cut through the hush of the crowd, a sound that spoke of life in the balance. And again, another shock, echoing like a distant thunderclap, its power reverberating through Chris's still frame.

"Come on, Chris," she whispered, more to herself than to the unresponsive man before her. She sensed the collective will of the crowd, their silent prayers joining her own, willing the young man back from the edge.

But fate, it seemed, had drawn its line in the sand. Chris's chest lay motionless, his spirit no longer tethered by the optimism that had once been his hallmark. His eyes, which had held the spark of hope even in adversity, now stared empty at the ceiling of a world that had turned its back on him one final time.

"Time of death," the older medic said softly, his voice carrying a weight that no words could lift. He looked around at the faces peering in, each etched with grief and disbelief. A whisper of fabric signaled the closing of Chris's eyes, a final act of dignity bestowed upon the fallen.

The room filled with the sound of weeping, the notes of sorrow mingling with the eerie remnants of celebration outside. The irony was not lost on those who remained—the jovial decorations a stark contrast to the tragedy that had unfolded within.

In that moment, the laughter that had once carried dreams across the cityscape seemed a cruel joke; the costumes and masks, mere facades that could not shield them from the harsh truths of their existence. Chris, the resilient optimist, had become a symbol of all that was broken, his pursuit of justice now a story left untold, an ending written in the book of what could have been.

"Justice," someone murmured, the word hanging heavy in the air, a question, a challenge. It echoed through the room, a reminder of the flaws in the system that had allowed things to go so terribly wrong. As the medical team packed away their tools, their movements slow and somber, they knew this scene would replay in their minds, a haunting memory of a night where redemption slipped through their fingers like grains of sand.

Chapter 13

The neon glow of the Las Vegas strip spilled into the cavernous hall, where ghosts and ghouls reveled under pulsating lights. Chris Matthews, dressed as a vintage detective with a fedora angled just so, slipped through the throng of Halloween enthusiasts, a wry smile on his lips. The scar under his eye—a stark reminder of darker times—was hidden by makeup, but his spirit remained unmasked, bright as the jack-o'-lanterns grinning from shadowed corners.

"Quite the shindig, huh?" Chris said to a partygoer clad as Frankenstein's monster, who nodded with a clunky tilt of his head. Chris's laughter mingled with the eclectic symphony of chatter, his optimism an infectious melody that few could resist. He had weathered storms and emerged not just standing but dancing, finding joy in these moments of whimsy and warmth.

From across the room, beneath the looming silhouette of a faux haunted mansion, David Brown's eyes were fixed on Chris. His body was still as stone, save for the white-knuckle grip he had on his drink. With every jovial gesture Chris made, David's jaw tightened. His muscles, honed from years in the ring, coiled with a protective fury that had long since become second nature. David's temper, notorious as a summer storm, simmered beneath his politician's veneer.

"Easy, Dave," he muttered to himself, a mantra to stave off the heat bubbling inside him. His gaze never wavered, tracking Chris through the costumed crowd like a hawk zeroing in on its prey. There was something about Chris, a flicker of defiance or perhaps a shadow of accusation, that clawed at David's insides.

"Keep it together," he breathed again, the words lost amid the din of celebration. David's dark suit, a sharp contrast to the revelry around him, seemed to absorb the light, as if foreshadowing the storm that brewed within him, waiting to break free at the slightest provocation.

Chris wove through the maze of costumed revelers, his laughter a bright thread in the tapestry of merriment. The air was thick with the scents of spiced punch and melting wax from jack-o'-lanterns lining the walls. It was in this blur of celebration that Chris found himself inevitably drifting closer to the brooding figure of David Brown.

"Matthews," David's voice cut through the din, cold and sharp as a knife's edge.

Chris turned, his easy smile faltering for a heartbeat. "Brown," he acknowledged, maintaining his composure. "Didn't expect to see you here."

"Lot of things you don't expect," David growled, a vein pulsing at his temple.

"Look, if this is about the campaign—" Chris began, but David's snort cut him off.

"Save it. I know you've been talking. Spreading your stories."

The festive atmosphere curdled around them, partygoers steering clear of the brewing storm. Chris held his ground, though. "If by 'stories' you mean the truth, then yeah, I've been talking. People deserve to know what's going on."

David's laugh was devoid of humor, a bitter sound that echoed off the fake cobwebs and plastic skeletons. "You call it truth. I call it slander."

"Truth hurts sometimes," Chris shot back, standing tall despite the tension ratcheting up between them.

"Enough!" David barked, the word slicing into the gaiety of the room like a siren's wail. In one swift motion, fueled by fury, he closed the distance. The crowd gasped as David's large, tattooed hands gripped Chris's shirt, the fabric straining against clenched fists.

"David, don't—"

There was no stopping the tempest now. With a primal roar, David Brown launched himself at Chris Matthews, the two men crashing to the floor with violent force. Pain flared across Chris's body as they collided with the unforgiving ground, the impact resonating like a drumbeat in the stunned silence that followed.

Around them, the party became a backdrop, the vibrant colors bleeding into a blur as David's rage unleashed. Shadows danced grotesquely on the walls, mimicking the chaos as David pinned Chris beneath him, the product of years spent grappling opponents now turned toward a different kind of fight—one not bound by rules or referees.

The air was electric with shock, the crackle of tension palpable as the confrontation reached its boiling point. And above it all, the haunting echo of a Halloween playlist played on, a sinister soundtrack to the violence unfolding amidst the festivities.

Shouts erupted from the crowd, their revelry morphing into a chorus of alarm. Faces drained of color, hands reached out only to recoil as if scorched by the fury before them. A woman's scream sliced through the din, a beacon of panic.

"Stop it!" someone yelled, his voice cracking under the strain of witnessing such raw aggression.

Chris writhed beneath David, adrenaline surging through his veins. He bucked against the weight, his palms pushing at the wrestler's unyielding chest. Chris's breath came in ragged bursts, each exhale a battle cry for survival. Fists flew, precise and sharp, but David was an immovable force, his muscular frame honed through years of combat.

"Get him off!" The plea echoed, desperate and futile, as bodies circled the scuffle, a ring of horror too stunned to act effectively.

A hand grabbed at David's shoulder, attempting to pry him away, but it was like trying to uproot a mountain. David's focus never wavered; his grip on Chris tightened.

"David, enough!" The command was lost amidst the cacophony of the fray, the thuds of fists against flesh punctuating the soundtrack of chaos.

Chris's knuckles connected with jaw and temple, fleeting victories in a losing battle. His resilience shone through the struggle, even as David's relentless assault threatened to extinguish it.

The floor vibrated with the impact of the skirmish, partygoers' feet shifting uneasily on the periphery. They were witnesses to a spectacle that had no place among jack-o'-lantern grins and fake cobwebs—reality clashing violently with the night's masquerade.

"Call 911!" The urgency in the cry was palpable, a stark reminder that the stakes were real, the danger immediate.

Through it all, Chris fought. Not just for physical dominance, but for justice, for truth. His very being seemed to defy the brute force that sought to silence him. Each block, each evasive maneuver, spoke of a spirit that refused to be broken, a testament to the man who had already faced adversity and emerged with hope still intact.

The air was thinning for Chris, each gasp a shallow snatch at life. His chest heaved under the onslaught, eyes wide with the dawning terror of a man realizing the fight was slipping from his grasp. The pain etched across his features told a story of endurance meeting its match. Somewhere in the melee, his hope flickered, caught between the hammering pulse in his ears and the tightening vise of David's fury.

"Get off him!" a voice shouted, edges frayed with panic. Hands reached out, grasping at David's hulking form, trying to haul him back. But their efforts were like leaves against a storm, futile and fleeting against the solid mass of muscle and rage that was David Brown.

"Stop this madness!" another screamed, as fingers clawed helplessly at David's arms. A woman's plea cut through the din, but it was met only by the relentless sound of struggle, the guttural grunts of exertion mingling with the sharp intakes of Chris's dwindling breaths.

"Chris, hold on!" urged an onlooker, close enough to see the fight draining from Chris's limbs, his resistance waning like the last light of day. The crowd surged, a collective will pushing against the immovable object that was David's wrath, yet they might as well have been pushing against the very walls of the venue itself.

"Someone do something!" The desperation climbed higher, infecting the mob with a frenzied need to act, to save a life that hung precariously in the balance.

But amidst the shoving and pulling, the cries and commands, Chris felt the world narrowing, his focus sharpening on the singular task of survival. Each strained inhalation was a battle won against the dark tide threatening to pull him under. Even as his body cried out for respite, his spirit raged against the dying of the light, an ember of defiance in the encroaching shadow of defeat.

David's grip tightened, his hands like iron shackles closing relentlessly around Chris's throat. The festive music that once filled the venue was now drowned out by a symphony of terror—sharp gasps and horrified cries from the onlookers. Chris clawed at David's thick wrists, his fingernails scraping uselessly against the skin. His lungs burned for air, eyes wide with the primal fear of a man staring into the abyss.

"Let go!" someone shouted, voice laced with panic, but David was deaf to the pleas, his face contorted in a snarl of fury. He was a storm personified, unyielding and merciless, driven by an anger that had shattered its restraints.

"Stop, you're killing him!" Another voice cracked through the chaos, futile against the onslaught. But David's only response was to tighten his grip, the muscles in his arms bulging, veins like rivers of wrath pulsing beneath his skin.

Chris's struggle began to fade, his movements growing sluggish, arms dropping to his sides. His resilience, the very fiber of his being that had carried him through so much, was slipping away under the crushing force of David's will. The world blurred at the edges, sounds muffled, as if he were sinking into deep water, the surface growing distant with each passing second.

And then, without warning, the fight left Chris's body altogether. It went limp, the last vestiges of resistance melting away. The violence came to a halt as suddenly as it had erupted, leaving behind a silence that smothered the room. It was a heavy silence, pregnant with disbelief and dawning horror. Time seemed to stutter, the Halloween decorations—a grotesque backdrop to the tragedy that had unfolded.

As Chris lay motionless on the ground, the reality of what had transpired hung over the crowd like a dark cloud. David stood, chest heaving, the red mist of rage slowly dissipating from his eyes as he surveyed the still form before him. The echo of their confrontation reverberated through the stunned onlookers, a chilling reminder of how quickly life could be extinguished, how swiftly justice could be twisted into something unrecognizable.

Panic rippled through the crowd like a shockwave. The Halloween revelry turned to chaos as shrieks and shouts filled the air. People pushed away from the scene, costumes brushing against each other in frenzied disarray. Still others converged on Chris's lifeless form, their faces ghostly pale beneath festive makeup.

"Call 911!" someone yelled, voice cracking with urgency.

A woman dressed as a nurse knelt beside Chris, her hands trembling as she checked for a pulse. Her costume suddenly seemed a cruel irony as she looked up, shaking her head slowly. "He's not breathing," she gasped out.

David stood frozen, his broad frame heaving. For a moment, the wrestler-turned-politician appeared lost, his usual commanding presence giving way to something more vulnerable and exposed. But as the sirens wailed in the distance, the reality of the situation bore down on him like the weight of his past opponents in the ring.

"David Brown, you need to stay right here!" an off-duty officer, who had been attending the party, ordered, stepping forward with authority. David's hands, still curled from the assault, began to open, surrendering to the circumstance he could no longer control.

Within minutes, police lights strobed through the venue's windows, casting eerie shadows that danced across the walls. Officers stormed in, their commands slicing through the murmur of the crowd. They moved with practiced precision, securing the area around Chris while paramedics rushed in with their equipment, a futile dance of hope where it was clear there was none left to give.

"Step aside, give them room," directed one officer, guiding the bystanders back with firm hands. The paramedics worked over Chris, but their movements were mechanical, perfunctory—a grim mime of rescue where salvation had slipped away too soon.

"Who did this?" an officer demanded, his eyes scanning the shocked faces for answers.

"David Brown," several voices echoed in unison, fingers pointing toward the man whose reputation now teetered on the edge of ruin.

"David Brown, you're under arrest for assault," the officer pronounced, his words heavy with the weight of consequence. The handcuffs clicked into place around David's wrists, a stark contrast to the applause that once celebrated his victories.

As David was led away, the gravity of his actions settled on the room, a palpable force that seemed to make the very air heavy. The authorities swiftly issued a warrant for his arrest, the legal gears turning in motion with a speed that matched the racing hearts of all who witnessed the tragedy.

The chapter closed with Chris's still body being wheeled out, the flashing lights painting the scene in surreal strokes of red and blue. The warrant for David Brown's arrest marked the beginning of a new battle—a legal struggle that would be scrutinized and debated, a fight for justice amidst a system fraught with imperfections. It was the end of one ordeal and the start of another, a journey that would test the resilience and optimism of all involved, especially that of Chris Matthews, whose fight for truth had come at the highest cost imaginable.

The siren's wail sliced through the clamor of the Halloween party, its shrill cry announcing the arrival of emergency services. In their wake, a sea of costumed figures parted to reveal Chris on the floor, his chest still and silent amidst the cacophony. Paramedics rushed in, their movements efficient and practiced as they knelt beside him, their hands working with urgent precision.

"Stay back, give us room!" one shouted, her voice cutting through the murmurs and gasps that filled the air like fog.

Detective Ramirez stood at the edge of the chaos, his seasoned gaze taking in every detail—the discarded witch's hat trampled underfoot, the jack-o'-lantern's grin flickering in the dim light, the unease that clung to every person like a second skin. He made a mental note of the bystanders' faces, each one etched with shock or fear, knowing they could hold the key to what happened.

"Ramirez," Laura Simmons called out, pushing through the throng with an urgency that matched the detective's own. "We need to secure the scene, make sure we get statements from everyone."

"Already on it," he grunted, signaling to the officers who began ushering people away, their voices calm but firm against the backdrop of confusion.

"Where's Brown?" Samuel Bennett asked, arriving with Carol Thompson close behind. Their expressions were grave, the weight of the incident pressing down on them like the heavy hand of fate.

"Taken into custody," Ramirez replied, the words terse and clipped. "He won't be hurting anyone else tonight."

Carol nodded, her eyes reflecting the resolve that had become her armor since losing her daughter. "Good. Now let's make sure justice is served this time."

Amid the turmoil, Angie Thompson found herself rooted to the spot, her gaze locked on Chris's unmoving form. She fought against the tide of panic that threatened to engulf her, reminding herself of the strength she'd cultivated in the face of adversity. Her breath came in short bursts, a stark reminder of life's fragility.

"Angie, come on." It was a friend, tugging at her arm, urging her towards reality. "They'll take care of him. We need to clear out."

As the crowd dispersed, leaving only the echo of their whispers behind, the paramedics lifted Chris onto the stretcher, his body limp as a marionette with cut strings. The moment stretched thin, like the last thread of hope about to snap, before they moved him into the ambulance.

"Will he—" Angie started, unable to finish the question that clawed at her throat.

"We're doing everything we can," the paramedic said, not unkindly, before closing the doors.

The ambulance lights painted the night in stark strokes of urgency as it pulled away, leaving behind a tableau marked by the absence of its main character. Detective Ramirez watched it go, the red and blue hues reflecting in his eyes, which held the promise of a relentless hunt for answers.

"Let's get to work," he muttered to Laura, who nodded in silent agreement.

The chapter ended with the fading sound of sirens, a poignant reminder that while the party had been shattered by violence, the fight for justice was just beginning. Chris's journey would continue, through the corridors of hospitals and courtrooms, a path paved with resilience and the unwavering pursuit of truth.

A fist cut through the dim light of the bar, quick and fierce, crashing into the side of Chris's face with a sickening crack. Pain exploded across his cheekbone as he stumbled backward, his hand instinctively reaching up to assess the damage.

"Keep your lies off my sister!" David snarled, his voice a growling undertone lost amidst the Halloween din. His eyes blazed with a dangerous fire, the protective fury of an older brother laced with something darker, more volatile.

"David, wait—" Chris's plea was cut short as another punch landed, this time in his gut, folding him over like a closing book. The room spun around him, a whirl of costumed revelers suddenly morphing into spectators of their unscheduled brawl.

"Get off him!" Angie's voice sliced through the chaos, her words sharp with fear. But David was beyond reason, his fists continuing their assault as if trying to exorcise his own demons with every blow.

Chris tried to shield himself, to parry the punches that came with relentless rhythm. His resilience—so often his armor—was now being tested, battered by the weight of David's rage. He gasped for breath, fighting not just for air but for clarity against the encroaching darkness.

"Stop this madness!" Carol's anguished cry broke above the noise, but it was like throwing water on oil, ineffective against the flames of violence.

Hands reached out, grabbing at David's flailing arms, trying to pry him away. "Enough, David! You're killing him!" someone shouted, but it was like speaking to a storm, expecting the wind to obey.

The sharp scent of fear mingled with the sweet tang of spilled drinks, as David's grasp tightened around Chris's throat. Eyes wide with terror, Chris clawed at the hands cutting off his life, his kicks growing weaker, his struggle dimming.

"David, let go!" The command, loud and authoritative, might have come from Detective Ramirez or Laura Simmons; Chris couldn't tell. It scarcely mattered. The arm's vice-like pressure around his neck didn't yield.

Then, as sudden as a blown-out candle, the pressure lifted. Air rushed into Chris's lungs, ragged and burning. His vision, clouded with spots, slowly cleared to reveal David being hauled back by several strong hands, his chest heaving with exertion and unspent anger.

"Call 911!" The urgency in the voice matched the racing of Chris's heart, pounding a reminder that he was still alive.

As Chris lay there, the cold floor grounding him, the clamor of the party seemed distant, replaced by the ringing in his ears and the thud of his own pulse. The silence that followed was not peace but the aftermath of a storm, leaving destruction in its wake.

"Stay with me," Angie murmured, her hand gripping Chris's, a lifeline amidst the wreckage. Her touch was both comforting and a stark contrast to the violence that had just passed.

In the distance, sirens wailed, a crescendo growing louder until they stopped right outside. The flashing lights cast a surreal glow, painting the scene in stark relief. The chapter of confrontation may have closed, but the pages of justice were yet to be written.

Chapter 14

The glass doors of the Las Vegas hospital whooshed open with urgency as Jenny Mitchell barreled through, Carol Thompson a half-step behind. The sterile, antiseptic smell of the hospital did nothing to alleviate the sour twist of anxiety in Jenny's stomach. Her eyes, searching and frantic, were a storm-dark grey, the usual steely resolve within them now replaced by waves of dread.

"Please," Jenny implored the first person in scrubs she could find, her voice breaking the clinical quiet of the lobby. "We need to know about Chris. Chris Henderson."

Carol's hand found Jenny's elbow, a silent plea for calm, but Jenny barely registered the touch. Her gaze was locked onto the nurse's face, watching as a shadow passed over the woman's features—a harbinger of the news they feared.

"Ms. Mitchell, Ms. Thompson?" A man in a white coat approached, his kind eyes not quite meeting theirs. His badge read 'Dr. Lewis,' but the formality of his title provided no comfort.

"Is he...? Tell us, please," Carol's voice held a tremor that seemed to speak of countless nights spent worrying and days spent hoping.

"Let's go somewhere private," Dr. Lewis said, his tone gentle, guiding them away from the curious looks of other visitors.

They walked down the hallway, passing rooms where life hung on a delicate balance, the silence growing heavier with each step. When they reached a small room with two chairs and a box of tissues set out on a side table, the unspoken truth was almost palpable.

"Chris fought hard," Dr. Lewis began, his words slow, measured. "But his injuries... he didn't make it."

The finality of those words settled in the room like dust after destruction. Carol's hand gripped Jenny's now, seeking solace in shared strength. Jenny felt her breath hitch, her direct and assertive nature momentarily lost in a sea of grief. She wanted to scream, to challenge fate, to demand a different outcome, but the truth had been laid bare before them—cold and undeniable.

"Take your time," the doctor continued. "I'll give you both a moment."

As the door clicked shut, leaving them enveloped in a cocoon of sorrow, neither woman spoke. What words could possibly fill the chasm that Chris's departure had left? Jenny's athletic frame, usually poised for action, slumped slightly, the fight in her temporarily extinguished.

Outside, the world moved on, indifferent to the void that now existed in the lives of two women bonded by loss and the pursuit of justice. But inside this room, for this moment, there was only stillness—a silent tribute to a friend whose fight had ended too soon.

Jenny's fingers clutched at the fabric of Carol's blouse, her nails digging into the material as if trying to anchor herself in a reality that refused to stand still. Her chest heaved with the effort to keep her sobs at bay, each breath a battle against the tide of anguish that threatened to spill over. The cold air of the hospital corridor brushed against her skin, a stark contrast to the warmth of Carol's presence beside her.

"Jenny," Carol murmured, her own voice quivering with emotion, "we'll get through this together."

The words, gentle and firm, were like a lifeline tossed into the tumultuous sea of Jenny's despair. She leaned in closer, the two women forming a pillar of shared grief amidst the swirling chaos of the hospital.

Their sorrow was reflected back at them as they became aware of the others gathered in the hallway. Friends and supporters of Chris, faces drawn and eyes red, stood huddled in small groups. Their expressions echoed the pain that twisted inside Jenny—a silent symphony of heartache. Chris's optimism, his fight for justice, had touched each of them, binding them in a common thread of respect and admiration for the young man who had become their cause.

Among them was Mike, Chris's roommate, usually quick with a joke or a witty retort, now silent and stoic. His arms were crossed over his chest, his jaw set hard, the spark in his eyes dimmed by the news they had all received. Beside him, Sarah, who worked alongside Chris in the community center, dabbed at her eyes with a tissue, her usually animated features stilled by shock.

"Chris... he would've wanted us to keep fighting," said Mike finally, his voice barely above a whisper, yet it cut through the heavy air like a beacon of resolve.

"Always," Jenny agreed, her tone steadier as she absorbed the strength from those around her, each person's presence a testament to Chris's legacy. They stood together, a united front formed in the face of tragedy, ready to uphold the values Chris had embodied.

For a moment, the corridor seemed to shrink, the walls embracing them in solidarity, as if the building itself recognized the gravity of loss within its confines. Jenny felt the weight of Chris's absence settle on her shoulders, but also the weight of responsibility—to honor his memory with action, to continue his fight for a just world even when the path ahead seemed shrouded in darkness.

"Justice," Carol whispered, as if reading Jenny's thoughts. "For Chris."

"Justice," Jenny echoed, her resolve reigniting like a flame coaxed back to life. And together, they began to weave a tapestry of memories and determination, a promise to carry on Chris's work, to make sure his relentless spirit lived on in the battles they would face.

Jenny and Carol found solace in the sterile silence of the private room, a stark contrast to the whirlwind of emotions that raged within them. Side by side they sat, two figures cast adrift on an ocean of unspoken sorrow. The hum of the hospital receded into the background, leaving an oppressive quiet that hung between them like a curtain too heavy to draw back.

Outside, the world continued its ceaseless motion, indifferent to the stillness that had claimed this small corner of Las Vegas. Inside, time seemed to stand still, each second elongating as it passed—a cruel reminder of the permanence of their loss.

The walls, painted in what must have been intended as a soothing shade of blue, felt cold and impersonal. In any other circumstance, Jenny might have found the color calming, but now it only served to underscore the chill of absence, the void where Chris's warm presence should have been. She turned slightly, her gaze catching Carol's profile—strong yet etched with lines of grief.

Carol's hands lay folded in her lap, knuckles white from the grip she had on herself, her composure a fortress against the tide of despair threatening to engulf her. She had always been the rock, the source of strength for others, but even rocks could crumble under too much weight.

Jenny's own hands trembled slightly, her athletic frame no match for the emotional exhaustion that clawed at her insides. Her black hair, usually so carefully styled, fell in disarray around her face, framing the battle she fought to keep her composure. She remembered Chris's words, spoken with such earnest conviction, and how his eyes would light up when he talked about making a difference. Now, those same eyes would never see the change he had fought for.

A small gesture, yet fraught with significance, Jenny reached out, her hand hovering momentarily before coming to rest upon Carol's. It was a silent offering of solidarity, of shared pain and unyielding support. Their fingers intertwined, a physical manifestation of the bond that had formed not just in friendship, but in the pursuit of a cause greater than themselves—a cause Chris had lived for.

"Jenny," Carol's voice broke the silence, a gentle yet firm whisper that seemed to carry the weight of the world. "We can't let this end here."

"No," Jenny replied, her voice matching Carol's in its quiet intensity. "We won't." Her grip tightened, a tangible promise that they would continue to fight, to seek justice, in honor of a man whose spirit had ignited a flame within them both—a flame that no darkness could extinguish.

In the simplicity of that touch, the exchange of grief and resolve, there was an unspoken understanding that this was not the end of Chris's story. It was a new chapter, one written in the language of perseverance and hope, a narrative that they would pen together as they stepped forward into an uncertain future, united in purpose.

The air in the room grew denser, each breath a struggle against an unseen force. It was as if Chris's absence had become a tangible presence, its weight pressing down on Jenny and Carol like a boulder upon their chests. The quiet that surrounded them seemed to echo with the silent scream of injustice—the kind that Chris had dedicated his life to fighting against.

Jenny felt a quiver in her heart, a sense of sinking as though she were being pulled into an abyss of sorrow. She looked at Carol, whose eyes mirrored the storm of emotions that raged within both of them. Anger flickered there, bright and fierce, fuelled by the thought of how a beacon of hope like Chris could be extinguished by the very darkness he sought to dispel.

"Can you believe it?" Jenny's voice cracked, the words barely squeezing past the lump in her throat. "Chris... he was supposed to..."

"Change the world," Carol finished for her, her tone laced with a bitterness that tasted like bile. "He was going to make things right." Her hands clenched into fists, the knuckles white as bone. She was a portrait of a warrior in grief, ready to transform her mourning into a battle cry.

Jenny nodded, her own anger rising like a tide within her. "It's not fair," she whispered, her eyes stinging with unshed tears. "He fought so hard, and for what? To be taken by senseless violence?"

"Violence that he stood against," Carol added sharply, her gaze fixed on some distant point, as if peering into a future that had been stolen from them. "We can't let his fight die with him."

A profound sadness cloaked the room, weaving itself between the threads of anger and disbelief. It was the kind of sadness that settled in the bones, heavy and unrelenting. For a moment, they sat in silence, each lost in the labyrinth of their thoughts—a silent tribute to a fallen hero who had walked among them, striving to mend the fractures of a flawed justice system.

Jenny squeezed Carol's hand once more, a lifeline amidst the tempest of emotions. In this touch was a shared determination to carry the torch Chris had left behind, to illuminate the path toward a justice that would not falter, would not fail. Together, they would keep the flame alive, for Chris, and for all those who had been wronged by a world that sometimes seemed too broken to fix.

A nurse entered, her footsteps a soft shuffle against the sterile linoleum. She approached Jenny and Carol with a tray bearing two cups of coffee, the steam curling up like wisps of hope in the cold room. "I thought you might need this," she said, her voice a low hum of compassion. The warmth from the cup seeped into Jenny's hands, a small comfort against the chill of loss.

"Thank you," Jenny murmured, taking a careful sip. The bitterness on her tongue was a stark contrast to the sweetness of the memories that began to surface.

Carol glanced at the nurse, offering a tired but grateful smile. "You all knew Chris, didn't you?" she asked, her voice carrying the weight of shared history within these walls.

"Everyone here did," the nurse replied, her eyes reflecting the collective grief of the staff. "He left an impression, always advocating for patients' rights, always the first to volunteer for community outreach." Her voice cracked slightly. "He made a difference."

As the nurse excused herself, leaving them in their cocoon of sorrow, Jenny turned to Carol, her eyes brightening with the flicker of a memory. "Remember how Chris used to say he'd change the world one case at a time?" she began, a faint smile tugging at her lips despite the ache in her heart.

Carol chuckled softly, nodding. "And he believed it with every fiber of his being. He had that stubborn streak—once he set his mind to something, there was no turning back."

Their laughter was brief, a fleeting reprieve from the gravity of their loss, but it filled the room with a reminder of Chris's vitality. "Even when he was little, he had that same conviction," Jenny continued, her voice steadying as she recalled their childhood. "He stood up to those bullies in fourth grade, remember? Said if he let them pick on him, they'd just go after someone else."

"Always the protector," Carol agreed, wiping away a tear that had escaped down her cheek. "His courage... it was contagious." Her words were wrapped in admiration, the legacy of a man whose resilience had touched so many lives.

They sat there, side by side, sharing stories that painted a picture of Chris's essence—a mosaic of moments that showcased his relentless pursuit of justice and unwavering optimism. Each anecdote was a brushstroke of light against the dark canvas of the present, a testament to a life that, while cut short, burned brightly enough to leave an indelible mark on the world.

"His laugh," Jenny said suddenly, the sound almost tangible in her mind. "It could light up the darkest corners of a room."

"Like a beacon," Carol added, her eyes glistening. "He was our beacon, Jenny."

In that private room, with each recollection, they wove together the threads of Chris's story, ensuring that even in death, his spirit would continue to inspire, to challenge, to advocate. It was an unspoken promise between them, a pledge to honor his memory not just in words, but in action, in the continuous fight for a justice system that Chris had so passionately believed could be better, should be better.

And as they rose to leave, fortified by shared memories and steely resolve, the echo of Chris's laughter seemed to follow them, a subtle reminder that some lights never truly go out—they simply take on a different form.

The shuffle of footsteps broke the hushed reverence enveloping the hospital's private room where Jenny Mitchell and Carol Thompson sat, immersed in their silent tribute to Chris. Two uniformed officers appeared at the threshold, badges glinting under the sterile fluorescent lights, their faces solemn.

"Ms. Mitchell, Ms. Thompson," one officer began, his voice steady but not unkind. "We're here to inform you that an arrest warrant has been issued for David Brown in connection with the death of Chris Matthews."

The air seemed to thicken with tension, the gravity of the officers' words sinking into the hearts of everyone present. Jenny's grip on Carol's hand tightened, her knuckles white with the force of her emotions.

Carol met Jenny's gaze, and in that exchange, a silent pact was forged. The grief that pooled in their eyes was underscored by a flint-like hardness, a shared determination that spoke louder than any words could. They would not let Chris's fight for justice end with his last breath; they would carry it forward, a torch passed from his hands to theirs.

"Thank you, officers," Carol said, her voice a fusion of gratitude and steely resolve. "Please keep us updated. We want to be involved every step of the way."

"Of course," the second officer replied, nodding with respect. "Chris was one of the good ones. We'll do everything in our power to bring justice for him."

Jenny's jaw clenched, her mind ablaze with memories of Chris—his conviction, his drive, the spark in his eyes when he talked about reforming a system fraught with flaws. It was that very system they now had to navigate to honor him, to make certain his death would not be just another statistic.

"Justice for Chris," Jenny whispered, more to herself than anyone else, her voice barely audible but laden with a weight that matched the resolve in her heart.

Carol gave Jenny's hand a reassuring squeeze, affirming their unspoken vow. Together, they would stand against the tide of injustice, just as Chris had taught them, just as he would have wanted. It was the least they could do for a man who had dedicated his life to the pursuit of what was right and fair.

Jenny and Carol stepped out of the sterile white corridors of the Las Vegas hospital, the sliding glass doors closing behind them with a soft whoosh. The Nevada sun hung low in the sky, its light casting long shadows that stretched across the parking lot like dark fingers. Their footsteps echoed on the pavement, slow and deliberate, each one a testament to the sorrow that weighted their limbs.

"Can't believe he's gone," Jenny murmured, her voice a hoarse whisper that fought against the silence enveloping them.

"Neither can I," replied Carol, her eyes fixed on the horizon, where the city's neon lights would soon flicker to life. "But we owe it to Chris to keep fighting. He wouldn't want us to give up now."

Jenny nodded, feeling the burn of unshed tears stinging her eyes. She wrapped her arms around herself, seeking solace in the small comfort it provided. They reached Carol's car, and for a moment, they simply stood there, the cool metal of the door a stark contrast to the warmth still radiating from within them—a warmth kindled by memories of Chris.

"Chris was more than just our friend," Jenny finally said, her resolve hardening with each word. "He was a beacon for all those lost in the shadows of injustice."

Carol unlocked the car and they slid inside. As the engine hummed to life, a quiet determination settled over them. Carol gripped the steering wheel tightly, as if willing her own strength into the vehicle that would carry them forward into battle.

"His fight won't end with him," Carol stated, her voice firm. "We'll make sure of it."

The car pulled away from the curb, merging into the steady stream of traffic. In the rearview mirror, the hospital shrank into the distance, but the purpose it represented loomed ever larger. Chris had been a tireless advocate for change, always pushing against the rigid confines of an often unforgiving system.

"Remember how he used to talk about reform? About fixing the broken parts?" Jenny asked, gazing out the window at the city passing by.

"Like it was yesterday," Carol replied. "He believed that justice wasn't just about punishment; it was about healing, about making things right again."

"Then let's continue what he started," Jenny said, her tone resolute. "For Chris, and for everyone else who's been let down by the cracks in the system."

Carol nodded, a silent vow passing between them. They both knew the road ahead would be fraught with challenges, but they also knew they weren't alone. Across the city, across the country, a movement was growing—a collective uprising demanding reform and accountability.

As they drove on, the night began to settle over Las Vegas, the city's famed Strip lighting up in a dazzling display of defiance against the darkness. It seemed a fitting parallel to the path Jenny and Carol were embarking upon—a journey through the night toward a dawn of greater justice and a hope that Chris's legacy would inspire lasting change.

"Chris's story will be heard," Carol whispered, more to herself than to Jenny. "It has to be."

And with that, the two women drove on, their grief a powerful fuel feeding the flames of a movement ready to challenge the very foundations of the criminal justice system.

Jenny clutched the steering wheel, knuckles white as the car hummed softly in the darkness of early morning. The desert air was cool against her face, a stark contrast to the heat that simmered in her chest. She glanced at Carol, who sat silently beside her, the neon glow from the Strip casting shadows across her determined features.

"First thing Monday, we talk to the DA," Jenny said, breaking the silence. Her voice was steady, but beneath it lay a tremor of anger and sorrow.

Carol nodded, her gaze fixed on the road ahead. "We need to gather everyone—every friend, every ally Chris ever made."

"His voice was silenced," Jenny continued, her words gaining strength, "but ours won't be. We'll make sure of that."

A pale light began to seep over the horizon, heralding the dawn of a new day. It was symbolic, thought Jenny, of the beginning of their own fight for justice—a fight that would honor Chris's memory and everything he stood for.

In her mind's eye, she saw Chris as he had been, full of conviction and hope. His belief in a fairer system was infectious, and it had ignited something within both women that would not be extinguished by his loss.

As the first rays of sunlight touched the sky, painting it with hues of orange and pink, Jenny felt a renewed sense of purpose. The path before them was fraught with obstacles, but she knew that the truth was on their side. Together with Carol, and the support of others who had been touched by Chris's passion for justice, they would take on the legal system that had failed him.

"Chris always said it was about more than just winning a case," Carol murmured. "It was about setting a precedent, about creating a ripple effect that could bring about real change."

"And so we'll start a wave," Jenny affirmed, her eyes reflecting the dawn's early light. "One that will crash through barriers and wash away injustice."

The car turned onto a quieter street, leaving the pulsing heart of Vegas behind. Ahead lay the courthouse, its stately facade a symbol of the law—a law that Jenny and Carol were ready to challenge in the name of their fallen friend.

"Let's do this," Carol said, a fire igniting in her eyes as they parked the car.

"Let's do this," echoed Jenny, stepping out into the cool morning air. With each step toward the courthouse, their resolve solidified. Today marked the beginning of a relentless pursuit for accountability and reform—a pursuit that Chris Matthews had lived for and that they would continue in his honor.

Chapter 15

The morning sun cast long shadows on the steps of the Las Vegas courthouse as Laura Simmons ascended them, flanked by Chris Matthews' family. They moved with a collective rhythm, each step seeming to pulse with their shared resolve. Uncertainty etched lines into their faces, but their eyes held onto a glimmer of hope, like the last stars fading in the dawn's light.

Inside, the cool hush of the court's marbled interior wrapped around them. Laura led the way, her heels clicking a steady beat against the floor, a metronome to the silent symphony of their tense breaths. The group found their way to a cluster of hard wooden benches where they settled, a tableau of anticipation.

Laura excused herself and slipped into a quieter corner of the room. She perched on the edge of a table, her posture straight, an island of calm in a sea of legal chaos. With practiced hands, she flipped open her briefcase, its contents organized with meticulous care, each document a soldier in her battalion of evidence.

She reviewed her notes, each page a familiar friend, their edges worn from constant consultation. Her red hair, usually a vibrant flame, was pulled back in a disciplined bun, and her blue eyes moved methodically over the papers. In her mind, she constructed the day's strategy, envisioning the chessboard of the courtroom, her moves calculated and precise.

Chris's resilience seemed to hover at her shoulder, urging her on, his voice almost audible in the rustle of papers. She remembered the first time she'd met him, how even in the shadow of false accusation, he had spoken with unwavering conviction. Laura knew that speaking for him now required every ounce of her own determination.

"Justice," she whispered to herself, a quiet affirmation. It was more than a word; it was a promise she intended to keep.

The clock on the wall ticked down the minutes until the trial would begin, its sound a heartbeat in the stillness. Laura closed her briefcase with a soft click and rose, her motions deliberate. She was a figure of strength carved from years of battles in rooms just like this one.

Returning to Chris's family, she offered them a nod that held both assurance and empathy. They looked up at her, finding an anchor in her steadfast gaze. In those few seconds, they drew from her a courage that fortified their spirits for the ordeal ahead.

"Let's go," Laura said, her voice low but clear, cutting through the tension. "It's time."

The prosecutor stood, a pillar of confidence in the sea of wood and marble that was the Las Vegas courthouse. His voice boomed through the chamber as he painted a grim portrait of David Brown.

"Members of the jury," he began, his tone laced with both authority and solemn duty, "you will see that this man,"—he pointed directly at David—"is nothing less than a tempest of violence. A danger to society who unleashed his fury on an innocent victim."

He recounted the night of the incident, each word chosen to etch an image of David as a predator driven by rage, his descriptions vivid enough to cast shadows across the courtroom.

"His past is riddled with aggression, his present marked with brutality," the prosecutor concluded, his gaze sweeping across the jurors like an accusing finger.

Silence hung in the wake of his words, thick and heavy, until Laura Simmons rose from her seat, her red hair a flame against the sterility of the room. She stepped forward, her blue eyes locking onto the jury with an intensity that seemed to pull them closer into her orbit.

"Truth," she said, her voice carrying a conviction that resonated off the walls. "It's a simple concept, yet it stands as the very foundation of justice—a beacon we must follow if we are to navigate the darkness of accusation and presumption."

Laura paced before the jury box, her movements measured, her presence commanding attention. "Chris was more than the victim you've heard described today. He was a man whose life was cut short, and now his story demands our unwavering commitment to uncovering what really happened."

She turned slightly, directing a fleeting glance toward David, not as an adversary but as a human being. "David Brown deserves a fair trial, not a narrative woven from fear and bias. The evidence will show that the truth is far more complex than the tale of unchecked anger you've been presented."

"Throughout this trial," Laura continued, her voice rising with passion, "I ask you to consider each piece of evidence, each testimony with an open mind. For in the end, it isn't just about proving guilt or innocence—it's about ensuring that justice is served, and that the true story of Chris's untimely death comes to light."

As she concluded, the weight of her words lingered in the air, an unspoken vow echoing in the hearts of everyone present. It was a promise that Laura Simmons intended to keep, no matter the obstacles in her path.

The courtroom hushed as the first witness took the stand, a middle-aged woman from the neighborhood where the tragic incident unfolded. She wrung her hands nervously, her gaze flickering over the crowd before settling on the prosecutor.

"Please state your name for the record," the prosecutor instructed.

"Susan Reynolds," she replied, her voice barely above a whisper.

"Ms. Reynolds, can you tell us what you heard on the night in question?"

Susan nodded, swallowing hard. "It was late, and I was in bed when I heard shouting coming from outside. It was loud, angry. Scared me half to death."

"Can you describe the shouting?" prodded the prosecutor.

"It was two men's voices. One was louder, full of rage. I remember thinking, 'Someone is going to get hurt.'"

"Did you recognize the voices, Ms. Reynolds?"

"I—I think one was Chris's voice... and the other must've been David Brown's."

"Thank you, Ms. Reynolds." The prosecutor's tone conveyed satisfaction, as if her words were the final nails in a coffin long prepared.

Laura Simmons rose, her posture unyielding, her eyes sharp as she approached the witness. "Ms. Reynolds," Laura began, her voice steady but not unkind, "you mentioned hearing two voices. Were you able to clearly identify them as belonging to Chris and Mr. Brown?"

Susan hesitated, fidgeting with the hem of her blouse. "Well, it was dark, and I didn't see them. But it had to be them."

"Isn't it true that you've never actually spoken to Mr. Brown? That you wouldn't recognize his voice?" Laura's inquiry was gentle but pointed.

"Uh, yes, that's true. But—"

"Furthermore," Laura continued, pacing subtly, "you stated it was very dark, correct? How could you be certain of what you heard or who you heard it from without visual confirmation?"

Susan's certainty seemed to waver under Laura's scrutiny. "I suppose I couldn't be completely sure..."

"Ms. Reynolds," Laura said, locking eyes with the juror closest to the stand, "your fear on that night is understandable. But fear can also cloud judgment. Without visual confirmation, isn't it possible that you may be mistaken about what you heard and who was involved?"

The neighbor's confidence crumbled, her shoulders slumping. "Yes, it's possible."

"Thank you, Ms. Reynolds." Laura gave a respectful nod before returning to her seat, leaving a trail of doubt lingering in the air, as tangible as the tension that gripped the room.

The courtroom air carried a charge, a silent current of anticipation as the next witness took the stand. Dr. Eleanor Hayes, a forensic expert with an impressive array of accolades, stepped forward, her expression one of calm professionalism. Laura Simmons watched intently from her seat, her sharp eyes tracking every move the witness made.

"Dr. Hayes," began Laura, "could you please explain your findings regarding the evidence collected at the crime scene?"

"Of course," Dr. Hayes responded, her voice clear and confident. "Upon analyzing the blood spatter patterns and the distribution of other forensic materials at the scene, I concluded that the prosecution's theory does not align with the physical evidence."

Laura nodded, encouraging the expert to elaborate. "The angle and direction of the blood spatter suggest that the assailant was shorter than Mr. Matthews. Additionally, the presence of a specific type of fiber, not matching anything owned by Chris, points towards another individual's involvement."

These statements seemed to reverberate through the courtroom, casting ripples of doubt upon the prosecution's case. Laura could feel Chris's family members leaning forward, their hope rekindled by the expert's confidence.

However, the prosecutor stood up sharply, his gaze fixed on Dr. Hayes. "Isn't it true, Dr. Hayes, that you've been criticized in the past for your unconventional methods?" he asked, voice dripping with skepticism.

"Objection, Your Honor," Laura interjected before Dr. Hayes could respond. "The prosecution is attempting to discredit the witness without cause."

"Overruled," the judge responded, a hint of curiosity in his voice. "The witness may answer the question."

"Indeed, some of my methods have been questioned," Dr. Hayes acknowledged. "But they have also been peer-reviewed and validated.

The evidence speaks for itself, regardless of personal opinions about my techniques."

Laura watched as the prosecutor's attempts to rattle the witness fell flat, each question parried with the same unflappable logic. When her turn came once more, she rose, her stance steady and her tone respectful yet firm.

"Dr. Hayes, in your expert opinion, is there any doubt that the evidence at the crime scene suggests someone other than Chris Matthews was the aggressor?"

"None whatsoever," Dr. Hayes replied, her certainty unshakable.

"Thank you, Dr. Hayes." Laura's words were succinct, the weight of truth behind them palpable in the hushed courtroom.

As Dr. Hayes stepped down from the stand, Laura turned to face the jury, her blue eyes conveying a silent message of trust in the facts, the science, and the unwavering pursuit of justice.

A solemn hush fell over the courtroom as the next witness, a sturdy man with a wrestler's build and a faded tattoo peeking from under his collar, took the stand. He was an old friend of David Brown, one who'd been in the crowd during many of his bouts and had seen the flash of triumph and temper in equal measure.

"Mr. Carter," Laura Simmons began after the prosecutor finished, her voice cool and controlled, "you described David as someone who 'doesn't back down from a fight.' Could you clarify what you mean by that?"

"Sure," Mr. Carter replied, shifting uncomfortably in his seat. "David's a fighter, always has been. If he believes he's in the right, he won't just let things slide."

"Did you ever witness him being the aggressor in situations that were not related to wrestling?" Laura pressed, locking eyes with the witness.

"Umm, well, there were a few bar scuffles," he admitted, his gaze flickering away.

"Bar scuffles," Laura echoed, writing a note before looking up again. "Would you say these incidents point to a pattern of violence outside the ring?"

"Objection," the prosecutor interjected, but the judge waved him off, signaling for Mr. Carter to answer.

"Guess so," he muttered, and Laura nodded, thanking him for his honesty.

The next witness, a former acquaintance of Chris, stepped forward—a young woman with nervous eyes and hands clasped tightly in her lap. The prosecutor painted a picture of Chris as a peacemaker, someone always ready to defuse tensions.

"Miss Johnson," Laura addressed her with a gentle firmness, "you mentioned Chris was an advocate for justice. In your experience, did he ever seek confrontation or resort to violence?"

"Never," she answered quickly, "Chris was all about talking things out. He didn't believe in fighting unless there was no other choice."

"Thank you, Miss Johnson." Laura turned to the jury, her gaze sweeping across their attentive faces. "What we see here is a consistent character trait—Chris Matthews sought peace, not conflict."

Witness after witness took the stand, each bringing fragments of truth shaded by personal bias. Some spoke of David's protective nature turned possessive, others of Chris's dedication to righting wrongs, even when it put him at odds with those around him. But Laura noticed the discrepancies, the small details that didn't add up.

"Mr. Phillips," Laura said to another of David's friends, a man who claimed David had been with him at the time of the incident. "You initially told investigators you weren't sure of the exact time David left your house that night. Now you're certain it was before the altercation?"

"Uh, yes," Mr. Phillips stammered, "I remembered later on."

"Convenient memory," Laura remarked dryly, scribbling another note. With each inconsistency she unearthed, the narrative woven by the prosecution frayed a bit more, the threads of doubt weaving through the minds of the jury.

As the day wore on, the air in the courtroom grew thick with tension and unspoken questions. Laura Simmons stood as a beacon of resolve, her every question and observation chipping away at the façade of certainty the prosecution had attempted to construct. She knew Chris's hope and determination lived on through her efforts, and she was unwavering in her mission to see justice served.

Laura Simmons rose from the wooden bench, her posture rigid with purpose as the courtroom hushed in anticipation. Her notes were a roadmap to justice laid bare on the lectern before her, each word a step closer to the truth. The jurors leaned forward, their eyes locked onto her as she began to weave together the strands of evidence, her voice steady and clear.

"Members of the jury," Laura started, commanding the room's attention, "you've heard testimonies that paint a picture with conflicting hues. You've seen evidence that doesn't just suggest but loudly declares that things are not as simple as they may seem."

She gestured to the exhibits displayed, photographs, and reports that told a silent story of their own. "The evidence shows us that Chris was not merely a victim of circumstance, but of a deliberate act that shattered many lives. We cannot ignore the pattern of violence that David Brown has exhibited, nor can we overlook the factual discrepancies raised during this trial."

As Laura spoke, she held the gaze of each juror, ensuring her words resonated not only in their ears but also in their conscience. "We must seek the truth, for it is the very foundation upon which justice stands. To honor Chris's memory, we must hold accountable those responsible for his untimely demise. It is your duty to sift through the layers of hearsay and uncover the core of what happened that fateful night."

Her closing argument was a crescendo of reason and passion, each sentence punctuating the solemn atmosphere. As Laura took her seat, a palpable sense of gravity settled over the courtroom, leaving an echo of her words lingering in the air.

The prosecutor, a seasoned figure who had weathered many such battles, stood up to deliver his final plea. With an air of confidence that bordered on arrogance, he addressed the jury, his voice smooth and practiced.

"Let's not be swayed by emotional rhetoric," he cautioned, casting a dismissive glance at Laura's notes. "The defense wants you to believe in coincidences, in conveniently timed recollections that defy logic. They ask you to question hard evidence and to discount the testimony of law-abiding citizens."

He paced before the jury box, hands clasped behind his back as he continued. "David Brown is a man known for his fiery temper, yes, but that does not make him a killer. What we have here is a tragic accident, one that has been twisted into a malicious act without a shred of conclusive proof."

"Remember," he concluded, pausing for dramatic effect, "a shadow of a doubt is all it takes to uphold the sacred principle of innocence until proven guilty. And there are shadows aplenty in this case."

With the weight of his words hanging in the balance, the prosecutor returned to his seat, his gaze locking with Laura's for a brief moment—a silent acknowledgment of the battle waged and the verdict that hung in the balance.

The courtroom hushed as the heavy door creaked open, and the jury filed back in. Laura Simmons' gaze followed their solemn procession, her heartbeat echoing the ticking of the courtroom clock. Chris's family sat rigid, hands grasped in silent prayer, each breath they took a silent plea for justice.

Laura studied their faces: the creased brow of Chris's father, worn from years of hard work and now etched with worry; the pallor of his mother's face, where hope fought to shine through the fear; the clenched jaw of his younger brother, trying to emulate Chris's resilience. Each one was a reflection of the man they lost, a testament to the hole his absence had left in their world.

As the foreperson handed a piece of paper to the judge, a suffocating stillness enveloped the room. It was the kind of silence that spoke volumes, heavy with implications and the weight of impending resolution.

"Will the defendant please rise?" the judge commanded, his voice cutting through the tension like a verdict itself.

David Brown stood, the lines of his suit sharp, but his composure betraying nothing. Laura's eyes stayed fixed on him, reading the subtle shifts in his stance, the restless flicker of his gaze.

"Members of the jury," the judge began, and that familiar spark in Laura flared—a mix of dread and defiance, "have you reached a verdict?"

"We have, your honor," the foreperson replied, a tremble in her voice revealing the burden of the choice they'd made.

"Please read the verdict," the judge instructed.

Chris's mother leaned forward, a silent gasp parting her lips as the words spilled into the space between them:

"We, the jury, find the defendant, David Brown, guilty of manslaughter."

A collective sigh rippled through Chris's family, a wave of relief crashing over the shore of their grief. His father's shoulders slumped as if unburdened by an immeasurable weight, and his mother's hand flew to her mouth, stifling sobs of gratitude. The brother's eyes glistened with unshed tears, a mirror of the optimism and determination that Chris had always embodied.

"Order in the court," the judge's voice boomed, but it couldn't mask the murmurs of astonishment and the shuffle of movement as people absorbed the gravity of the decision.

Laura allowed herself a moment, just one, to close her eyes and let the tide of emotions wash over her. For Chris, for truth, for justice—this was what they had fought for. When she opened her eyes again, they were clear, resolute, reflecting the flame of victory that burned quietly within.

"Justice has been served today," Laura whispered to Chris's family as they clutched each other, a fortress amid the storm of human fallibility and the quest for redemption. They nodded, their expressions a mosaic of sorrow and solace, knowing that this verdict was not an end but a beginning—the first step on the long road to healing.

Laura Simmons led the way as the courthouse doors swung open, her heels clicking a steady, purposeful rhythm against the marble floor. Behind her, Chris's family followed, their arms linked in an unspoken pact of solidarity. The afternoon sun was setting, casting long shadows that stretched across the steps like fingers reaching out for the day's end.

"Where to now?" Chris's father asked, his voice rough around the edges, yet steadier than it had been inside the courtroom.

"Home," Laura said, turning to look at them. "You need rest, and time to let today sink in."

Chris's mother nodded, dabbing at her eyes with a crumpled tissue, the lines of strain on her face softening in the golden light. Her gaze lingered on the courthouse, a monolith of both their greatest fears and newfound hope.

"Will things get easier?" Chris's brother murmured, more to himself than to anyone else. His eyes searched the horizon as if expecting to find answers etched into the fading sky.

"Justice doesn't erase the pain," Laura replied, her voice carrying the weight of her experience, "but it paves the way for healing."

They descended the steps slowly, a silent procession marked by quiet sobs and hands clenching hands. A gentle breeze whispered through the air, a small comfort against the heat of the desert city.

"Ms. Simmons," Chris's mother said, halting their descent, "thank you for believing in him, in us."

"Always," Laura responded, her blue eyes meeting theirs with an intensity that spoke volumes. "This isn't just my job; it's my calling. We've made strides today, but the fight continues."

"Then we'll keep fighting," Chris's father stated with resolve, anchoring the family with a resilience that echoed Chris's own spirit.

"Exactly." Laura's lips curved into a resolute smile. "Because the truth matters, because Chris's legacy deserves nothing less."

The last rays of sunlight dipped below the city skyline, and the coolness of evening began to settle around them. They turned away from the courthouse, each step a testament to their unwavering commitment to justice—a journey far from over but buoyed by the strength they found in one another.

Chapter 16

The heavy wooden doors of the courtroom creaked open, and a hush fell over the gallery. Eyes darted toward the sound—the jury was returning. Chris's family sat shoulder to shoulder, a solid line of shared hope and fear. They leaned forward as if drawn by invisible strings toward the twelve people who held their collective breath in a manila envelope.

Laura Simmons stood like a pillar among them, her posture rigid, yet not unkind—a lighthouse guiding ships through a stormy night. The sharp lines of her suit seemed to cut through the tension that filled the room. She did not look at the jury; instead, her gaze stayed on the judge's bench, her mind likely running through every possible outcome with the precision of a chess grandmaster contemplating the board.

Chris's mother clutched a tissue between her fingers, twisting it absentmindedly. Her eyes, so much like Chris's—once vibrant with mischief, now dimmed with grief—never left the foreperson's face. Next to her, Chris's father's hand shook ever so slightly, the only sign of the turmoil churning beneath his stoic surface.

"Remember what I said," Laura whispered, leaning in close to them. "No matter what happens next, we've done everything we could." Her voice was a steady thrum, a bass note grounding the melody of murmurs that rippled through the courtroom.

The Matthews nodded, holding onto her words like a lifeline. The rest of Chris's friends, a small contingent of loyal supporters, sat behind the family, a patchwork of somber attire and clenched jaws. They exchanged glances, silent communication passing between them—a language built on months of waiting, hoping, and supporting one another.

A young woman, Chris's college roommate, bit her lip hard enough to draw blood. A metaphorical dam against a flood of emotions, she willed herself to stay strong for the family, embodying the resilience Chris himself had always shown.

And then, as the jury took their seats, the world seemed to contract to this single point in time. Every breath held, every heartbeat a drum roll to the moment of truth.

"Look at me," Laura whispered again, her tone soft but commanding. Chris's family turned to her, finding an anchor in her resolute blue eyes. "Whatever they say, remember you're not alone."

Her words were a salve, but the wound would remain. This was a scene etched in stone—a tableau of those left behind, standing on the precipice of justice, teetering between the agony of uncertainty and the hollow relief of resolution.

The gavel's sharp rap cut through the clamor like a scythe, and the courtroom snapped to attention. A hush fell over the spectators, thick with tension and heavy expectation. The judge's eyes swept over them all, a silent command for silence and respect.

"Order," the judge intoned, his voice reverberating against the high ceilings. He nodded toward the jury foreperson, a signal unseen by most but felt by all.

Chris's sister gripped the wooden bench beneath her, knuckles white, as if bracing against a storm. Laura Simmons stood tall beside them, a pillar amidst the swirling emotions of the room.

The foreperson rose, a solemn figure. Her lips parted, and the words that followed would carve the future into history.

"We find the defendant, David Brown, guilty of the murder of Christopher Matthews."

As the verdict pierced the room, it unraveled the tightly wound threads of anticipation. A collective sigh, laden with sorrow and relief, rippled through Chris's family and friends. They had walked through fire to get here, their path singed with loss and pain, but now the flames gave way to embers of justice.

A friend of Chris's, a young man who'd known him since childhood, closed his eyes. The sound of the foreperson's voice echoed in his ears, a solemn bell tolling the end of one journey and the beginning of another.

Next to him, Jenny Mitchell, her arm still encircling Chris's sister, let out a breath she didn't realize she'd been holding. It was over. The truth Chris had championed had not been buried with him; it had risen, a phoenix from the ashes of tragedy.

In the gallery, heads bowed and hands clasped, some seeking solace in prayer, others in the quiet acknowledgment of a battle fought and won. But the victory was bittersweet—no verdict could return what they had lost.

The room remained locked in its tableau of mixed emotions, a canvas painted with broad strokes of human experience—pain, joy, defeat, and triumph. And at the center of it all, a sense of finality, the closing of a chapter penned with heartache and inked in the somber hues of justice served.

David's knuckles whitened as he gripped the edge of the table, his tattooed arms tensing like coiled springs. The buzz-cut hair that once spoke to a disciplined life now seemed an ironic contrast to the chaos brewing within him. His broad chest heaved, and for a fleeting moment, his imposing figure looked vulnerable in the face of the jury's damning words.

"Guilty," echoed in his ears, the single word collapsing the future he had envisioned. In disbelief, he scanned the courtroom, desperate to find an ally in a sea of faces that held no solace. David's jaw clenched so tightly it ached, the muscles working angrily beneath the surface of his skin. He was a man undone, trapped in the web of his own making, and the realization came crashing down upon him with a weight that threatened to crush his spirit.

Across the room, the slow drip of silent tears traced the contours of a mother's grief-stricken face. Chris's mother, her features etched with sorrow, sat hunched as though bearing the weight of the world on her slender shoulders. Her hands trembled lightly, a physical testament to the storm of emotions raging inside her.

"Mrs. Jenkins," Laura Simmons whispered, her voice a soft anchor in the tumult.

The simple utterance cut through the haze of despair, and Chris's mother turned towards the lawyer who had become her steadfast advocate throughout this ordeal. With eyes blurred by tears, she reached out, her fingers brushing against Laura's hand, seeking the contact as a lifeline. Their touch bridged the gap between professional and personal, a silent communion in a place where words often fell short.

"Thank you," Mrs. Jenkins managed to murmur, the gratitude mingling with the raw ache of her heart.

Laura's grip on her hand was firm and reassuring, conveying a shared resolve. It was not merely the end of a case but the closure of a chapter that had been written in the darkest ink. Laura's blue eyes, usually sharp with focus, now softened with empathy as she stood beside the woman who had entrusted her with more than just a legal battle—she had handed over her shattered hope for justice.

"Chris would have been proud," Laura said, offering a small, sad smile that carried the promise of remembrance and respect for the son taken too soon.

As the judge called for order again, the verdict's echo began to fade, leaving behind the indelible mark of lives changed forever. David, still seated, stared at the handcuffs that would soon bind him, while Chris's mother, supported by Laura, prepared to navigate the world that lay beyond the courtroom doors—a world without Chris but one where justice had, at last, been served.

Jenny Mitchell's heart raced as the foreperson's words still echoed in her ears: "Guilty." She felt a surge of relief, tightly mingling with sorrow. She turned to Chris's sister, who stood beside her like a slender pillar on the verge of crumbling. Without a word, Jenny reached out and wrapped her arms around her friend. The embrace was more than a gesture—it was an unspoken promise that she would be there, just as Chris had always been for them.

"Everything's going to be okay," Jenny whispered, her voice a steady stream amid the rising tide of emotions flooding the courtroom. Chris's sister clung to her, her body shaking with silent sobs.

As if the verdict had flipped a switch, the room erupted. People's feelings, held at bay during the tense hours of waiting, now burst forth unrestrained. Tears of relief washed over some faces, while others contorted in anger. Shouts of "Justice!" punctuated the air, tangling with cries of outrage from those who couldn't accept the outcome. The collective voice of the crowd swelled into a chaotic symphony, each note carrying the weight of the pain, the hope, and the fractured dreams that had gathered within these walls.

Jenny tightened her hold on Chris's sister, feeling the tremors that coursed through them both. They were waves in the same storm, finding solace in their shared anchor of friendship. Jenny knew that even amidst the clamor of justice served, the quiet void left by Chris's absence would echo the loudest.

The gavel's sharp rap cut through the tumult, once, twice, three times. The judge's voice, stern as the law he represented, boomed for attention. His eyes swept over the room, demanding silence with an unwavering gaze. Slowly, the storm of voices ebbed into a hush, the last murmurs fading like ripples in a still pond.

"Order," the judge commanded, and the word resonated with the power of finality.

Laura Simmons stood up from her seat, her spine straight as the pillar of justice she embodied. The red waves of her hair seemed to catch the solemn light of the courtroom as she stepped to the podium. Her hands, usually steady as bedrock, betrayed a faint tremor — not of fear, but of profound gravity.

"Your Honor," Laura began, her voice clear as a bell in the newly quieted room. "Members of the jury," she continued, turning slightly to address the twelve citizens who held Chris's legacy in their hands. "On behalf of Chris Matthews' family and loved ones, I want to express our deepest gratitude for your service."

Her eyes, two pools of cerulean sincerity, locked on each juror, conveying more than words ever could. "Your careful consideration and dedication to justice have not gone unnoticed. Today, you've honored Chris's memory by ensuring that truth prevails."

A murmur of assent rippled through the onlookers, many heads nodding in respect for the sentiment she shared. Laura paused, gathering her composure as emotion swelled within her chest. Chris's resilience, his unyielding spirit, seemed to infuse her with the strength to speak on.

"Though nothing can bring Chris back to us," she said, her voice thickening with emotion yet never losing its steady cadence, "the verdict you've rendered today is a testament to the belief that in our society, no wrong should endure without consequence."

In the silent aftermath of her words, something shifted in the atmosphere — a sense of something achieved, something approaching peace.

The courtroom buzzed, a low hum of whispered conversations snapping to silence as the heavy clink of shackles echoed through the space. Eyes darted towards the sound, converging on David Brown as two guards began escorting him away. His broad shoulders were tense, hands clenched into fists at his sides, the steel bracelets glinting coldly around his wrists.

In the gallery, Chris's mother squeezed her eyelids shut for a moment, a silent prayer fluttering from her lips before she opened them again to witness the end of this chapter. Across the aisle, Stephanie Brown's gaze lowered to the floor, the weight of her stepfather's sentence pressing down on her like the heavy air before a storm.

Chris's friends, a tapestry of faces etched with grief and relief, exchanged muted looks. Here was justice — raw and unflinching — yet it offered little comfort in the shape of their friend's absence. The resilience that Chris always carried seemed to manifest subtly among them, an invisible thread binding their collective sorrow and fortitude.

"Justice served," one of them murmured, almost to themselves, and the words were both a balm and a barb.

David's imposing figure shrank incrementally with each step he took towards the door, defiance etched into the harsh lines of his jaw. He turned his head slightly, catching the eye of his family one last time; the charismatic spark that once animated his face had dulled, leaving behind the stark reality of consequence.

"Never forget who you are, Steph," he said, his voice a gruff whisper meant only for her. She nodded, her eyes brimming with tears that refused to fall, a testament to her internal struggle between familial loyalty and moral clarity.

Chris's mother watched the exchange, her heart a turbulent sea of empathy for the young girl caught in the wake of tragedy. Laura stood beside her, a pillar amid the storm, her presence a promise of support for the long road ahead.

"Let's go home," Laura said gently, her hand resting on the shoulder of Chris's mother, guiding her away from the scene unfolding before them—the final act of accountability that closed the curtains on one story, while outside the courthouse, life's relentless narrative continued unabated.

The wooden benches creaked as they stood, their bodies worn from the relentless pace of the trial. Relief was a lightness in their chests, lifting the grief that had settled there like a stone since Chris's death. They lingered for a moment, glancing at the empty seat where David Brown had sat, now just another hollow space in a room full of them.

"Can you believe it's over?" Jenny Mitchell whispered, her voice carrying the tremble of subdued sobs.

"Part of it, at least," Chris's sister replied, her words threading through the newfound stillness of the courtroom like a needle mending torn fabric. "He would've wanted this... Justice."

Outside the courthouse doors, the world rushed to meet them. Flashes sparked like fireflies caught in the midday sun, and microphones bobbed on the sea of hands that reached towards them. Reporters' questions pierced the air, each one sharp and hungry for a sound bite of sorrow or satisfaction.

"Mrs. Matthews, how do you feel about the verdict?"

"Is this the outcome you hoped for?"

"Any words for other families seeking justice?"

Chris's mother raised a hand, not to answer but to shield her eyes from the glare. Her lips were a tight line, sealing away the flood of emotions that no sentence could ever truly appease.

"Let's just get through this," Laura Simmons urged softly, her gaze protective as she guided them forward.

"Chris would've been proud today," a friend murmured, nodding to no one in particular. In his mind, he saw Chris's determined smile, the kind that once lit up even the darkest of rooms.

"Excuse us, please," Laura said firmly to the reporters, her voice a clear note in the clamor. She steered Chris's loved ones through the throng with the skill of someone who had navigated many such storms.

"Remember what he stood for," Chris's mother finally said, her voice steady despite the chaos around them. "Truth, love, and never giving up. That's his legacy. That's our comfort."

One by one, they passed through the gauntlet, their hearts heavy with loss but buoyed by the weight of justice that had, after all this time, tipped in their favor.

Laura placed herself between Chris's family and the relentless barrage of microphones, her body a barrier to the probing questions. The scent of stale coffee and sweat hung in the air as she ushered them forward, her voice a low whisper soothing the turmoil around them.

"Keep moving," she said, her tone steady like a beacon guiding ships through fog.

"Stay close," she instructed, her hand lightly touching the small of Chris's mother's back, steering her through the sea of chaos. The clicking cameras and shouted queries formed a discordant symphony, but Laura's presence was a mute button, silencing the noise just enough for them to find their way.

The courthouse steps loomed ahead, a path back to a world that would continue spinning despite the gravity of what had just transpired within its walls. Laura glanced back to ensure no one lagged behind, her blue eyes scanning for any signs of distress.

"Almost there," she assured them, the corners of her mouth lifting ever so slightly in encouragement. It was a bittersweet smile, acknowledging both the victory and the void left by Chris's absence.

As they reached the bottom step, the fresh air was a brief respite from the stifling courtroom and its afterbirth of emotion. Laura turned to face the crowd one last time, her stance firm, a silent sentinel who had fought fiercely for this moment.

"Thank you," she said, addressing the throng with polite finality. "But we ask for privacy now." Her words were not a request but a gentle command, and the message was clear: This chapter was closed.

With each step away from the courthouse, the noise faded into a distant buzz, and the group found solace in the shared silence, a collective exhale marking the end of their long ordeal. They had come together through pain and now walked shoulder to shoulder, bound by a justice hard-won and a memory forever cherished.

Chapter 17

Samuel Bennett stepped onto the stage, his silhouette framed by the modest lighting of the small community center. The buzz of conversation that had filled the room quieted as eyes turned towards him, drawn by an almost gravitational pull of presence. There was something about Samuel—perhaps the measured confidence in his stride or the way his gaze swept over the crowd—that commanded attention without a word.

"Good evening," he began, his voice steady and clear. It cut through the silence, reaching every corner of the room. "We're here tonight because we believe in justice—a justice that's blind to bias and deaf to lies."

A murmur of agreement rippled through the audience. People leaned forward, as if trying to catch every nuance of Samuel's speech, their faces reflecting the shared flame of determination that his words kindled.

"Chris Matthews' story is not just a tale of wrongful conviction; it is a rallying cry for all of us," Samuel continued, invoking the name that bound everyone together.

In the back of the room, Jenny Mitchell stood with a group of Chris's friends, each one wearing a button emblazoned with Chris's smiling face. They were the torchbearers of his legacy, a tight-knit circle of loyalty and sorrow transformed into action.

"Can you believe the turnout?" whispered Jenny to the person beside her, her expressive eyes scanning the crowd. Her voice, though low, vibrated with a fervor that resonated deeper than the hushed tones she used.

"Chris would've been amazed," came the reply, equally soft but edged with the rawness of grief not yet dulled by time.

Jenny nodded, swallowing hard against the tightness in her throat. She then stepped forward, mingling with the listeners, sharing fragments of memories like precious gems. "Chris always stood up for what was right," she told an elderly woman who clutched her hand with surprising strength. "Now, it's our turn to stand up for him."

"Join us," Jenny urged, her voice now louder, emboldened by the nods and words of encouragement from the people around her. "Help us carry on this fight, so no one else has to endure what Chris did."

As Samuel spoke of redemption and the path forward, Jenny and the other supporters moved through the crowd, their personal stories bridging the gap between abstract injustice and palpable reality. Their words, simple but heartfelt, left imprints on the minds of those listening, stirring emotions and awakening a collective need to act.

"Change doesn't happen overnight," Samuel said, his tone a mixture of realism and hope. "But with every voice that joins our cause, we move closer to a future where truth prevails."

The air in the room seemed to thrum with newfound energy, charged by the union of personal loss and public resolve. As Samuel concluded his address, the applause that erupted was not just one of appreciation, but of solidarity—a sound that seemed to promise that the fight for justice, Chris's fight, would continue to echo far beyond the walls of the community center.

Samuel Bennett stood in the glow of the spotlight, the faces before him a tapestry of hope and grief. The hum of the community center had vanished, replaced by a silence heavy with anticipation. He cleared his throat, and each word he spoke carved through the stillness, resonating deeply within the rapt audience.

"Every day, innocent people wake up behind bars," Samuel began, his voice steady and resolute. "Families are torn apart, dreams are shattered—all because of a system that is fundamentally flawed."

He recounted stories of those wrongfully convicted, painting vivid pictures of their struggles. A young artist who sketched birds across prison walls, wings spread as if in flight from his cell. A mother who whispered bedtime stories to her child through the cold prison phone, each word a lullaby of resilience.

"Like Chris Matthews, they were robbed of their futures," Samuel said, invoking Chris's name like a sacred invocation. The mention of Chris sent a ripple through the crowd, a collective breath held and then released in quiet acknowledgment of the loss.

"Chris was more than a statistic; he was a beacon of hope in a system plagued by shadows," Samuel declared, the fire in his eyes mirroring the passion in his voice.

The scene shifted as the campaign for justice reform swelled, moving to an auditorium where hundreds had gathered, drawn by the promise of change. The larger venue vibrated with energy, each person a live wire connected by a shared purpose.

Samuel ascended the stage once again, his presence magnified by the sea of expectant faces. He spoke of Chris's legacy—not one of defeat, but one of enduring courage.

"Chris believed in justice, even when it failed him," he said. "Now, we carry that belief forward. We fight not just for him, but for every soul ensnared by injustice."

The room hung on his every word, a collective heartbeat pulsing through the space. When Samuel raised his hand, it wasn't just a gesture; it was a call to arms—a signal to rise, to act, to transform a shared vision into reality.

"Let us be the architects of a future where truth is the cornerstone of our justice system," Samuel proclaimed, his words echoing off the walls and into the hearts of those assembled.

The applause that followed was not merely a response to a speech well-delivered; it was the sound of conviction, of solidarity, of an unwavering commitment to turn the tide of injustice. It reverberated through the auditorium, a sonic testament to the power of Chris's story and the movement it had sparked.

In the bustling heart of a small conference room, a group huddled around a table strewn with pamphlets and sign-up sheets. Chris's friends and supporters, their faces etched with determination, orchestrated the hum of activity that filled the space. Each one took on the role of mentor and guide, offering practical steps to the eager attendees now scribbling notes and asking questions.

"Remember, it's about making our voices heard," one of them advised, pointing to a flowchart that mapped out how to reach local representatives. "Your phone calls, your letters—it all adds up."

The room buzzed with energy, a hive of shared purpose, as personal stories wove through the air, binding strangers in common cause. They spoke of Chris with reverence, their words painting him as a beacon, illuminating the path toward advocacy and action.

Amidst the workshops and panel discussions, Jenny Mitchell stood at the periphery, her short black hair catching the light as she observed the impact they were making. Her eyes, usually so full of fire, held a softness as she prepared for her own moment on the stage.

When Jenny's turn came, the room fell into an expectant hush. She walked up, each step measured, her athletic frame poised but revealing a tremble of vulnerability. Taking a deep breath, she gazed out at the sea of faces, finding solace in their attentive silence.

"Chris was more than my friend—he was my inspiration," Jenny began, her voice steady yet laced with emotion. "His fight became our fight. And even though he's gone, we owe it to him to keep going, to be the change he dreamed of."

Her words, raw and heartfelt, struck chords within the listeners. Some nodded, others wiped away discreet tears, but all felt the gravity of her loss, the weight of the mission they shouldered together.

"Chris taught me resilience," she continued, her hands gripping the podium as if drawing strength from its solid form. "He used to say, 'Darkness is just a space waiting for light.' It's up to us to be that light."

When she finished, the applause was not thunderous, but warm and supportive, enveloping her in a collective embrace. Jenny's journey of grief and resilience had bridged a gap, connecting hearts, urging them forward in the relentless pursuit of justice.

As the event wound down, the conversations lingered, charged with newfound resolve. Chris's story, told through the voices of his friends and immortalized by Jenny's courage, was more than a memory. It was a rallying cry, a promise of relentless advocacy, echoing far beyond the walls of the community center.

The hum of conversation filled the air as Samuel Bennett meandered through clusters of attendees during the break. His presence was a beacon, drawing eyes and sparking whispered recognition. In the warmth of the community center's faded yellow walls, he listened intently to each story, his blue eyes reflecting empathy that reached into the soul.

"Mr. Bennett," a young woman approached, her voice tinged with both respect and urgency. "How can we truly make a difference if the system is so broken?"

Samuel leaned in, his salt-and-pepper hair catching the light as he shared words that were equal parts wisdom and motivation. "Change begins with awareness," he assured her, his tone imbuing her with a sense of importance. "Every voice that joins the chorus makes it louder. Yours is needed."

Nods of agreement rippled through the onlookers, a sense of community and shared purpose knitting them together. The energy was tangible, a current that charged the very air with the power of collective resolve.

As the day waned, the scene shifted from the intimacy of the community center to the expansive grounds of a university campus. The keynote address was set in a grand auditorium, its vaulted ceilings echoing with the footsteps of hundreds of students filing in, their faces alight with enthusiasm.

Samuel took the stage, surveying the sea of youthful faces before him. Their passion was palpable, a living force that fed the flame of his own commitment. He cleared his throat and began, his voice resonant, carrying to the farthest corners of the room.

"Chris's story is not just a tale of tragedy; it is a beacon, illuminating the path toward justice," Samuel proclaimed, his hands punctuating the air with each point. "Your presence here today is a testament to the belief that change is possible—that together, we can right the wrongs etched into the lives of the innocent."

Murmurs of assent swept through the audience, an undercurrent of eagerness to learn and to act. As he spoke of redemption and the flaws of the criminal justice system, heads nodded, pencils scratched notes furiously, and eyes remained fixed on the man whose words seemed to carve hope out of despair.

"Let us carry Chris's legacy forward," Samuel urged, his voice swelling with conviction. "Let it be the spark that ignites reform, the story that awakens conscience, the memory that fuels our fight for justice."

The applause that followed was not merely polite acknowledgment. It was the sound of awakening, of barriers breaking, of young minds resolved to dismantle injustice, brick by brick. Samuel's message had taken root, and from it, a garden of activists would grow—each bloom a vibrant promise for a more just tomorrow.

The air was different in each city, yet the purpose united them all. In a bustling town hall, where the scent of polished wood mingled with the fervor of the locals, Samuel Bennett's voice echoed with the same resolve that had captivated the students. Here, workers with rough hands and hearts worn on their sleeves nodded, understanding the weight of Chris's story, seeing parts of their own struggles reflected in his fight for justice.

Under the harsh fluorescent lights of a community church basement, the audience was sparse but no less passionate. A single mother wiped away a tear as she spoke of her son, another life entangled in the merciless gears of the system. Jenny Mitchell stood beside her, hand resting on the woman's shoulder—a silent vow of solidarity.

In a modern library conference room, awash with the glow of sleek screens and hope, tech-savvy advocates tweeted #JusticeForChris, their digital voices amplifying the call for reform. The click-clack of keyboards punctuated Samuel's speech, a staccato rhythm of progress.

At a historic auditorium, its walls laden with the whispers of past orations, elders with memories of justice long-denied leaned forward in their seats. They listened, eyes gleaming with the fire of youth reignited, as Samuel wove tales of injustice with threads of resilience from Chris's life.

Each setting was a unique chorus in the anthem of change, diverse voices rising in harmony to sing the melody of justice.

Behind the scenes, connections sparked like synapses firing in a collective brain. In coffee shops and quiet corners, Jenny and other friends of Chris huddled with local leaders, activists' eyes meeting in mutual recognition of the journey ahead. They shared strategies and stories, piecing together a patchwork quilt of advocacy stitched with purpose.

"Your outreach program is impressive," Jenny remarked at a roundtable discussion, admiration clear in her tone. "We can integrate our efforts, amplify our impact."

"Absolutely," replied a seasoned organizer, her handshake firm and her resolve firmer. "Chris's story will be heard in every household, every street corner. We'll make sure of it."

City by city, the movement grew, fed by the fertile soil of collaboration. New alliances blossomed, roots intertwining, forming a sturdy network that spread far beyond the confines of any single venue.

Chris's spirit, emboldened by the tenacity of his friends and the dedication of strangers-turned-comrades, became an enduring symbol, a shared dream of what could be achieved when many acted as one.

The ripple effect of his tale, once a solitary pebble dropped into the vast ocean of the world, now surged as a powerful wave, reshaping the shores of justice.

Samuel Bennett stood still for a moment, his gaze sweeping over the sea of faces before him. The hush of anticipation in the community center was palpable, as if every breath held a story, every heartbeat a shared purpose. He cleared his throat, and when he spoke, his voice was tinged with gravity.

"Friends," Samuel began, his words deliberate, "our path is strewn with obstacles, much like the one Chris courageously tread. We've seen the justice system falter, watched innocent dreams crumble under its weight." Murmurs of agreement rippled through the crowd, and some nodded, their own battles reflected in their eyes.

"Yet here we stand," he continued, "united by a resilience that Chris himself embodied. Each setback, each challenge, is but a test of our perseverance. Remember, it's in our steadfastness that we honor Chris's legacy."

Jenny Mitchell stood to the side, her hands tightly clasped as she absorbed Samuel's message. Tears glistened at the edges of her eyes, not just for the loss of her friend, but for the truth in Samuel's words. They needed to be as unyielding as the concrete walls that once confined Chris, yet as hopeful as the sky above them.

As the day waned, Samuel's speech gave way to an evening of poignant remembrance. The small community center transformed into a sanctuary of sorts, candles flickering in the dimming light, casting shadows that danced upon the walls. People gathered, some holding pictures of Chris, others simply clutching onto the memories etched in their hearts.

"Today, we come together to remember a life that sparked a movement," Jenny announced, her voice steady despite the emotion clogging her throat. "Chris's laughter, his unshakeable spirit, they live on in our actions, in every step we take toward a just tomorrow."

Around her, heads bowed in silent tribute, and the air became thick with the weight of collective sorrow and determination. A quilt hung in the background, a patchwork of messages and images symbolizing the lives touched by Chris Matthews' story.

"His fight is now our fight," Jenny declared, lifting her gaze to meet those of the assembly. "And each of us carries a piece of his hope, his courage. Together, we will continue to push forward, because that's what Chris would have done."

The room resonated with a solemn promise, an oath taken by every heart present to see the battle through. There was strength in their unity, power in the commitment that simmered within each individual. It was a force that could weather any storm, a beacon that would shine through the darkest hours.

As the memorial drew to a close, the once-still room buzzed with renewed energy. Conversations ignited, plans were made, and the spirit of advocacy was rekindled. Chris's story had bound them together, a narrative stronger than the chains of injustice, a legacy that would continue to inspire change long after the candles had burned out.

"Let's walk this journey for Chris," Samuel said, his words echoing Jenny's sentiments. "For every Chris that comes after. Our resolve will not waver, for it is grounded in truth and righteousness."

And with that, the event came to an end, not with a sense of closure, but with the opening of countless doors, leading to paths of action and advocacy. Chris's memory was a flame, and each person there carried away a spark, ready to ignite a future where justice prevailed.

Samuel Bennett stood outside the community center as a cool breeze swept past, carrying with it murmurs of hope and determination from the crowd inside. He watched as people streamed out into the evening, their faces alight with a fire that Chris's story had kindled—a fire that would not be extinguished by the winds of opposition or the rain of challenges yet to come.

"Did you see them in there?" Jenny Mitchell approached Samuel, her eyes reflecting the same flame. "It's like Chris woke something up in everybody."

Samuel nodded. "He did more than that. He started a movement. And it's only gaining strength." Around them, groups formed spontaneously, discussing what they could do next, how they could contribute to the cause for justice reform. Chris's legacy was taking root, growing stronger with every shared story, every resolved stance against the system's flaws.

As the night deepened, the anticipation of what lay ahead settled on Samuel's shoulders like the weight of his own resolve. The fight was far from over. There were legal battles looming on the horizon, the most immediate being the confrontation with David Brown. His reputation for being impulsive and confrontational was well-known, and Samuel knew that facing him wouldn't be simple or straightforward.

"Samuel, the road ahead is going to be tough," Jenny said, drawing him back to the present. "David won't go down without a fight. You ready for this?"

"Ready as I'll ever be," Samuel replied, his gaze steady. "Chris taught us resilience. We'll need that and more when we step into court."

The two stood in silent camaraderie, understanding the gravity of the struggle for justice that awaited them. Yet, despite the heaviness of the upcoming conflict, there was an undercurrent of excitement—an eagerness to champion the cause that Chris had believed in so fiercely.

The chapter closed not with the finality of an ending but with the charged energy of a beginning. Chris's friends and supporters were bonded by a shared purpose, each ready to do their part in the ongoing fight for justice reform. They knew the journey would be fraught with obstacles, but they also knew that together, they were unstoppable.

With a sense of hope lighting the path forward, Samuel looked towards the future, towards the courtroom where the next chapter would unfold, where David Brown awaited. It was there that they would continue to honor Chris's memory—not just with words, but with action and unwavering commitment to change.

Samuel Bennett stood at the edge of the stage, his eyes sweeping over the sea of faces that had gathered for the final event of the speaking tour. The auditorium was a mosaic of determination and empathy, each person's presence an echo of Chris Matthews's spirit. As he watched them, Samuel could almost feel Chris standing beside him, his resilience and optimism as palpable as the warmth in the room.

"Tonight," Samuel began, his voice carrying the weight of their shared mission, "we close this chapter, but not the story. Not Chris's story."

A hush fell over the crowd, their attention fixed on Samuel. He spoke with a simplicity that belied the complexity of their cause, each word a testament to the journey they had embarked upon together. The speaking tour had been more than a sequence of events; it was a lifeline that connected them all to Chris and to each other.

"Chris always said, 'It's not about the fall; it's about how you rise,'" Samuel continued, invoking Chris's words like a sacred mantra. The audience leaned in, as if the very air they breathed was laced with the promise of reform.

"His legacy is not etched in sorrow but in the actions we take from here." Samuel gestured towards the crowd, including them in the narrative unfolding before them. "Because of this tour, because of your voices, Chris's memory is a beacon that will guide us through the fight ahead."

There were nods throughout the room, a silent pledge from each person to carry the torch that Chris had lit. They had learned about the cracks in the system, the innocent lives shattered by wrongful convictions, and now they held the glue to mend those fissures - awareness, advocacy, and unyielding perseverance.

As the evening waned, Samuel felt the collective heartbeat of the movement they had built. They had sowed seeds of change in every city, town, and community center, leaving behind fertile ground for justice to flourish.

"Let Chris's courage be the wind beneath our wings," Samuel concluded, his gaze fierce with resolve. "We honor him not just in memory, but in action. We continue the fight for justice, together."

The applause that followed was not merely a reaction to a speech well delivered; it was the sound of commitment, the reverberation of a movement gaining momentum. Each clap was a vow to keep pushing forward until the day the criminal justice system reflected the fairness and truth Chris had so ardently believed in.

And as Samuel stepped off the stage, the chapter closed with a quiet yet profound certainty: Chris Matthews's story would live on, inspiring change and challenging injustice, one heart, one mind, one voice at a time.

Chapter 18

The morning sun filtered through the stained glass windows of the church, casting a mosaic of color over the somber faces gathered within. Rows upon rows were filled with those who had known Chris Matthews—friends, family, and the many touched by his unyielding spirit. Their expressions, etched with sorrow, held a silent vow to honor his legacy.

In the front pew, Sarah clutched Michael's hand, her knuckles white against the dark wood. They stood shoulder to shoulder, their stance a testament to years weathered together, now facing the inconceivable task of saying goodbye to their son. Before them lay a casket, simple yet dignified—a heartbreaking contrast to the vibrant life it represented.

Sarah's gaze lingered on the photograph perched atop the casket—their boy, captured in a moment of laughter, the very image of resilience and hope that had defined him. A tear escaped her eye, tracing a solitary path down her cheek to fall silently onto the polished floor below.

"Sarah," Michael's voice barely rose above a whisper, thick with unshed tears, "he brought so much light."

She nodded, her arm slipping around his waist, holding him together as much as herself. In their embrace, they found a shared fortitude amid the grief—two pillars of strength amidst the storm of loss.

"Chris fought for what was right, always," Michael continued, his words a lifeline cast into the swell of memories. "We'll keep fighting, too. For him, for justice."

"His dream won't end here," Sarah affirmed, her voice steady despite the tremor she felt inside. It was a promise made not just to Chris but to a world still needing the change he had championed.

Jenny Mitchell threaded her way through the hushed crowd, a solitary figure with purpose etched into her stride. Her heart was heavy, yet in her eyes, there flickered the same flame that had always connected her to Chris—a shared resolve that injustice could not be allowed to stand unchallenged. She reached Sarah and Michael, who seemed like anchors amidst the sea of mourners.

"Sarah, Michael," Jenny said softly, her voice imbued with an empathy born of countless shared battles against life's cruelties. Her arms extended, enveloping them both in an embrace that spoke volumes more than words ever could. It was a silent pledge—a vow that the fight Chris had dedicated his life to would endure, even as he had departed from theirs.

"Thank you, Jenny," Sarah murmured, drawing back just enough to meet her gaze. "He loved you like family."

"Because we are family," Jenny replied, the corner of her lips lifting in a faint, sad smile. "We all are."

As if on cue, the gathered assembly of friends and fellow advocates moved closer, their presence a tangible testament to the bonds forged in the trenches of advocacy. Their faces were canvases of sorrow, each stroke of pain underscored by a resolute determination that mirrored Chris's own spirit. The quiet murmur of conversation was punctuated by solemn nods and clasped hands; a community united not only in mourning but also in an unwavering commitment to continue the work that had given Chris's life its purpose.

They formed a circle around Sarah and Michael, a barrier against the chill of loss, their collective strength offering a warmth that no cold whisper of despair could penetrate. They were the living embodiment of Chris's legacy—diverse voices harmonizing in a song of hope for a future where truth and justice prevailed.

"Chris showed us the way," someone whispered, and heads bowed in silent agreement. A shared breath was drawn, and in that moment, the air seemed charged with a renewed sense of mission. Chris may have fallen, but the mantle he carried would be lifted again, passed from hand to hand among those he had inspired.

The circle tightened, a symbol of the unity that grief had only served to strengthen. Here, in this gathering of souls, the echoes of Chris's resolve reverberated, a call to action that none present could ignore. And Jenny, standing shoulder to shoulder with those Chris had called his allies, felt the weight of responsibility—and the lightness of hope—as they prepared to carry forward the torch of justice he had lit.

Carol Thompson's presence was like a steadfast oak in the throng of mourners, her short brown hair a quiet testament to the storms she had weathered. She stood beside Sarah, close enough to share the sorrow that seemed to ripple through them both with every breath they drew. Their eyes locked for a moment, and without words, there was a silent communion of shared loss—the kind that only those who have had their world irrevocably shattered could understand. In that glance, there was an unspoken vow: Chris's legacy would not fade into the shadows of forgotten causes.

The shuffle of feet and soft clearing of throats brought a communal focus to the front of the room where a simple podium awaited the voices that would echo Chris's life. Jenny Mitchell, her black bob a stark contrast against the solemn attire of the crowd, made her way forward. She wasn't just a figure of youthful vigor among the grieving; she was the embodiment of the resilience that Chris had championed.

"Chris... he was more than a friend to all of us," Jenny began, her voice steady despite the ocean of faces before her. "He was our rock when the tides of injustice tried to sweep us away." A collective nod swept through the crowd, as if her words conjured their own memories of Chris's tireless spirit.

"Even when the world told him to move, he planted his feet firmly and said, 'No, you move,'" she continued, her tone rising with conviction. "Because that's who Chris was—a man who knew the meaning of justice, who lived it with every fiber of his being."

Murmurs of assent rippled through the air, a chorus of affirmation for the truth in Jenny's words. She spoke of late nights pouring over case files, of marches in the biting cold, of laughter that cut through tension like sunlight through storm clouds. With each recounted memory, it was as though Chris's essence animated the room, reminding everyone of the undying commitment to the cause he had held so dear.

"His laugh could shatter walls, and his resolve could move mountains," Jenny said, a wistful smile fleeting across her face. "But what I'll remember most is how he never gave up—on people, on justice, on hope. And neither should we."

There was a palpable shift in the air, as if the weight of grief had been momentarily lifted and replaced with a buoyant determination. Jenny stepped down from the podium, her speech not just a eulogy but a call to arms, a reminder that the fight for justice didn't perish with Chris—it was carried in the hearts of all who believed in the cause he had so fiercely defended.

The hushed murmurs of the crowd began to fade as Samuel Bennett took his place at the podium, his presence commanding the room with a quiet authority. He adjusted the microphone, casting a solemn gaze over the sea of faces gathered in memory of Chris Matthews—an advocate gone too soon but never forgotten.

"Chris's story," Samuel began, his voice resonating through the chapel, "is one that demands we pay attention. It's a narrative that speaks of resolve in the face of injustice, of courage against insurmountable odds." He paused, allowing his words to sink in, tapping into the shared sorrow and purpose of those assembled. "But let us not forget—it is also a call to arms, a reminder that our work is far from over."

Samuel spoke of systemic flaws, of battles fought and won, and those still raging. His speech was peppered with anecdotes of Chris's dogged pursuit of truth, each tale underscoring the young man's impact on the fight for justice reform. "He was more than just an advocate;

he was a beacon of hope for those who felt they had none," Samuel declared, his tone imbued with both reverence and fervor.

As Samuel concluded, offering a silent nod of respect toward Chris's family, there was a collective breath held within the chapel—a space filled with the gravity of his message and the responsibility it carried.

Then, Laura Simmons rose gracefully from her seat, the rustle of her skirt barely audible as she approached the stage. There was a steely resolve in her eyes, a reflection of the determination that had driven her career and the cases she'd championed alongside Chris.

"Chris taught me that the law isn't just about rules," Laura stated, her voice clear and unwavering. "It's about people—about their stories, their struggles, and their right to be heard." Her hands gripped the edges of the podium, her knuckles white with the intensity of her emotions.

She recounted the early days of her journey with Chris, how they had been united by a common vision: a world where truth prevailed and the scales of justice were balanced. "I remember the late nights," she said, "the fierce debates, the tireless research. But most of all, I remember the unyielding belief Chris had that every voice mattered."

Laura's speech was a powerful homage, threading her personal narrative with the larger tapestry of Chris's legacy. "Today, we mourn a remarkable soul," she continued, her gaze sweeping the room. "But tomorrow, we rise—carrying the torch that Chris lit, vowing to illuminate the dark corners of our justice system."

The raw emotion in Laura's words echoed the sentiments of all present. Each syllable was a testament to the enduring bond between the advocate and the attorney, between a fallen friend and the cause that bound them together.

"Chris's fight is now our own," Laura concluded, her promise hanging in the air, filled with conviction. "We will seek the truth. We will demand accountability. And we will never cease in our quest for justice."

As Laura stepped back, the silence was palpable, a moment of collective reverence for the path ahead—a path paved by Chris's indomitable spirit, now entrusted to those he had left behind.

The hushed murmurs of the crowd shifted, giving way to a more personal testament as one by one, individuals rose from their seats. They spoke of Chris, each voice a thread in the rich tapestry of his life's work.

"Chris once spent an entire weekend helping me pore over case files," a middle-aged man recalled, the timbre of his voice heavy with reminiscence. "Said it was our duty to leave no stone unturned."

A young woman stood up next, her hands trembling slightly as she clutched a crumpled tissue. "He believed in me when nobody else did," she said, her words catching on a sob. "Taught me that justice isn't just a lofty ideal, but something you fight for every day."

As stories unfolded, snapshots of Chris's unwavering dedication and infectious optimism materialized before the congregation. His influence was palpable, etched into the lives he touched, each memory a beacon of his spirit.

The atmosphere was thick with emotion, a palpable mix of sorrow and reverence hanging in the air. Tears fell freely, yet amongst the grief, there were smiles too—fleeting and fragile, like sun breaking through clouds. It was as if Chris himself was present, his resilience echoing in the quiet strength of his mourners.

"His laughter was the light in dark times," someone chuckled through tears, eliciting a wave of soft, bittersweet laughter in return.

"Chris fought harder than anyone I've ever known," another voice added, steady and sure. "He'd stand with us now, urging us to keep pushing forward."

There was determination in these shared tales, a collective resolve to honor Chris's legacy not just with words, but with action. The pain of loss was interwoven with the fortitude to continue his crusade against injustice. He had left an indelible mark on the world and the flawed system he so fervently sought to change.

As the service drew to a close, the blend of grief and grit settled over the attendees like a mantle. Chris might have been gone, but the fight for truth, the quest for justice—he had sparked in each heart would carry on. His story, his dreams, did not end here; they were merely passed on, entrusted to those who would walk the path beside him, even in his absence.

As the final words of remembrance hung in the air, a silent signal seemed to pass among the crowd. One by one, people began to rise from their seats, their movements slow but deliberate. In the quiet church, footsteps whispered across the stone floor, carrying the weight of a shared sorrow and purpose.

Sarah, her eyes red-rimmed but steady, extended her arms as Jenny approached. Their embrace was tight and long, a physical manifestation of the bond that had only grown stronger through hardship. Michael joined them, his hand resting on Jenny's back—a silent thank you for standing with them, for embodying the spirit of their son Chris.

"Chris would've been proud," Jenny murmured, her voice a soft beacon of hope in the dimness of the church.

"Of all of us," Sarah agreed, pulling back just enough to look into Jenny's eyes. "He brought us together for a reason."

Around them, the room was a tapestry of connection; every touch, every hug, each clasped hand wove a deeper sense of unity. Carol Thompson stood shoulder to shoulder with Sarah, their shared loss a silent undercurrent that connected them beyond words.

"His fight isn't over," Carol said, a steel thread running through her hushed tones. "Not as long as we keep fighting."

The nods that followed were solemn, heads tilting in agreement. Advocates, friends, family—all who had gathered here were bound by a mutual dedication to the cause that Chris had championed.

As the group slowly dispersed, pockets of conversation emerged, each one laced with the fervor that Chris had inspired. Laura Simmons leaned in close to Samuel Bennett, her voice firm and filled with conviction.

"We'll take this forward," she promised, echoing the sentiment that simmered in everyone's hearts. "Chris's work, his passion—it lives on through us."

Samuel's response was a nod, his gaze sweeping over the crowd. "We owe him that much, and more. We owe it to ourselves to fix what's broken."

The church doors opened, letting in a stream of sunlight that seemed to chase away the remnants of grief. As the attendees stepped out into the brightness of the day, their faces lifted not only in remembrance of Chris but also in recognition of the road ahead. They were more than mourners; they were torchbearers, each carrying a spark of the change Chris had envisioned.

"Justice," a voice called out, strong despite the lump of emotion behind it, "for Chris, for all those still waiting for it."

"Truth," another answered, equally resolute.

And with these words, the chapter came to a close. The gathering may have ended, but the collective resolve remained, pulsing like a heartbeat among them. Chris's life and struggle had kindled a fire that would not be easily extinguished. It was a fire that would light their way, fuel their steps, and guide them in the unrelenting pursuit of justice.

Chapter 19

The modest community center buzzed with murmurs and the shuffling of chairs as Carol Thompson took her place at the front of the room. Her gaze swept over the gathering — a patchwork of concerned faces, some etched with the same kind of pain that had become her constant companion. Today, she would transform that pain into purpose.

"Good evening," Carol began, her voice steady and strong. "We're here because we believe in justice — true justice — and right now, our system is failing us." She paused, letting her words hang heavy in the air before continuing. "I stand before you not just as a mother who lost her daughter but as someone who refuses to stay silent while innocent lives are destroyed."

A hush fell over the crowd; Carol's passion was palpable. "The Innocence Project is fighting to overturn wrongful convictions, but they can't do it alone. We need to be their allies in this battle for change."

After the meeting, Carol didn't allow herself a moment's rest. She pulled out her phone, her fingers flying across the screen as she drafted emails to local businesses, asking for their support. Her determination was like a well-oiled machine, propelling her forward, as she meticulously crafted each message.

"Hi Jim, hope the bakery is thriving," she typed with familiarity, knowing that personal touches went a long way. "I'm reaching out about an important cause — the Innocence Project..."

Carol's efforts didn't stop at emails. She hit the pavement, her comfortable sneakers a testament to her readiness to do whatever it took. Local café owners, bookstore managers, even the florist down on Main Street — all heard Carol's earnest plea for donations, for space to hold events, for anything they could spare to help the cause.

"Anything helps, really," Carol would say, her eyes conveying the depth of her resolve. "We're working to bring justice to those who have been silenced."

Her voice never wavered, her mission clear. The community recognized her dedication, responding with nods and promises of checks, gift baskets for raffles, and offers of venue spaces.

"Thank you, truly," Carol expressed her gratitude time and again, her sincerity touching hearts and opening wallets. She was the embodiment of single-minded pursuit, a beacon guiding others toward the light of justice reform.

As the sun dipped below the horizon, painting the sky with strokes of purple and orange, Carol reflected on the day's achievements. She allowed herself a small smile — not one of contentment, but of acknowledgment. There was much to do, but every step forward was a step toward honoring Angie's memory and righting the wrongs of a flawed system.

Carol stood resolute outside the courthouse, the cool breeze brushing against her cheeks as she clutched a handmade sign that read "Justice for Angie and Chris" in bold, black letters. The morning sun cast long shadows on the steps where a sea of protesters gathered, their voices merging into a chorus demanding change. Conversations buzzed around Carol, each one like a heartbeat pulsing with purpose.

"Can you believe how long it's been since Angie's case was first ignored?" a woman beside Carol asked, her tone a mix of frustration and disbelief.

"Too long," Carol replied, her grip tightening on the sign. "And every day is another that Chris spends without justice. We're here to make sure their stories aren't forgotten."

Nods of agreement met her words, and Carol felt the shared resolve of those around her, a community united by a common cause. They stood together, a tapestry of determination woven from their individual strands of pain and hope.

As the protest continued, they chanted, held up signs, and shared stories, each one an indictment of the system's failures. Carol spoke earnestly with fellow activists, her voice steady yet impassioned as she outlined the missteps and oversights that had ensnared Angie and Chris in a web of injustice.

"Change comes when we stand together," Carol declared, her words echoing off the courthouse walls. Her conviction resonated with others, sparking discussions about reform and accountability. It was more than just a gathering; it was a movement brought to life by the need for truth and fairness.

Later, as the crowd began to disperse and the echoes of their voices faded into the afternoon, Carol returned home to a silence that enveloped her like a shroud. She climbed the stairs, each step a reminder of the daughter who once bounded up them two at a time. Pushing open the door to Angie's room, she stepped inside, her heart heavy with both sorrow and love.

Angie's room remained untouched, a frozen moment in time. Photographs of Angie with her sunlit smile adorned the walls, her laughter almost audible in the stillness. A teddy bear sat perched on the pillow, its worn fur testament to years of bedtime stories and whispered secrets.

Carol sank onto the edge of the bed, running her fingers over the quilt Angie had chosen herself, vibrant patches of color that seemed to hold fragments of her spirit. Memories swirled around Carol, a torrent of joy and loss so intertwined that one could not be separated from the other.

"Sweetheart, I'm doing all I can," Carol whispered to the empty room, her voice breaking the silence. Tears brimmed in her eyes, but she let them fall freely, each one a testament to the depth of her grief.

Surrounded by these mementos of a life too brief, Carol found strength in her resolve. Angie's absence was a void no amount of time could fill, but it was also a wellspring of determination. Carol would fight — for Angie, for Chris, for every soul entangled in injustice's cruel grasp.

She rose from the bed, her resolve solidifying like steel tempered in fire. Carol knew the road ahead was fraught with obstacles, but she carried within her the unshakable belief that the battle for justice was worth every step, every tear, every raised voice.

"Your memory will be a beacon, Angie," Carol vowed, her reflection firm in the mirror amidst the photos of happier times. "I'll fight until the world knows your story, and the stories of all those wronged by a system meant to protect them."

Carol's fingers danced across the keys of her laptop, her gaze unwavering as she composed a message to a group of families bound by a shared tragedy. The email list had grown over the months, each name representing a heartache in need of solace. With gentle words, Carol extended an invitation to a support meeting she had organized—a space for those torn apart by wrongful convictions to find comfort and community.

"Your experiences matter," she typed, her voice threading through each sentence. "Together, we can shoulder this burden and transform our pain into purpose."

As she hit send, Carol leaned back in her chair, allowing herself a brief moment to absorb the soft hum of the computer, the quiet solidarity that filled the room. They were more than just names on a screen; they were lives upended, futures stolen, and to Carol, they were kindred spirits woven into the fabric of her mission.

A chime from her phone signaled the arrival of a text message. It was from a lawyer at the Innocence Project, confirming their meeting later that day. Carol's heart thrummed with a familiar cocktail of anticipation and resolve as she prepared to leave. She slipped into her coat, its fabric worn from countless rallies and gatherings, yet it still held the protective embrace of a warrior's armor.

The office of the Innocence Project was a place where hope battled despair, where the weary found renewed vigor. Carol's steps echoed through the hallway, each stride carrying the weight of stories yearning to be righted. As she entered the room, the lawyers greeted her with a respect born of shared battles, their faces etched with lines of dedication.

"Carol, thanks for coming," said one lawyer, his voice a warm welcome.

"Thank you for fighting the good fight," Carol replied, taking a seat at the round table that seemed to symbolize their unity in purpose.

They delved into strategy, pouring over case files like cartographers charting a path through treacherous terrain. Carol listened intently, interjecting with questions that cut to the heart of the matter, her mind working to piece together a mosaic of action and awareness.

"We need to shine a light on these stories," Carol asserted, her hands gesturing emphatically. "We have to make the public see the people behind the statistics—the lives derailed by a single stroke of injustice."

The lawyers nodded, their expressions a mix of admiration and understanding. One of them placed a hand on a stack of affidavits, his touch reverent.

"Absolutely, Carol. Your voice amplifies theirs. Let's talk about ways we can bring this to the forefront, maybe start with a series of community talks?" he suggested, his eyes seeking hers for agreement.

"Let's do it," Carol said firmly, a spark igniting within her. "And let's not stop there. We'll organize events, engage with local leaders, use every platform we have to call for change."

As the meeting progressed, plans took shape, each idea a thread in a tapestry of advocacy. Carol's presence anchored the discussion, her insights and fervor infusing their efforts with a sense of urgency. By the time they concluded, a blueprint for raising awareness lay before them, brimming with potential.

Walking out of the office, Carol felt the weight of the task ahead, yet it was a burden she bore willingly. For Angie, for Chris, for every wrongly accused soul, she would be a beacon of hope in a system shrouded in shadow. Their cries for justice would not go unheard, not while Carol Thompson had breath in her body and fire in her spirit.

Carol Thompson took her seat at the long, drab table, flanked by fellow panelists in a modestly lit community center. Her heart thrummed with an amalgamation of nerves and determination, the audience's expectant eyes upon her like spotlights. She adjusted the microphone, her fingers tapping against the cool metal before she leaned forward, her voice steady but rich with emotion.

"Every story has its shadows," she began, "and ours is no different. Angie, my vibrant daughter, became a victim not only of a heinous crime but of a system that faltered when we needed it most." The room fell into a hush, the air thick with anticipation as Carol wove the tale of Angie's tragic loss and the wrongful accusations that followed.

"Organizations like the Innocence Project shine a light on these dark corners of justice," Carol continued, her words painting a vivid picture of struggle and hope. "They fight to reclaim stolen lives, and supporting them isn't just an act of charity—it's an act of humanity."

As Carol spoke, her gaze never wavered from those gathered before her. Their faces, etched with empathy and concern, reflected back at her the power of her message. She concluded with a plea that resonated through the hall, "Let us be the bearers of change, for Angie, for Chris, for all whose innocence was their only crime."

The applause that followed felt like a warm embrace, validating Carol's mission and fuelling her resolve.

Later that afternoon, under the comforting canopy of an old elm tree, Carol sat across from Chris Matthews' parents on their well-worn porch swing. A gentle breeze carried the faint scent of jasmine as she listened intently to their account of Chris's resilience, his optimism unwavering despite the iron bars that unjustly confined him.

"I see so much of Angie's spirit in your son," Carol said softly, her hand reaching out to clasp Mrs. Matthews', a lifeline between two mothers entwined by fate. "His strength gives me hope that we can right these wrongs."

Mr. Matthews nodded, his voice a gravelly whisper, "Your work, Carol...it's lighting a fire. We can't thank you enough."

"Chris is family now," Carol replied, her smile bittersweet. "We are bound by a pain that few can comprehend, but together, we'll forge a path to justice."

They sat there together, united in a silent vigil, the setting sun casting long shadows that seemed to acknowledge their shared journey—a relentless quest for a dawn where truth would prevail.

Carol Thompson perched on the edge of a chair, phone pressed to her ear, in the cramped office of the local radio station. The morning sun filtered through the blinds, casting striped patterns across the desktop cluttered with flyers and notes.

"Absolutely, we'll run the story," said the voice on the other end, one of the station's hosts. "Your initiative speaks volumes about the community spirit here."

"Thank you," Carol replied, her tone imbued with gratitude but underscored by urgency. "It's vital that people understand the human cost of wrongful convictions—real lives are being shattered."

"Consider it scheduled. We'll have you on air first thing Monday morning."

Carol scribbled the details in her notebook, her handwriting a mix of loops and quick strokes—a testament to her resolve. She ended the call and allowed herself a moment to breathe, feeling the warmth of the sun on her face as she mentally prepared for the next task at hand.

Days later, Carol stood at the heart of the community center, bustling with volunteers and the quiet hum of anticipation. Banners adorned the walls proclaiming "Innocence Matters" and "Justice for the

Wrongfully Convicted." Each table was meticulously arranged, covered with literature and clothed in hope.

"Everything looks wonderful, Carol," remarked a volunteer, admiration evident in his voice.

"Thank you, Tom," Carol responded, scanning the room with a critical eye. "We need this to be perfect. People need to hear these stories."

The doors opened, and a trickle of attendees swelled into a stream. The room filled with murmurs and movement as people gathered, drawn by a shared cause. Carol took her place at the podium, the microphone an old friend in her hand.

"Good evening, everyone," she began, her voice steady and clear. "We're here today because we believe in justice, and we know our system is far from perfect. Tonight, you'll hear from those who've lived the nightmare of wrongful conviction."

As the first exoneree took the stage, a hush fell over the crowd. The man spoke of years lost, of the fight to reclaim his name, of the resilience of the human spirit. His words were raw and edged with pain, yet they soared with triumph, too. The audience listened, rapt, their expressions a tapestry of empathy and outrage.

Carol watched from the sidelines, her heart aching with each account, yet swelling with pride at the courage on display. This event, born from her tireless efforts, was not just a gathering—it was a clarion call for change.

When the last story had been shared, and the applause had faded, the conversations began. Attendees clustered around the exonerees, offering words of support, expressing shock at the injustices described. Carol moved among them, her presence a beacon of solidarity, her voice a gentle force urging action.

"Think of what you heard tonight," she implored a group of listeners. "Carry these stories with you, become advocates for reform. Together, we can mend the fractures in our justice system."

As the night drew to a close and the community center emptied, Carol remained, picking up scattered chairs and folding tables. Her body felt the weariness of the day, but her spirit was undiminished. The seeds of awareness had been planted, and with care, they would grow into a movement strong enough to transform the very bedrock of justice.

Carol adjusted the stack of files under her arm, each one brimming with statistics, case studies, and heartfelt testimonies. She paused outside the polished oak doors that led to the city council chamber, gathering her resolve like armor. Today, she wasn't just a grieving mother; she was the voice for those who had been silenced by injustice.

"Mrs. Thompson, they're ready for you," a young aide said, gesturing toward the open door.

"Thank you," Carol replied, nodding as she stepped into the room, her shoes echoing softly on the marble floor. The council members sat in a semi-circle before her, their expressions ranging from attentive to indifferent. Carol's gaze met each of theirs, silently imploring them to listen, to understand.

"Thank you for allowing me to speak today," Carol began, her voice steady. "I stand here on behalf of the Innocence Project and countless families torn apart by wrongful convictions." She laid out the facts with precision, citing alarming rates of false imprisonment and the ripple effects on communities.

One councilman, his fingers tented in front of him, leaned forward. "But what exactly are you proposing, Mrs. Thompson?"

"Comprehensive reform," Carol answered without hesitation. "Better access to DNA testing. Support services for exonerees. Independent review boards." Her suggestions flowed, each punctuated by a firm nod or an affirming glance from some of the council members.

As the meeting progressed, Carol wove personal stories between the threads of data, including Angie's, to paint a vivid picture of the human cost. By the time she concluded, even the most reserved politicians seemed moved, their pens restless over notepads, eyes no longer glazed with indifference.

"Your points are well taken, Mrs. Thompson," said the council chairwoman, her tone reflecting newfound respect. "We'll certainly consider your proposal."

Exiting the chamber, Carol allowed herself a small smile. It was a step, a crucial one, on the long road to change.

***

The morning sun spilled across Carol's kitchen table, casting light on a newspaper folded to the local section. Front and center was a photograph of her at the protest, holding her sign high, determination etched into her features. The headline read: "Local Advocate Awarded for Justice Reform Efforts" and below it, a recounting of her tireless work for the Innocence Project.

Carol traced the words with her fingertip, each sentence affirming that her message was resonating, spreading beyond whispered conversations and closed-door meetings. She thought of Angie then, of how her fight was now intertwined with so many others.

Her phone buzzed, breaking the moment. It was a text from a fellow activist: "Saw the paper. You're making waves, Carol. Proud to stand with you."

She set the phone down, her heart swelling with a mix of sorrow and gratitude. This recognition wasn't just for her—it was for Angie, for Chris, and for all the lives touched by the shadow of doubt cast upon the justice system.

With a renewed sense of purpose, Carol folded the newspaper, placing it in a drawer with other clippings and mementos. They were not just records of her journey but fuel for the continued fight. There was much to be done, and Carol Thompson would not rest until the scales of justice balanced true.

Carol Thompson stood at the front of the bustling town hall, her eyes scanning the room filled with community members who had come to voice their concerns. The air was thick with the hum of conversations, each one a thread in the tapestry of collective yearning for justice reform. Carol's short brown hair caught the light from the overhead fluorescents as she called the meeting to order with a gentle tap of the microphone.

"Thank you all for coming," she began, her voice firm and soothing, reaching every corner of the room. "Tonight is about finding our voice and using it to inspire change."

One by one, residents stepped up to the makeshift podium, sharing stories of how the criminal justice system had failed them or their loved ones. Each account was a sharp reminder of why Carol had dedicated her life to this cause. She listened intently, nodding in empathy, her eyes sometimes reflecting back the pain she saw before her.

"Let's talk solutions," Carol guided the discussion, encouraging proposals from the floor. Ideas flowed, from police body cameras to legal aid funds, and Carol ensured each suggestion was met with respect and consideration. Her ability to facilitate was like watching an expert weaver at a loom, threads of disparate thoughts being pulled together into a fabric of potential action.

As the evening wore on, the room felt charged with determination, and when the meeting drew to a close, Carol knew they had taken a step toward something powerful. A sense of accomplishment warmed her as she packed away her notes.

The following week found Carol at a conference on justice reform, surrounded by advocates who shared her passion. They gathered in a spacious auditorium, badges around their necks marking them as warriors in the same fight. Carol's presence was magnetic; as she moved through the crowd, others were drawn to her warmth and resilience.

"Your work has inspired so many of us," a fellow advocate said, shaking Carol's hand with both of theirs.

"Thank you," Carol replied, her heart full. "It's not just my work. It's our work. Together, we'll make a difference."

Throughout the day, Carol attended panels and workshops, absorbing new strategies and statistics that would bolster her efforts. But more than that, she forged connections with people who understood her journey, who knew the kind of grief that could fuel a lifetime of advocacy.

During a roundtable discussion, Carol shared her own story, her words painting a vivid picture of Angie's absence and the gaping hole left in the wake of injustice. The attendees listened, rapt, their faces a mirror of the sorrow and strength that defined Carol's narrative.

"When we stand united, our voices are louder, and the truth cannot be ignored," Carol concluded, her tone imbued with impassioned fervor. Heads nodded in agreement, a silent vow shared among them to keep pushing until the scales of justice were balanced once again.

As the conference came to an end, Carol exchanged contact information with new allies, her network of support expanding with every handshake and hug. There was solace in knowing she wasn't alone, that across the country, there were others like her fighting the same battle.

The camaraderie of the day lingered as Carol made her way home, the weight of her purpose both heavy and uplifting. Each connection, each conversation, they were all vital pieces in the larger puzzle of reform. And as the sun dipped below the horizon, casting long shadows across the city streets, Carol felt the familiar stir of resolve within her.

Justice might be a flawed system, but with enough hands to mend it, change was more than just a possibility—it was inevitable.

The evening air was cool as Carol Thompson locked the door to her modest home, the click of the deadbolt resounding with finality. She paused for a moment on her doorstep, letting the quiet of the night wrap around her like a cloak. The streetlamps cast a gentle glow on the pavement, their light guiding her path to the small bench in her garden.

Sitting down, she drew her knees up and wrapped her arms around them, gazing at the stars that twinkled above, indifferent to the trials of mortals below. The day's conference had left an indelible mark on her spirit, the shared stories of struggle and triumph echoing in her mind. Each face she had seen held its own tale of pain and perseverance.

As the cool breeze whispered through the leaves, Carol let out a slow breath, feeling the weight of her own story pressing against her chest. Angie's memory was a constant companion, a reminder of what had been lost and what still needed to be fought for.

"Change is like these stars," she murmured to the night, "distant but within reach if you're willing to stretch far enough." Her voice was a tender thread in the tapestry of the evening's stillness.

With each event she organized, each person she comforted, Carol knew she was adding links to a chain that would pull them all toward a brighter future. It wasn't easy—injustice was a stubborn foe, its roots deep and gnarled. But Carol's resolve was ironclad, forged in the fire of her daughter's tragedy.

She thought about the families she had met, the hands she had held, and the promises she had made. They were more than just words; they were lifelines thrown across the chasm of despair.

"Angie," Carol whispered, "your light guides me. It always has." A tear traced a path down her cheek, catching the soft light from the stars. Her grief was a river that never ran dry, but it also fueled her relentless push for justice.

Rising from the bench, Carol looked back at her home, its windows dark yet warm with the life she had built. Tomorrow she would meet with more lawyers, plan more events, and write more letters. The fight for justice was far from over, but Carol Thompson was not one to shy away from a challenge.

"Let them say it's impossible," she said to herself, a wry smile tugging at her lips. "I'll show them what's possible."

With a firm step, she walked back inside, her heart steady and her mind clear. She would rest, but only for a moment. There was much to do, and Carol would not rest until the scales of justice were evenly balanced.

"Change is coming," she promised the silence of her home, the walls bearing witness to her vow. "And I'll be there to meet it."

Chapter 20

The room hummed with low conversations as Samuel Bennett leaned against the edge of a cluttered desk, his eyes scanning the dedicated faces of his team at The Innocence Project's office. A stack of case files teetered beside him, each a life story waiting for a new chapter. Clearing his throat, he commanded the room's attention.

"Everyone," Samuel began, his voice steady and sure, "I've been thinking a lot about Chris Matthews's story." He paused, allowing the weight of that saga to settle among them. "Chris showed us the true meaning of resilience. His optimism in the face of injustice is nothing short of inspirational."

A murmur of agreement rippled through the room, punctuated by nods and solemn glances.

"His fight isn't just his own," Samuel continued, locking eyes with several team members. "It's our fight too. Every file in this room," he gestured to the precarious stacks around them, "represents not just a case, but a life snared by the very system meant to protect it. We're here to untangle those knots, to shine light on the truth."

Heads bowed in a collective moment of gravity, acknowledging the mission that bound them together.

"Let's review the new cases we've taken on," announced Sarah, one of the lead attorneys, as she clicked her pen and opened a bulky folder. "First up, we have Maria Lopez, convicted of a crime with evidence so flimsy it would crumble under scrutiny."

"DNA?" asked a junior researcher from the back, squinting at the notes projected on the wall.

"Non-existent," Sarah replied with a shake of her head. "And alibi witnesses never called to the stand. We need to dig deeper."

"Next is Jameson Clarke," another attorney chimed in, his voice tinged with frustration. "Arrested for a burglary based on a single eyewitness who now admits uncertainty. There's potential here for an appeal."

The team leaned in, scribbling furiously on their legal pads, their brains already churning with legal strategies and investigative leads.

"Then there's Ella Mae Robinson," Sarah said, her tone softening. "Imprisoned for two decades over a coerced confession. No physical evidence linked her to the scene. We've got to find the real story."

"Absolutely," Samuel affirmed, nodding with resolute determination. "Each of these cases is a person counting on us to restore their stolen years. We can't—and won't—let them down."

The team murmured their assent, their commitment to justice as fervent as ever. They knew the road ahead was fraught with challenges, but together they were undaunted, ready to peel back the layers of doubt and fear until innocence shone through.

Samuel Bennett stood in the drab visitation room, his eyes settling on the man across from him. Michael, with his worn face and tired eyes, looked nothing like a criminal. He was just a man caught in the unforgiving gears of justice.

"Michael," Samuel started, his voice steady, "tell me about the day of the robbery."

The man leaned forward, hands clasped together as if holding onto hope itself. "I was at work, Mr. Bennett. I clocked in at 9 AM, didn't clock out till late. But they say the store was robbed at noon."

Samuel nodded, scribbling notes. "And the evidence against you?"

"Shaky at best," Michael replied, bitterness creeping into his tone. "A witness claimed to see me there. But she's mistaken, sir. I've never been to that store."

"Any surveillance footage?" Samuel probed.

"None that shows me. Because I wasn't there," Michael insisted, his frustration palpable.

"Alright," Samuel said, closing his notebook with purpose. "We'll pull your work records, re-interview witnesses, and see what we can find. We're going to get to the bottom of this."

Exiting the room, he felt the weight of Michael's gaze on his back—a silent plea for redemption.

Back at the office, the atmosphere was charged with determination as the team gathered around clusters of desks, dividing themselves by case files. Samuel watched as they settled into their groups, each person fueled by a shared mission—to unravel the knots of injustice.

"Maria's group, check on those alibi witnesses. Jameson's team, get a statement from that eyewitness," Samuel directed, pacing among them, his presence grounding yet invigorating.

"Sarah, any luck tracking down alternative suspects for Ella Mae's case?" he asked, pausing beside her workstation.

"Working on it," she answered, eyes fixed on her screen. "There's a lead I'm chasing."

"Good," Samuel encouraged. "Keep pulling that thread."

Each group buzzed with activity, phones ringing as they arranged meetings with experts, tapped keys composing requests for evidence, and voices rising and falling in passionate debate. The air was thick with the scent of coffee and the hum of printers spitting out documents.

"Let's also revisit the forensic evidence for Michael," Samuel added. "There could be something missed, something to crack the case wide open."

"Will do," a determined voice responded from across the room, one of the researchers already on the move, his steps quick with purpose.

Samuel surveyed the scene, the cacophony of justice-seeking a symphony to his ears. This was more than a fight for the wrongfully convicted; it was a crusade against a flawed system. And they were the champions at the vanguard, armed with truth as their weapon, ready to strike at the heart of injustice.

Samuel leaned over a cluttered table, his hands splayed across a sea of case files like a captain steadying his ship in rough waters. The Innocence Project's office was a hive of quiet intensity, with Samuel at its heart, his piercing blue eyes scanning the room for updates.

"Progress reports, everyone. Let's hear where we stand," he called out, his voice an anchor in the bustle.

One by one, his team members raised their heads, sharing snippets of hope and hurdles from their cases. There was talk of breakthroughs, of doors opening where windows had been slammed shut. But with each victory, challenges loomed—a missing piece of evidence here, a reticent witness there.

"Patience and persistence, folks," Samuel reminded them, a smile tugging at the corner of his mouth. "We're in this for the long haul."

It was Sarah's turn, her voice a soft but strong ripple in the air. "I've found someone—a potential witness for the Thompson case. They were never approached during the initial investigation."

"Interesting," Samuel mused, stroking his salt-and-pepper beard thoughtfully. "How credible is this witness?"

"Seems solid," she replied. "They were at the scene but somehow overlooked. Could be the break we need."

"Excellent work, Sarah. We need to get their statement, pronto," Samuel said, his tone conveying urgency without panic. "Every voice matters, especially those silenced or ignored."

Heads nodded in agreement around the room, their shared mission clear: to unearth truth and mend the cracks in justice's foundation. Samuel watched as Sarah returned to her computer, her fingers already dancing across the keyboard. This was more than work; it was a calling, and every lead pursued meant another step toward redemption.

"Keep digging, team. Every case, every client, deserves our best," Samuel concluded, his gaze lingering on the framed photo of Chris—a constant reminder of why they fought so hard.

"Justice will prevail," he whispered, as much to himself as to the room, before turning back to the task at hand.

Samuel Bennett leaned over the cluttered table, fingers brushing against the day's mail. Amid the usual stack of legal documents and case files, a cream-colored envelope stood out, handwritten and sealed with care. He plucked it from the pile, the weight of its significance heavy in his hands. His team watched, a collective breath held as he slid a finger under the flap, breaking the seal.

"Who's it from?" asked Sarah, her curiosity echoing the sentiment in the room.

"Jameson," Samuel replied, unfolding the letter with reverence. The team had spent countless months untangling the web of Jameson's wrongful conviction, and now, his words lay before them—a tangible sign of hope.

Samuel cleared his throat and began to read aloud. "Dear Team, I never thought I'd have a reason to smile again behind these walls, but your belief in my innocence has brought light to my darkest days..." As he continued, Jameson's gratitude resonated through the office, each word a testament to their perseverance.

The room fell silent as the final phrases lingered in the air. They were a reminder, a beacon affirming their purpose. Samuel let the silence sit for a moment, letting the impact of Jameson's words sink in. Then, with a nod to his team, he folded the letter and placed it beside the photo of Chris.

"Let's keep this going," Samuel said, warmth flooding his voice. "We're making a difference—one life at a time."

With renewed vigor, he turned to his next appointment. A lawyer specializing in forensic evidence awaited him in the small conference room, her presence promising new avenues for justice.

"Ms. Carter," Samuel greeted her as he entered the room, offering a firm handshake. Her reputation for meticulousness preceded her, and Samuel hoped that her expertise could unlock the truth they desperately sought.

"Mr. Bennett," she nodded, returning his handshake with equal resolve. "I've been reviewing the DNA evidence you sent over. There's potential here for retesting with the latest technology."

"Tell me more," Samuel urged, gesturing for her to take a seat. His blue eyes fixed on hers, ready to absorb every detail.

"Advancements in genetic sequencing could give us the clarity needed to differentiate between samples that were previously indistinguishable," Ms. Carter explained, spreading out diagrams and reports across the table.

"Would that be enough to clear our client?" Samuel probed, his mind racing with possibilities.

"It's promising," she admitted. "But we'll need to move carefully. The court will want definitive proof."

"Understood," Samuel nodded. "We'll provide everything you need. Our client's future—his very freedom—depends on it."

As they delved deeper into the strategy, the room filled with the hum of focused conversation and the rustle of papers. Here, in the heart of The Innocence Project's office, science and determination intertwined, each discovery a step closer to redemption.

"Let's get to work then," Samuel declared, his voice steady with the weight of responsibility. "It's time to bring the truth to light."

And with that, they set forth, united by a common goal: justice for the wrongfully accused, no matter the odds.

The air in the conference room bristled with tension, each member of The Innocence Project's team perched on the edge of their seats. Samuel Bennett stood at the helm, his piercing blue eyes scanning the room as he led the discussion on a particularly knotty case.

"Rebecca's alibi is solid," one lawyer argued, tapping her pen against the stack of affidavits. "We need to push for that security footage that was supposedly 'lost.'"

"Footage can be dismissed," another countered, his brow furrowed in thought. "What about the eyewitness? If we can prove the lineup was suggestive, it could discredit the identification."

Samuel rubbed his chin, weighing each word carefully. He appreciated the fervor of his team, their eagerness to unearth the truth like detectives combing through the shadows for that elusive glint of light.

"Both points have merit," he acknowledged. "But we need to consider the risks. Challenging the footage might lead us into a procedural quagmire. On the other hand, attacking the eyewitness could cast doubt on Rebecca's innocence if we're not careful."

Voices rose and fell, ideas clashing like waves against a stubborn shore. With every suggestion came a volley of what-ifs and buts, the team navigating through the complexities with the precision of surgeons and the passion of crusaders.

"Let's focus on the lineup issue," Samuel decided, his voice cutting through the cacophony. "It's direct, and it speaks to a systemic problem that needs addressing. We gather more evidence, get expert testimony on improper police procedures, and shine a light on the flaws in the system."

Nods of agreement rippled across the room, a collective breath released as they settled on their course of action. Samuel's leadership had once again steered them through stormy waters, his magnetic presence a beacon of calm amidst the tempest of debate.

Just as the team began dispersing into their respective tasks, Samuel's phone buzzed sharply on the table. Glancing at the caller ID, he saw the name of a well-known journalist flickering on the screen. A sense of opportunity gripped him as he answered the call.

"Samuel Bennett speaking," he said, his tone professional yet inviting.

"Mr. Bennett, this is Alex Reynolds from The Justice Tribune. I've been following Chris Matthews' story and your work with The Innocence Project. I'd love to do a feature interview with you."

Samuel's heart quickened at the mention of Chris, the young man whose resilience had become a symbol of their mission. "That sounds like an excellent idea, Alex. It's crucial that we keep these stories in the public eye. It's how we inspire change."

"Exactly," Alex agreed, her voice crackling with excitement. "Chris's perseverance has moved many of our readers. Your insight could help people understand the importance of justice reform and possibly encourage others to support your cause."

"Let's set it up, then," Samuel replied, already picturing the ripple effect this exposure could generate. "I look forward to discussing how we can turn a tragic narrative into a catalyst for change."

As he ended the call, Samuel felt the invigorating promise of progress. Each interview, each case, each exoneration was another step toward mending the fractures within the criminal justice system. And with the unwavering spirit of his team, bolstered by the strength of individuals like Chris Matthews, Samuel knew that the fight for justice would continue, relentless and undimmed.

The cork popped from the champagne bottle with a festive burst, and a cheer erupted through The Innocence Project's office. Samuel watched as his team, a collective of dedicated souls, each raised a glass filled with bubbling liquid. Their faces, usually etched with concern and concentration, now glowed with the light of victory. It was a small win in the grand scheme, but to them, it felt monumental.

"Here's to second chances," Sarah exclaimed, her voice brimming with joy.

"Second chances," the team echoed, clinking glasses in solidarity.

Samuel couldn't help but smile at the sight. Each victory, no matter the size, was a testament to their unwavering commitment to justice.

He could see the reflection of their triumph in the sparkle of their eyes—a mixture of relief and renewed determination.

"Listen up, everyone," Samuel's authoritative voice cut through the celebratory murmurs, commanding attention. His team turned toward him, glasses poised mid-air, ready for his words. "Today's victory is not just ours; it belongs to every soul we fight for, every life we strive to mend. This new trial means another shot at freedom, another crack in the wall of injustice that stands before us."

He paced slowly in front of the room, the weight of his purpose grounding his steps. "Our mission is far from over. But let this be a reminder of the power we hold when we unite in our pursuit of truth. With each case, with each life touched, we are weaving a tapestry of hope—hope that one day, justice will no longer be a privilege but a promise fulfilled for all."

His gaze swept over the team, locking eyes with several members who nodded in silent agreement. "Your dedication, your hard work... it does not go unnoticed. You pour your hearts into these cases, and today, that devotion has paid off."

A hush fell over the room as they absorbed the gravity of his words. It was more than just a job for them; it was a calling—a relentless drive to right the wrongs written into too many stories.

"Thank you," he concluded, his voice softened by emotion. "Thank you for believing in second chances, for fighting the good fight. Together, we are changing lives—and that, my friends, is the greatest victory of all."

The team responded with nods and murmurs of agreement, the understanding of their shared purpose reflected in their expressions. As they sipped their champagne, the fizz tickling their tongues, they didn't just taste success—they savored the sweet flavor of hope reborn.

Samuel Bennett leaned forward, his hands pressed flat against the oak conference table that bore the weight of countless case files and hopes. The room was abuzz with a kind of electric energy, each team member ready to channel their recent victory into fresh endeavors.

"Alright, everyone," Samuel's voice cut through the chatter, "let's harness this momentum. We have new cases waiting—people counting on us to shed light where there's been darkness." He began passing out folders, his movements precise and deliberate.

Eyes scanned documents, absorbing the fates typed out in black and white. Dates, names, alleged crimes—a litany of lives derailed by a system that had failed them. There was Thomas, accused of a murder with no physical evidence; Maria, sentenced based on a coerced confession; James, whose alibi went inexplicably ignored.

"Sarah, I want you on Thomas's case," Samuel directed, tapping the folder. "His trial was riddled with inconsistencies. We need to dig deeper."

"Got it," she replied, her pen already scribbling notes in the margins.

"Mark, Maria's confession doesn't add up. Revisit the interrogation tapes, look for discrepancies," he continued, distributing tasks like a commander outlining a battle strategy.

"Will do, Samuel," Mark nodded, determination etched across his face.

"We need to be thorough, leave no stone unturned," Samuel reminded them. "Collaboration is key. If you hit a wall, reach out. We're a team—that's our strength."

Heads bobbed in agreement, the shared commitment to justice binding them together. As they dissected their responsibilities, the collective resolve grew palpable, their synergy a force to be reckoned with.

Amidst the fervor of planning, Samuel pulled a letter from his jacket pocket, the paper slightly creased from his careful handling. He held it aloft, and the room quieted, all eyes on him.

"This," he began, his voice tinged with warmth, "is why we do what we do."

Unfolding the letter, he read aloud, "Dear Innocence Project, I never thought I'd see the world outside my cell again. You believed in me when the system didn't. Because of your tireless efforts, I walked free last Thursday—after twenty years for a crime I didn't commit."

A collective breath seemed to hold in the room as Samuel continued, "I watched the sunrise this morning, felt the sun on my face, and it was like being born again. My family—we hugged and cried for hours. You didn't just give me back my life; you restored a father to his children, a son to his mother. Thank you for fighting for me, for giving me back my future."

As he finished reading, the silence was profound, weighted with the significance of their mission. It was more than just overturned convictions; it was about mending shattered realities, about hope rekindled in place of despair.

"Let's keep going," Samuel said finally, the letter gripped gently in his hand as if holding someone's very heart. "For him, for all the others still waiting—our work is far from over."

Nods of renewed purpose rippled through the team. They were ready to take on the world, one case at a time, armed with nothing but the truth and an unwavering belief in second chances.

Samuel closed the letter, tucking it into his jacket pocket like a talisman of hope. He looked around at the small sea of faces before him—each one etched with the same determination that had carried them through countless hours of meticulous work. The air in the room felt electric, charged with an unspoken promise to keep pushing against the tide of injustice.

"Alright, team," Samuel began, his voice steady and resolute. "We've got our marching orders. Let's get to it."

In an almost choreographed motion, chairs scraped back against the floor, papers shuffled, and laptops snapped shut as the team mobilized. Laura, with her keen legal mind, began organizing files for the next round of appeals, her red hair catching the light every time she turned her head to consult with her colleagues. Chris, whose own story was a beacon of their collective cause, huddled with Jenny, discussing the finer points of witness statements with an intensity that belied his youth.

Carol stood by the window, her gaze momentarily caught by the bustle of the city below—a world that continued to spin, oblivious to the battles fought within these walls. She turned back to the room, her eyes meeting Samuel's. There was a silent exchange between them, a shared history of loss and the unyielding urge to prevent others from experiencing that same pain.

"Samuel, do you think we're making a dent?" Carol asked, her voice a mixture of hope and weariness.

"Every case we crack open, every life we touch... it's more than a dent, Carol. It's a seismic shift for them," he replied, a hint of warmth breaking through his typically firm demeanor.

Angie's laughter bubbled up from the corner where she was brainstorming outreach strategies with Sarah. Her energy was infectious, and even in the most solemn moments, her spirit served as a reminder that there was joy to be found in their purpose. They weren't just fighting against something; they were fighting for someone—for many someones.

"Hey, did anyone reach out to that forensic lawyer yet?" Jenny called out, her athletic frame leaning forward with urgency.

"On it," Laura responded without missing a beat. "I've got a meeting lined up for tomorrow."

"Good, that DNA evidence could be the key we've been looking for," Samuel noted, pleased with the team's synchronicity.

As the day waned, the office hummed with activity. Phone calls punctuated the air, computers clicked in a steady rhythm, and the occasional high-five signified a small victory in the vast ocean of their endeavor.

The sun dipped below the horizon, casting long shadows across the room. Nobody seemed ready to call it a day—not when there was still so much to be done. The challenges ahead were numerous, the path to exoneration fraught with obstacles, but the resolve within The Innocence Project's office was palpable.

"Remember, folks," Samuel said, gathering his things, "every step we take is a step towards justice. We owe it to those counting on us to never lose sight of that."

"Here's to righting wrongs and setting the innocent free," Chris chimed in, raising an imaginary glass.

"Here's to justice," echoed the rest of the team in unison.

They left the office that evening with a quiet strength, the kind that comes from knowing the worth of one's fight. Tomorrow, they would meet again, ready to face whatever challenges lay ahead with the same unwavering conviction. For now, the night belonged to the city, but come morning, they would resume their relentless pursuit of justice for the wrongfully convicted.

Don't miss out!

Visit the website below and you can sign up to receive emails whenever Shane Reed publishes a new book. There's no charge and no obligation.

https://books2read.com/r/B-A-LSDAB-EESFF

BOOKS 2 READ

Connecting independent readers to independent writers.

Did you love *Unjust Conviction*? Then you should read *Voices Of Deception*[1] by Shane Reed!

[2]

In a world where the line between sanity and madness blurs, Vince was just an ordinary Canadian man—until the day a sinister voice claimed to be his god. Tasked with a divine mission to protect humanity from an impending alien threat, Vince spirals into a nightmarish quest where reality twists and darkness reigns.

As the voice drives him deeper into paranoia, Vince becomes convinced that extraterrestrial beings are disguised as ordinary people. His frantic search leads him to abandon his life, leaving behind a shattered marriage and a desperate wife who can no longer comprehend the man he has become.

On a fateful bus ride, Vince's delusions reach a horrifying climax when he identifies a fellow passenger, Tim, as the very alien he was meant to destroy. What follows is a brutal act of violence that will haunt him forever—a gruesome murder fueled by an unrelenting command from a god of his own making.

In the aftermath, Vince faces the consequences of a mind unraveling under the weight of untreated mental illness. Committed to a psychiatric facility, he spends seven agonizing years grappling with the echoes of his actions. Now, as he steps back into a world that once seemed so familiar, Vince must confront the chilling truth of his past and the haunting specter of the life he extinguished.

"Voices Of Deception" *is a harrowing tale of the fragile human mind, exploring the depths of delusion, the horror of unchecked mental illness, and the chilling intersection between faith and fanaticism. Will Vince ever find redemption, or is he forever bound by the shadows of his own creation?*

Also by Shane Reed

A Conning Couple Novel
Checkmate
The Great Escape
The Queen's Gambit
The Sicilian Defense
Fool's Mate
The Scottish Game
Stale Mate
The Conning Couple Books 1-5

True Crime
The Sniffing Dog Scam
The Vengeful Parent
The Psychic Scam
Conterfeit Capitalist
Innocence On Trial
Voices Of Deception
Shadows of a Perfect Life
Unjust Conviction